To Robin
With best wishes
and our thanks.

James Osborne
(aka - Jim)

The

Ultimate

Threat

James Osborne

The Ultimate Threat

ISBN – 13: 978-1514283943

First published in 2015 by Endeavour Press Ltd.,
London, UK

This novel is dedicated to the memory of

Judi Osborne

(January 8, 1948 – April 22, 2004)

Judi's courage, energy and humility were an integral part of her very being. Her selfless commitment throughout her too short life to helping those less fortunate was recognized in 1992 when she received the Canada 125 Medal, and in 2002 when she was awarded the Queen Elizabeth II Golden Jubilee Medal for outstanding citizenship. Her extraordinary spirit and life example are an inspiration to all who knew and loved her. Judi's legacy endures.

The Ultimate Threat

Forward

'The Ultimate Threat' is a work of fiction based upon the stark realities of the 21st Century. It is about the expanding campaigns by terrorists intent on destroying all of those precious joys we experience from life on this magnificent planet. Despite the threat from these sub-human psychopaths we should be encouraged that among us are people whose motives are based not upon misanthropic dogma, but on furthering goodwill and the dignity of humanity. These are the heroes of human kind we must encourage our youth to know and to emulate, particularly those vulnerable young people who are most susceptible to the seductive recruiting overtures of these barbarians.

We can choose as a society to not act in our own best interests. If we opt for that path, 'The Ultimate Threat' provides a glimpse into what the consequences might very well be.

-- James Osborne

The Ultimate Threat

Chapter 1

Candlewood Lake, CT

"I never thought I'd live in a lakefront estate like this!" Paige said.

Mark smiled at the pretty young woman he'd fallen hopelessly in love with.

Six months had passed since they'd moved in. The renovations were almost complete. He was bemused by Paige's enduring enthusiasm.

"Look around, Hon!" she persisted, pointing through the windows of the two-story great room. "Look at those gorgeous hills, the beautiful trees, the beach, the lake. It's spectacular!"

"Yeah. We can talk later," he said, enjoying the sparkle in her eyes. He had more intimate things on his mind. Mark had bought the house before they met, after returning from duty in Afghanistan with the Navy SEALS.

"It's no big deal for you," she said. Paige reached for his hand. "Your family's rich. But this is a really big deal for a humble little Latino girl and my kids.

"Our kids," she corrected herself.

It was a special time. Mark Tremblay and Paige Sanchez were embarking on a new life together. They were admiring the panoramic view through the huge great room windows across Candlewood Lake to tree-covered hills rising beyond in Pootatuck State Forest.

"Just a sec," he said, as they started toward the master bedroom. It was afternoon and sleep was not on their agenda. The kids wouldn't be back for a couple of hours. He stopped in front of a painting they'd just hung. "We didn't get this very straight."

Paige's hazel eyes followed him affectionately. He felt her gaze. Desire surged through his well-muscled body.

They continued toward the bedroom hand-in-hand. Paige took one more look over her shoulder, enjoying the view she'd come to love so much.

What she saw would change their lives.

"Mark! Who are those people?" she said stopping abruptly, frightened. Hooded men dressed in camouflage and carrying assault rifles were running up the sloping lawn toward them. "What are they doing here? What's going on?"

Mark turned around. He spotted a zodiac on the beach, 250 feet away, and then saw three men sprinting toward their huge back deck.

"Son of a bitch!" Mark muttered. "Son of a bitch!"

"Behind the bar! Now!" he shouted, grabbing Paige. "Get your head down! Hurry! Hurry!"

He wrapped her slender frame in his strong arms and pulled her down behind the bar, shielding her with his body. They heard 'Pop-Pop-Pop!' in rapid succession, again and again. He recognized the sounds . . . bullets fired from AK-47 assault rifles.

"Watch the flying glass!" he shouted, tucking Paige deeper under him. "Cover your face!"

Plate glass mirrors above them shattered. Bottles of liquor, drinking glasses and shelving became clouds of alcohol laced with razor-sharp glass.

Thank God for the renos, he told himself. He feared something like this might happen given his line of work. During the renovations, he'd installed 5/8-inch hardened steel plates behind the front facade of the L-shaped bar . . . just in case. The shields could withstand machine gun bullets.

Mark pushed a concealed button. A section of floor dropped. Powerful servomotors retracted it.

Paige looked up at him in disbelief, confused about the handsome man she'd fallen in love with. Tiny fragments of glass covered her hair and clothing. A narrow trickle of blood flowed down the left side of her face and neck, disappearing under her collar. There was a small cut beside her forehead.

*

East Harlem, New York City

"It should be done now," Abdul Rhamir said. He spoke over his shoulder to two men sitting behind him. "It's about fucking time those infidels felt the wrath of Allah . . . His wrath delivered by ISIS." He slammed his fist down onto the sill of a dirt-streaked window in his rundown apartment, three stories above a trash-littered courtyard.

A month earlier, he'd encountered a stubborn 'mob guy' who'd caused him grief. Rhamir had been trying to infiltrate the Caprionni mafia family's drug operations. The guy he needed help from wouldn't be bought off. In fact, the guy laughed at Rhamir, and told him to 'get lost'. That 'guy' was Mark.

No one talks to Abdul Rhamir like that, he thought angrily. He could barely control his fury.

Rhamir grew up a bully. Few had dared stand up to his fierce temper. He enjoyed intimidating others. It helped that he was over six feet, unusual for his culture. Hawk-like features reinforced his domineering presence. Rhamir had come to expect others would do his bidding. That hadn't happened this time.

"Damn it, I offered that infidel $20,000," Rhamir said to the other two. "That son of a camel refused me. Me! Abdul Rhamir."

Rhamir knew the New York mafia was taking in millions of dollars a week from drugs, cash he was determined to access. He needed money desperately to finance the jihad he was planning for ISIS. He was excited. Within weeks he would be sending teams of jihadists across America to set up sleeper cells that would attack three cities. A fourth attack would be an ISIS trademark, a public beheading. It would send an unmistakable signal that ISIS had brought Islamic holy war home to America.

"That infidel will not stop us," Rhamir said, "ISIS has invested much time and money providing our fighters with training and guns. Now, the rest is up to us. We shall triumph!"

"Allahu Akbar," the two men behind him said together.

"Allahu Akbar," he replied.

But Rhamir had a problem. His only income was a life annuity his elderly mother received after his father was killed in an accident. It was barely enough to support him and her, much less finance an ambitious holy war. And since US security forces had learned to intercept most of ISIS's money transfer schemes, the flow of cash had dropped to nothing. One day, he realized the mafia was scoring big on drugs, so he worked to become accepted by a mafia family. He even shaved off his beard so he could blend in better with other Mafioso.

"At least I've got one problem solved," he told his two visitors, a vicious smile flashing across his face. "I've fixed that infidel bastard!"

It pleased him to think that at this very moment, Mark, the stubborn barrier to accessing 'his' mafia drug money, was being removed. Three of his best fighters, the leaders of the three attack teams he'd set up, would be at Mark's home this very minute. Rhamir was tempted to have his men behead Mark and his 'shameless infidel' wife in front of their children and then behead the children, and post the gruesome killings on social media. However, he reasoned the murders would draw too much attention prematurely. He wasn't quite ready yet for that much notoriety. For now, with Mark dead, Rhamir knew he could bribe the mafia godfather's weak indulgent son into making the deal he wanted.

Rhamir turned and sat down at the littered kitchen table.

"It will be good to have that infidel out of the way," said Ali-Mumar Shahid, in a well-cultivated subservient tone. He silently resented being the 'junior' of Rhamir's two deputies and having to suck-up to Rhamir. "Have you decided on a date for the attacks?"

"Soon," Rhamir replied, glancing at his 'real' deputy, Iraq-born Frank Larigani, sitting across the table from him. "Very soon."

Larigani knew the date. It was just a few weeks away. Shahid caught the exchange between Rhamir and Larigani. They didn't trust him even though ISIS had sent him. It hurt. He resolved once again to do something about Larigani, to get him out of the way. Then he could begin planning to succeed Rhamir.

*

Candlewood Lake

"Quick!" Mark urged Paige. "Down the stairs! We'll be safe down there, for now."

Sheltered behind the bar, Mark knew they were seconds away from being discovered by the attackers. He could hear bullets ripping up the kitchen and hitting cupboard doors.

A trap door beside Mark and Paige had opened onto stairs. Mark scrambled part way down the stairs. Paige was frozen with terror. Mark reached up and carried her down. Flipping on the lights, he pushed a button on the wall. A heavily reinforced section of floor above then rumbled over and up, locking into place. The top of the trap door blended with the surrounding floor above. The heavy door itself was reinforced cement.

"What's going on?" Paige asked, squatting at the bottom of the stairs. "What is this place?"

She was shaking and crying softly. Her dark brunette hair screened her face.

Mark knelt, pulling her close to him.

"It's going to be okay, now," he said, releasing her. "Hold still, my love."

Mark gently dabbed blood from the side of her face with tissue. He pressed it to her wound and lifted Paige's hand to hold it in place. Mark put his arm around her, and guided her along a cement-lined tunnel to a brightly lit 20 by 20-foot chamber.

"Sit here," Mark said softly. He pointed to an upholstered bench built into the wall. He wrapped a soft wool blanket around her shoulders. The seven-foot-high room was painted light beige and brightly lit with LED fixtures.

"Where are we?" Paige repeated, looking around in fear, "What's going on, Mark?"

"We'll be okay here for now." He could see she was in shock. He wiped blood from the back of his own neck. "This is a secret safe-room, self-contained and soundproof. It's made of reinforced cement. We could stay here for a few days if we really had to."

Paige jumped to her feet, eyes wide with horror.

"My kids!" she screamed. "Oh my God, Mark! The kids! Where are they? They were going to the playground with Anashi. We've got to get them . . . right now! Oh God, Mark! We've got to go!"

She began running back toward the stairs, stumbling in her blind haste, a trickle of blood again running down the side of her face.

"Paige, we can't do anything for the children right now," Mark said, sprinting after her. He caught up and wrapped his arms lovingly around his petite wife, trying to calm her. "If we go back up there, they'll kill us. They came to do that. That's why they're here . . . to kill me . . . us.

"I'm really sorry, Paige," Mark said, still holding her. "Let's hope Anashi got them away in time. It'll be risky but we'll go look for them right away."

"I don't care Mark," she screamed at him. "We've got to get Edward and Caylyn right NOW!" She struggled to get free, her arms flailing. "Oh my God! My babies! What if they took them, Mark . . . or worse? Dear God . . . we've got to get up there right now!"

He held her gently but firmly against his athletic body . . . finally convincing her to return to the bench. Paige sat reluctantly. She struggled to calm herself.

"What're we going to do?" she said between hysterical sobs, tears streaming down her cheeks. "I don't know where they are, or even if they're all right. Oh, my God, Mark! We've got to do something . . . we've got to!"

"We'll get out of here in a minute," Mark replied. "I need to fix that cut first. And then we'll go look for them. Okay?"

She nodded reluctantly, her eyes still wide with fear "Hurry up!"

Paige had hired Anashi as a nanny after her first husband, Derek Sanchez, a US Marine sergeant, was sent to Afghanistan. She was in university. He was killed by an IED. Caylyn, now four, was born two months after her father died. Edward, six, had only vague images of his father. To Paige and Mark's immense joy, both children had taken immediately to Mark when they began dating.

"Okay, my love," he said as he dressed her cut. "Here's our situation. As you know, I bought this house before we met, after I got home and joined the FBI. Along with the renos, I had the garage built and this chamber dug under it as an escape route. I thought it might come in handy someday. Guess I was right."

Paige shook her head in confusion.

"We'll be going down a tunnel," Mark continued, pointing behind him. He unlocked a cupboard and took out a Glock .45 pistol, and tucked it in the back of his belt. "The tunnel comes out behind a hedge. I'll go first and make sure our way is clear. From there we'll slip down the highway to my uncle's farm. You've been there. I've got an old car in the barn. We'll come right back and look for the kids. Okay?"

"Tell me right now!" Paige demanded. "What's going on? Why can't you call someone for help?"

"There isn't time," Mark said. "And both of our cell phones are in the den. Besides, I can't have a bunch of local cops running around who've not been briefed and cleared."

"Who did this?" she demanded, as Mark finished work on her cut. "Why are these men after you? What's going on? How are you involved . . . why are you involved . . . with these terrible people?" Paige jumped to her feet and wiped at her tears. "Why didn't you tell me you were mixed up in something awful like this before . . . before we were married?"

"I wanted to, very much," he answered quietly. "But it wasn't quite that simple. Let me tell you what's going on, and then you decide."

Mark inhaled deeply. He began:

"After we were engaged, I told you I worked for the FBI. It was only fair. I couldn't tell you I'm assigned to an undercover team. When you thought I was away on training or overseas, I was working undercover in the city. I'm really sorry I couldn't be honest with you, but our project is top secret. I was under direct orders not to tell anyone about it, not even you."

"Good God, Mark!" Paige said. "I feel like I'm living a lie! What else haven't you told me?"

"Look, Paige. I'm going to tell you everything. I'm not supposed to, but here goes."

Paige shifted uncomfortably and shivered as if a cold breeze had suddenly caught her.

Mark continued:

"I worked my way into the fringes of an organized crime family. Its leader is a man called Giovanni, Joe, Caprionni. He must have liked something about me, because he picked me to become a business advisor reporting directly to him. It was a big surprise, and a huge break for our investigation. It got me working closer with Caprionni. He's trying to expand into legitimate businesses."

As Mark spoke, Paige's forehead wrinkled. Her hazel eyes opened wider. "Why in God's name, Mark, would you and the FBI help the mafia?" she exclaimed, "They're scum!"

"Yes, it's bizarre but things change," he said. "The FBI learned that ISIS is in the process of

16

bringing its war to America. And those crazies have been trying to infiltrate the mafia. That intelligence changed my job. ISIS has at least one sleeper cell in America that we know about, and probably more.

"Look, I'll tell you more about this later," he added. "We're wasting time. Let's go look for the kids. Ready?"

"Yes!" Paige said, jumping up before he'd finished. "Let's go!"

She looked around anxiously.

"This way," Mark said.

In 15 minutes, the couple was seated in a dusty 10-year-old white Subaru Outback that Mark kept in his uncle's barn half a mile down the road. He used it for backcountry fishing, kayaking and exploring. They drove toward their home. He parked the car well back from the driveway, shielded behind dense bushes.

"I'm going to check around the house," he said, "Just in case anyone's still here. Will you be okay or would you feel better coming with me?"

"I'm okay here," she replied uncertainly.

"Lock the doors," Mark said as he pulled a hunting rifle from the back of the . He tucked the Glock .45 into the back of his blue jeans, and then stuffed spare bullets and clips in his pockets. He handed Paige another Glock .45 he kept in the barn. She waved it away vigorously, her eyes wide with fear. She'd never fired a weapon in her life, and didn't want to listen as he told her how to fire it. He put the Glock on the floor beside her right foot and closed the door, waiting until she locked the doors.

Mark crept through the heavy bush along the side of the house and then around to the back. There was no sign of the attackers. Completing the circuit, Mark saw Anashi's empty car parked in front of the three-car garage. The driver's door and both rear doors were ajar. There was no sign of Edward, Caylyn or their nanny. He felt a nauseating ache in the pit of his stomach.

Mark crept through the house, his rifle poised.

Good God! He kept saying to himself as he surveyed the heavily damaged interior. *Son of a bitch!*

The assailants had shot up and virtually destroyed the kitchen, living room and dining room, and ransacked closets and three of the four bedrooms. For some reason they'd missed the master bedroom suite. It was at the end of a long hall, the door closed.

I wonder if they thought this was a door going outside? He thought as he entered their bedroom. It was untouched. He went next to their shot up den where he found both of their iPhones under a pile of rubble. He sprinted back to the .

"I'm really sorry love," he said, answering her distraught look, "There's no sign of the kids or Anashi. Her car is there. I don't know if they ran away in time or those bastards took them.

"We'll check out the playground right now," Mark added. "And then check with the neighbors. Okay?"

"Yes, yes!" Paige said.

The playground was deserted. Then, every neighbor gave the same negative response. With each stop, their fear grew for the safety of the children and Anashi.

Finally, Mark pulled the to the side of the road and called his boss Warren Mitchell about what had happened. Warren said he'd get an FBI kidnap team working on it, immediately and quietly.

Mark and Paige looked at each other, shared a silent understanding of dread, and headed for his aunt and uncle's home a few miles away.

*

Danbury, Connecticut

Mark rang the doorbell at the front door of his uncle's upscale home.

"Good Lord, are you two all right?" Douglas Winston said, seeing his disheveled nephew and wife. The fashionable home was in a gated community, part of an upscale suburb. It was early evening.

"What happened?" he added, stepping back to let them enter. "Where are the kids?"

"We've had some trouble," Mark said as they slipped through the door into an elegantly furnished living room.

"So I see." He'd noticed the blood on Paige's top, and the bandage on the side of her forehead. Her strikingly beautiful hazel eyes were red and swollen from crying. Light sparkled off tiny granules of broken glass in Mark's dark brown hair. The collar of his blue denim shirt displayed a sizeable bloodstain.

"We need your help," Mark said before his uncle could ask more questions. "Our kids were kidnapped, we were attacked at the house a couple of hours ago . . . by three men with AK-47's. Edward and Caylyn are gone . . . they're missing! So is Anashi. We've searched everywhere."

"Good God!" the distinguished business executive said. "What the hell's going on?"

"It's someone connected to the mafia," Mark said. "I've no doubt. It's not the Caprionni's . . . probably the Maniero's."

They exchanged knowing glances. Mark filled his uncle in on what had happened.

"Kidnapping the kids!" his uncle growled angrily when Mark finished. "Those bastards!"

Mark's iPhone rang. It was the smartphone Caprionni had given him for his work with the mafia family.

"Mark Trimonti," he said using his fake undercover name.

"Trimonti!" the male voice barked. "You want those brats and that infidel bitch back?"

"Yes, of course," Mark said cautiously.

"Then listen very carefully," came the reply. The deep aggressive voice had a subtle middle-eastern accent.

"We need a volunteer," the voice said with a sarcastic laugh. "You're gonna be it."

"Whad'ya mean?" Mark asked.

"You want your kids back, you're gonna volunteer! Listen. We got a job for a suicide bomber. You're volunteering!" the caller chuckled.

"We'll make you a martyr. But if you call the cops or tell anyone, the brats and that shameless whore are gonna die! You get that? They die! You're gonna get a call."

"How're we going to do this?" Mark asked. But there was a click. The call went dead.

"Shit!" Mark said, wondering how the caller got his phone number.

Mark described the call to Paige and Douglas, leaving out references to him becoming a suicide bomber.

"When can I get my children back?" Paige said, barely containing her emotions. "What did they say?"

"He's gonna call back with some demands," Mark replied. It was partly true.

The three sat down to prepare descriptions of the children and Anashi to give the FBI in the morning. Douglas explained that his wife Jennifer was at a conference in San Francisco. He'd called her while Mark was on the phone. She was flying back immediately on a company jet owned by Prescott Enterprises, where Douglas was executive vice-president. That eased Mark's mind. The two women had grown close. Paige would need Jennifer's support.

"Okay, Mark," Douglas said. "It's pretty damn obvious there's more to this than your mafia investigation. Let's hear it."

"Well, yes, there is, Uncle Doug," he said.

Mark confided in Douglas. He'd been estranged for years from his father, Douglas's brother. That's why his uncle was listed as Mark's primary emergency contact for the FBI.

"A few things are happening. First, I'm certain the Maniero family hired the attackers. We've reason to believe they may be part of a sleeper cell of extremists put here by ISIS."

"Holy shit!" Douglas exclaimed. "This is a far cry from what you signed up for, Mark. An anti-drug task force is one thing, but now you're getting into international terrorism."

"Yeah, I know," Mark said. "We know the leader is a guy called Abdul Rhamir. Shortly after I went underground, the FBI got an agent into Rhamir's group. He's providing some excellent intelligence. He found out Rhamir is building a network of jihadist fighters, many recruited right here and trained by ISIS in Syria and Iraq. As far as we know, it's pretty thin on the ground right now. But some of those militants have worked their way into influential positions in a number of organizations across the country.

"Remember that US Army major at Fort Hood that went on a killing spree? Well, ISIS trained him and he was a secret part of Rhamir's infiltration and intelligence strategy. Our guess is Rhamir got that officer so riled up with religious fervor he went berserk. As we know, ISIS, al-Qaeda and others have done the same thing in other countries. We're deluding ourselves thinking it can't happen here.

"Now, here's the worst part," Mark continued. He paused, sighed deeply, and then drew a deep breath.

"Our undercover guy recently overheard Rhamir tell his lieutenants that teams of ISIS-trained fighters are planning to attack several cities. We don't know where yet, or how many. You've seen the barbaric slaughters of innocents in Iraq, Syria and Africa. Well, the war is right here and right now."

Paige and Douglas said nothing, their eyes wide in disbelief.

"And my babies are caught up in all of this," Paige said, her voice breaking.

"Dear God!" Douglas added. "Are you absolutely certain?"

"I wish I wasn't," Mark replied.

Paige looked at Douglas and then at Mark, still trying to make sense of all the bizarre events unfolding in her previously well-ordered life.

"The only good news is this, for what it's worth," Mark continued. "Rhamir and his people are facing a big problem – money. Sanctions by America and other countries have cut the international flow of money to and from ISIS to a trickle. Rhamir seems to think he can fix that by taking over drug operations from organized crime. It's a stupid move, of course. And now, obviously, things are heating up and getting nasty.

"There's one more wrinkle I might as well tell you about while I'm at it," Mark sighed. "I'm facing a problem with the Caprionni's. The old man will be livid when he hears what I've been up to; that I'm an undercover agent for the FBI, and not a confidante working for him."

"Then don't tell him," Paige blurted out.

"Oh, I have to tell him, now," Mark replied, taking Paige's hand. "I'm going to need his help getting the children back. Besides, my role has to change now that we need to go after ISIS aggressively. The best chance I have of staying alive is to come clean with Caprionni before he finds out from somewhere else. And he will."

"Good God!" Paige exploded, her mind spinning. "I love you, Mark, but what are you doing to us? I don't want you going back to that mafia boss! It's too risky! And what about my children . . . our children?

"Where are they?" she added. "Shouldn't they be your very first priority?"

Her eyes flashed with fear and anger. "Who took them? The mafia or those . . . those terrorists? Who? I want Edward and Caylyn back now, Mark, right now! Before something awful happens to them."

"Of course, they're my first priority," Mark said. "I expect Rhamir's thugs kidnapped the kids. They probably did it when they couldn't find us. Rhamir wants me out of his way. I'm certain he's working with the Maniero family.

"I think Rhamir and his fanatics originally planned to target the Caprionni's drug operations. It's the biggest. When I refused to go against the Caprionni's I put myself in Rhamir's crosshairs.

"Here's what I think happened:

"Shortly after Mr. Caprionni assigned me to help expand their legitimate businesses, I met people from the Maniero family and some thugs I didn't recognize. Their leader tried to make a deal with me to betray the Caprionni's. I found out later from our undercover agent the guy I told off was Rhamir. He was not happy."

"But how did they know where to find us?" Paige asked.

"The Caprionni's know where we live," he replied. "The mafia can find out just about anything they want to know. It wouldn't be all that hard for the Maniero's to find out too. Mafia families spy on each other all the time. Besides, they can search public records of real estate transfers and building permits just like anyone else."

"Okay," Douglas said, stretching. "Enough for now. You two must be exhausted. Paige, I know this is a terrible experience for you. I hope you'll try to get some rest. You two will use our guest suite here for as long as you need while your house is being fixed.

"I promise you, Paige, tomorrow, we'll put all of the resources we can think of into getting your children back safely. Promise. See you two in the morning."

Chapter 2

Danbury, CT

Mark answered a knock on the door to the suite. He was on the phone.

"Hold on for a second," he said into his iPhone. It was 7:15 a.m. Douglas walked into the guest suite. "Good morning."

Mark waved over his shoulder as he turned toward the master bedroom to take the call.

"Morning Uncle Doug," Paige said. She got up wearily from the dining room table and gave him a hug.

Mark and Paige had spent a sleepless night. The worried couple agonized over their missing children and were impatient to begin searching for them.

"Trimonti here," Mark said into the phone, using his undercover name.

"It's Warren," his boss said. "Has anyone called you this morning from your house?"

"Good morning Warren," Mark said. "No . . . no one's called. What's up?"

"I just got a call from a Lt. Garrett Sanchez with the Connecticut State Police," Warren replied. "He's at your house. You need to get over there right away. Call me after you contact Sanchez. Okay?"

"What's up?" Mark repeated.

"I need you to confirm something," his boss replied, being vague. "Just call me back after you talk with Sanchez. And make that a priority, okay?"

Mark was puzzled. Warren's comment was more of an order than a request. Something was wrong. This was not like him.

On the way to Candlewood Lake, Mark kept mulling over Warren's comments. The three arrived at the shot-up home just before 10 a.m. The damage was worse than they feared. Paige took one look, burst into tears and turned away. Mark was holding her close, trying to comfort her, when he heard a deep voice boom out.

"Douglas! Over here! Comment ça va?"

"Hey, Emile," Douglas replied to the burly six-foot French Canadian striding over to greet them. They met in the destroyed kitchen/dining room. The strained look on Emile's face surprised him. Douglas expected Emile's usual boisterous friendly smile. He wondered.

"Great to see you again," Douglas said. "I want you to meet my nephew, Mark Tremblay and his wife, Paige. This is . . . was . . . their home. Mark, Paige . . . meet Emile Bilodeaux. He's the executive vice-president for Global Security. I asked his team to help with the investigation. He's an old friend. All of his guys are former cops."

While the two discussed the investigation, Mark excused himself and guided a tearful Paige down the hall toward the master bedroom suite, away from the damage. By some miracle it had been untouched by the attack.

"Try to rest for a few minutes, my love," Mark said, guiding Paige to the king size bed. She lay down reluctantly. Mark covered her with a duvet and tucked it in around her, hoping the warmth would help ease her discomfort. He kissed her gently and assured her he'd be back in a few minutes.

Meanwhile in the kitchen, Emile briefed Douglas about the investigation and the role Global Security personnel would be playing in cooperation with the state police and the FBI. Finally, the strained look on Emile's face became too much for Douglas' curiosity and patience.

"There's something else, isn't there, Emile?" Douglas asked. "Let's have it."

"Yes," Emile replied. "We might as well get to it. Our security people came over last night right after you called. They were here all night working with the Connecticut State Police for clues to the kidnappings. Anyway, just around dawn, a police sergeant from New Fairfield called to say a body was found early this morning floating in Squantz Pond."

Mark returned. They were joined by Global's director of executive security, Bill Hollingsworth, a former NYPD homicide detective, and Lt. Sanchez of CSP, who was in charge of the crime scene.

Lt. Sanchez turned to Mark.

"Mr. Tremblay, Emile probably told you that a body was discovered this morning in Squantz Pond, near the entrance to Candlewood Lake?"

Mark nodded.

"There's no ID," Sanchez said. "I've arranged with the coroner's office to bring the body here. I regret asking you this, but would you see whether you recognize the deceased? Are you up for this?"

"Yes," Mark replied, a knot of fear growing in his belly. "Is the body an adult or a child?"

"An adult female, likely in her mid-20s," Sanchez replied.

Mark was hit by conflicting emotions – relief that it wasn't Edward or Caylyn, but with foreboding. *Surely, it won't be!* he thought. Despite his experiences with death in Afghanistan, anticipation of whom he might see took a steely grip on his heart.

Sanchez led the group across the large wooden deck at the back of the house and around to the front driveway. A state coroner's van was parked behind Anashi's Ford Focus.

"I must warn you, gentlemen," Sanchez said, motioning them to a stop behind the van. "What you're going to see is unpleasant . . . gruesome, actually."

Sanchez opened the back doors. Mark, Douglas and Emile stepped forward. Mark saw a small black blanket. It obscured most of an irregular shape – the body. A slim arm, obviously female, poked out from beneath the near side of the blanket, its partly opened hand turned upward. The feet and lower half of two awkwardly bent legs stuck out from the far edge of the blanket.

"I guess this is up to me," Hollingsworth said, as he stepped forward and lifted the tarp back.

It was Anashi! Her body was badly bruised and naked, lying on its left side facing them. Her half-bent right arm was extended above her head. Her throat had been cut deeply, almost decapitating her. A torn strip of rag had been used to gag Anashi's mouth. Her once beautiful brown eyes were open and sightless.

The three men recoiled in horror.

"Subject to the inquest, the coroner believes she died within the past 12 hours," Lt. Sanchez was saying. Mark barely heard him. "It appears from the bruises and broken ribs that she was tortured and beaten severely first. We suspect the body was dumped in Squantz Pond near the entrance to Candlewood Lake sometime during the early morning hours."

Mark forced himself to look back at the body of a remarkable young woman. Blood was caked on Anashi's pretty face, around her open vacant dark brown eyes and on her long black hair.

He stumbled back from the van and fell to one knee on the lawn. He'd grown fond of Anashi. Her bubbly personality and obvious love for Edward and Caylyn had made her much more than an employee. Mark and Paige regarded her almost as a little sister. Despite frequent exposure to violent death in Afghanistan, the sight of Anashi like this became overwhelming. He gagged, struggled to keep from being sick . . . and failed.

"Oh, dear God!" he gasped, spitting vomit, barely able to breathe. "Anashi! What have they done to you . . . you poor girl! Oh my God!"

Lt. Sanchez walked over and squatted down beside Mark. Performing his official duties unwillingly, he said gently, "Mr. Tremblay, I'm very sorry but I must ask you if this is the body of a person you know as Anashi Jassim?"

Still on his hands and knees, Mark looked up, nodded between heaves of his stomach, and then managed, "Yes".

"Those sons of bitches!" Mark said, speaking to no one in particular. "Those miserable bastards! Why . . . why . . . do this to an innocent, defenseless young woman? My God, she's hardly more than a child? Why? She never hurt anyone!"

Forcing himself to his feet, Mark growled, "Those rotten sons of bitches . . . they're going to pay for this!"

"We found a note," Sanchez told the group. "Someone stuck a kitchen knife through it and then between the victim's ribs, just beneath the left breast.

"It was soggy, but we were able to decipher most of the note," Sanchez said. "From what I could make out, it said: 'Your brats are next.' I will assume, Mr. Tremblay, the note was intended for you."

Mark nodded, "I expect so."

"For what it's worth," Sanchez added, "in the 20 years I've been with CSP homicide, I've never seen anything this brutal, this barbaric."

"Son of a bitch!" Mark repeated. His fear for Edward and Caylyn had skyrocketed. He understood now why Warren did not want to be forthcoming on the phone.

"We've got to cover her better than this," Mark demanded through his grief. "This little blanket is way too small. I can't risk Paige coming out here. It would be too much for her."

"It's all we could find in the coroner's van," Hollingsworth said, apologetically.

"I'll go see what I can find inside," Douglas said.

"Yes, yes, of course," Mark said absently. "The linen closet in the hall."

Douglas gave his nephew a comforting hug and headed toward the house.

Mark walked over and gently adjusted the too-small blanket to cover as much of Anashi's body as possible. His emotions were shrouded in a dark, dense fog. Anger was boiling up through his grief. And he was worried about Paige. She would have heard them leave the house. He knew she'd wonder what was going on outside. Luckily, the bedroom windows overlooked the back yard and lake. He prayed she wouldn't come out to investigate before he got back to her.

Damn it all! Mark said quietly to himself, trying to comprehend this tragedy and reassure himself the children were still all right. After what he'd just seen, he wasn't sure at all.

"Will this do?" Douglas said, returning from the house. He unwrapped a pink sheet covered with frilly 'little girl' designs. Mark recognized the sheet with a jolt.

"Yeah, sure," Mark said. "It's from an extra set Paige picked up for Caylyn's new bed."

Mark remembered the day a year ago when Paige had arrived with loads of bedding. He knew then that Paige was sending him a message – she was committing fully to a life with him. It had made his heart soar. Now his heart was hurting.

"I'll do that," Mark said. He took the soft cotton sheet from his uncle and shook it open.

Douglas and Emile stepped forward to help. Mark held the little blanket in place as they leaned into the van and spread the sheet over Anashi's body. Mark stepped in and tenderly raised her body. He cradled her in his arms and wrapped the sheet closely around her, tucking it under her body. Finally done, Mark felt no need to hide his grief for Anashi, or his rising panic over the safety of Edward and Caylyn.

As Mark made his way into the house, despair ripped at his very being, knowing he must face his already troubled wife.

How am I ever going to tell Paige about this? he thought as he rinsed vomit from his mouth in the main bathroom sink and washed his hands as if trying to erase the horror he'd just witnessed. He sprinkled cold water on his face, trying to ease the redness in his eyes.

Mark looked in the mirror and saw with horror his light gray hoodie had traces of Anashi's blood. He ripped it off and threw it down the laundry chute to the basement. It would go into the trash later. He washed again vigorously, once more trying unconsciously to erase reality. He grabbed an old work shirt from the back of the door and headed down the hall to Paige. As he opened the bedroom door, he thought: *My God! She'll never want to come back here again.*

He was right.

Paige was almost hysterical when Mark told her about Anashi, and became even more panicked about the children's safety. Mark spent hours on the bed rocking her in his arms, trying to ease her grief and fear. Douglas brought them cups of herbal tea that he knew they both liked. Mark finally persuaded Paige to lie back down. She stayed there until mid-afternoon.

Paige found Mark at the dining room table with the other men: Sanchez, Hollingsworth, Douglas and Emile. Mark jumped to his feet.

She looked at him stoically, raising her hands slightly. He could see she had herself under control. He was impressed.

"Mark and Paige, let me say how terribly sorry I am about Anashi," Emile said. "It's the most barbaric thing I've ever witnessed. And the kidnapping; that's despicable. I want you to know, we're going to devote all the resources we have to help the FBI and CSP bring them back to you quickly and safely, and to track down whoever did these terrible things.

"There's something else we need to discuss," Emile added, pausing. "Your uncle asked me to discuss your personal safety. We really need your cooperation with this. First, you need to disappear for a while, once the authorities have finished with your interviews, of course. I'm suggesting you leave town for a week or so, until things settle down just a bit.

"I know you want to be here near the children. I understand that, but the people who attacked your home might try again. The truth is, there isn't anything more you can do to find your children than we're already doing. We'll stay in contact with you constantly . . . and I mean constantly. But right now, frankly, you'll just be in the way and our concern for your safety would be a distraction. You know that, Mark."

Mark nodded. His uncle, Hollingsworth and Sanchez added their nods of agreement.

Lt. Sanchez spoke up: "Our investigators are done with you for now. I agree with Emile. It would be best for you to keep a low profile for a few days."

"I'm not going anywhere!" Paige said, her eyes bright with anger. "Not until I get my children back!"

"Listen to me, please, Paige," Mark said, worried as much about his wife's safety as the children's. "I understand how you're feeling, but our being here could make recovering the kids more difficult. I know you want to make it easier for the authorities, not more difficult."

Paige looked at him. "Oh, God, Mark. I'm so scared!" she said. "Where are they? How are they? Are Edward and Caylyn all right? I need to know. How can I leave them and go away?"

"We'll be in constant touch with Uncle Doug and Emile," Mark said. "And we can be back in just a few hours. Uncle Doug said he's reserved the company plane for us, for as long as necessary."

Paige sighed, and reluctantly agreed.

"There's one other thing," Emile said. "Hollingsworth has brought in some guys from our New York office. They're highly trained in personal security. All six of them are ex-Marines and mafia-savvy. They're your bodyguards. They'll work in shifts. I've told them to stay out of your way as much as possible."

"What?" Paige said. "I don't want strangers following me around! How is this going to help get our children back?"

She looked at Mark. He was surprised too, but quickly seized on the necessity for their safety.

"Paige, please understand," Mark urged. "These are very nasty people we're dealing with. They've savagely murdered Anashi, and they've kidnapped our kids, just to get to me . . . to us. We're both in danger. I don't like this either. Will you at least try to put up with them until we get the kids back?"

The look on Paige's face was a mixture of annoyance and resignation. She started to walk toward the deck overlooking the lake. Paige thought of the happy times they'd spent on the big wrap-around wood deck, and the many more they'd dreamed of. Reality flooded back when she saw the broken glass, wrecked outdoor furniture and pieces of window frame. She glanced toward the lake then recoiled, remembering the black-hooded men who'd stormed their home. She whirled around and walked stiffly back to the living room, fighting for control, her teeth and fists clenched tightly. Mark followed her to their bedroom.

Thirty minutes later, Mark and Paige returned.

"We've talked it over," Mark said. "We'll go visit my grandparents in Kansas City for a few days."

They were introduced to their six bodyguards. Before returning to Danbury, Mark called Warren.

"That was sound advice," Warren said, "and you made a good decision, Mark. I know how to reach you, so just go. I'll see you when you get back."

Chapter 3

LaGuardia Airport, NY

"Is Paul Winston in, please?" Mark said into his iPhone. "It's Mark Tremblay calling."

"Oh hi, Mark," replied the friendly voice on the other end. "Good to hear from you. It's Karen. Your grandfather's out at a meeting. He'll be back soon. Are you in town? Can I help you with anything?"

The voice belonged to Karen Keetley, his grandfather's long-time executive assistant at Prescott Enterprises in Kansas City, MO. Paul was an energetic 75, and his wife Anne, a vibrant 71. Both still came to work every day, leading their multi-billion dollar merchant bank and holding company.

"Thank you for asking, Karen," Mark replied. "I'm at LaGuardia. We're flying over this afternoon to see Grandpa, if he's available."

Karen assured him that both his grandparents would be in their offices when he arrived. He would have preferred to not worry his lovable but feisty grandmother about what had happened; he knew better than to try keeping anything from her.

Mark's uncle, Douglas, was Executive Vice-President of Prescott Enterprises, based in New York, and had arranged the corporate jet for their trip. The plane made it possible to bypass commercial airline schedules at most airports, avoiding the delays caused by regular check-in procedures and baggage. It also provided better personal security.

Mark's iPhone rang as he walked through the executive aviation departure lounge with his bodyguard. Paige, his uncle and her bodyguard continued on ahead.

"Yes Vinny," Mark said. His caller ID showed the name and number of Joe Caprionni's son, who Mark found objectionable. "What's up?"

"More to the point, Trimonti," Vinny replied arrogantly, using Mark's undercover name. "What the hell's up with you? We heard your house got hit last night. What the fuck happened?"

"Thugs with AK-47s, Vinny," Mark said. As always, he struggled to be civil to the mafia boss's only child, a repulsive self-indulgent little pipsqueak Mark was obliged to work with in his undercover assignment.

"D'ya know who done it?" Vinny persisted.

"No, I don't," Mark said, growing impatient. "But I can guess. Those thugs left some useful clues behind, Vinny. And I'm damned well going to find out. So, what's up?"

"My father wants to see you, Trimonti," Vinny said. "You can tell us all about the hit then. He wants you over here right away."

"I'm at LaGuardia, Vinny," Mark told him. "I'm flying out to visit family on an important matter. Today's Monday, right? I'll be back Friday night. How about Saturday morning? Will your father be okay with that?"

"He's not going to be happy," Vinny said. "But he puts up with you for some fuckin' reason." Mark wasn't concerned.

Maybe Vinny was right for once, Mark thought. He suspected Joe Caprionni had grown to respect him if not actually like him in the short time they'd known each other. Besides, the Caprionni family had a firm rule; anything to do with family was to be respected.

"That's because I always tell him the truth, Vinny," Mark retorted. He knew that would annoy the conceited mafia don's offspring. Mark disliked that Vinny habitually lied to his father. It offended his sense of respect.

"I'll call when I get back," Mark told him. "We'll set a time."

"Yeah, sure," Vinny said. "I'll square it with my father. You're gonna owe me, man!"

The disingenuous tone in the younger Caprionni's voice came through loud and clear. Mark wondered what the scheming little screw-up would be up to while he was away.

"That'll be the day!" Mark shot back as he hung up. He and his bodyguard cleared airport security and left the executive terminal, heading for the Prescott Enterprises Learjet parked nearby.

Mark's phone rang a second time as he reached the steps to the aircraft. It was Warren. Mark was surprised. Just a few hours earlier, he'd briefed Warren on the latest details surrounding Anashi's death and progress on the investigation at their home.

What his boss said to him left Mark in shock.

"Maybe I shouldn't go," Mark said. "I'll just send Paige."

"No," Warren said. "But while you're away, I want you to think about some strategies to deal with this. See you when you get back."

Chapter 4

Kansas City, MO

"Mark, give your grandmother a big hug!" Anne Winston exclaimed, bursting through the closed door to her husband's private office. The nameplate on the door did nothing to deter the petite septuagenarian. It read: 'Paul Winston, CEO, Prescott Enterprises Inc.' and beneath it in bold letters, 'PRIVATE'.

Mark, Paige and Douglas had just sat down with Paul when Anne came charging into the office. Paul's door was rarely closed. This time it was.

"What's the meaning of this?" Anne challenged, hands on hips, her radiant smile evolving into a loving frown. "I go shopping for a bit and you sneak into town without telling me, and then hide out in your grandfather's office? You better have a good explanation!"

Anne rushed over to Mark as they all stood.

"Hi, Grandma," Mark said.

He leaned his muscular six-foot, two-inch frame over to hug his diminutive grandmother and give her an affectionate kiss on the cheek.

"We just got here."

Anne exchanged a warm hug with Paige and then with her son, Douglas. She noted the troubled looks on the faces of the three visiting family members, and then shot an annoyed glance at her husband. No one had told her they were coming.

"All right! What's going on?" Anne demanded, looking around the large oval rosewood table in Paul's conference room, and then fixing her gaze hard on her distinguished husband.

"You better ask Mark," Paul said, shifting uncomfortably in his chair at the head of the meeting table. Nodding sideways toward his grandson, he said, "This is his show, Anne."

Mark was not surprised his high-spirited grandmother was suddenly involved. Douglas's right eyebrow rose above a self-conscious grin as his mother glared at him.

"Have a seat, Grandma," Mark said. "You're going to need it."

First, he filled his astonished grandparents in on his work as an undercover agent for the FBI. He'd received Warren's approval to do so. Then, he told them about the attack on their home and the kidnapping of Edward and Caylyn, and Anashi's murder.

"Oh my God!" exclaimed Anne. "What is this world coming to?"

"Nothing matters right now more than getting Edward and Caylyn back quickly and safely," Mark said. "That's one reason why we're here. We need your help. Oh, and just so you know, those two fellows you saw in the lobby reading magazines and pretending to be waiting for appointments are bodyguards. A team of them will be shadowing Paige and me until this is over. That's the other reason we're here. We need to hide out for a few days."

His grandparents looked at each other, worry in their eyes, eyebrows raised.

"Have you told your parents about this?" Anne continued, looking hard at Mark and then questioningly at Paige. Both shook their heads, 'No'. Relations between Mark and his father had been strained since he'd joined the US Navy without telling his parents. His father, Philip Tremblay, was president and CEO of Continental Del Rio Oil and Gas, one of America's fastest growing integrated oil companies. For years, he'd had a plan in place for Mark to succeed him one day. The problem was, he hadn't bothered to consult with his only son. Mark had other plans.

"Until the attack," Mark told his grandparents, "My orders were to keep things on a 'need to know basis'. That's all changed now. Our families may be in danger. Law enforcement can't provide the needed protection. That's why they told Paige and I to disappear for a few days.

"We'll bring my parents up to speed this evening." Mark paused uncomfortably. "Paige and I are having dinner with them. We'll call Paige's parents in Costa Rica as soon as we're done here."

Mark expected the evening with his parents to be tense. He hoped his father wouldn't be there. Mark was counting on his mother, Catherine, who was Paul and Anne's daughter, to keep the peace if his father did show up.

Five years earlier when Mark told his family that he'd joined the Navy, his oilman father's disappointment erupted as angry rhetoric. The two strong-willed men argued loudly. His mother had intervened fearing father and son might come to blows. Mark and his father had not spoken since, despite attempts by his mother and his uncle at reconciliation.

The dinner at his parents' home would be the first face-to-face encounter between Mark and his father since then, and would be Philip's first meeting with Paige.

"We need to ask you two for a couple of favors," Paige said.

"Ask away," Paul replied, smiling warmly at his grandson's bright and beautiful young wife. Right from the moment they'd met her, Paul and Anne had been captivated by Paige's gentle nature and awed by her razor-sharp intelligence.

"We know Prescott provides executive security for you and your senior people," Paige said. "And I would imagine that applies also to Continental Del Rio and its top executives. Right?"

Paul, Anne and Douglas nodded, curious.

"We want you to increase your personal security to a much higher level," Paige said. "And we need to ask you to take charge of the same for Mark's parents and for my parents? As you know, my folks winter in Costa Rica. Mark will explain."

"Once word of my real work becomes known," Mark said, "the risk from both the mafia and those religious nutcases will increase sharply, potentially placing everyone in danger. And frankly, some of Continental's facilities, their interstate travel centers in particular, are vulnerable targets. I believe Continental now has the third largest network of highway travel centers in the country."

"That would be correct," Paul said.

Prescott Enterprises was a major shareholder in Continental, second only to Mark's parents.

"So, how do you want to do this?" he said.

"We need someone to oversee the executive security. We've hired Global to provide security personnel for this, including personal security for Paige's parents. We'll brief Paige's folks when we call them this evening. A team is on its way to Costa Rica as we speak. That leaves the two of you, as well as my parents and the two companies. Would you be willing to oversee the security requirements, Grandma and Grandpa?"

"Of course," they said together. "Consider it done," Paul added.

"But that's not all there is to this, is it?" the wily grey-haired entrepreneur said. "I get the feeling there's a lot more to this than you've told us, right? So, how about you fill your grandmother and me in on the rest?"

"I guess it'll be all right," Mark replied, glancing at Paige and his uncle. "It better be. Here goes.

"The FBI has reliable intelligence that we're on the verge of attacks across the country by those religious wing-nuts."

With reluctance, he described the FBI's urgent task of stopping Abdul Rhamir and his ISIS-trained religious fanatics.

"How could this happen?" Paul said, breaking the stunned silence. "I'm sorry but I have to ask . . . are you sure that your information is credible?"

"It's as good as we're going to get," Mark replied. "An undercover agent has managed to work his way into Rhamir's jihadists."

"Why haven't all these crazy people been arrested?" Anne asked. "Surely your agent has given you enough information to take action?"

"Yes and no," Mark replied. "Most of the information our agent provides is hearsay, legally. It helps guide our investigations but wouldn't qualify as evidence in court. Besides, it could tip off Rhamir and blow our agent's cover. We need him there for now.

"Oh, one other titbit," Mark added. "Those lunatics need a lot of money to finance what they're planning. That's how I came across them. They're targeting the mafia, hoping to get access to some drug money. As I mentioned, I was working undercover in a mafia family. In fact, the family still thinks I work for them."

Paul whistled softly under his breath while Anne raised her petite eyebrows.

"Anyway, just before we flew here, I got a call that Joe Caprionni, the godfather, wants to see me. It's probably about the attack on our house. I'll know more about that after we meet. I'm going to use the meeting to tell Mr. Caprionni what I really do."

"My God," Anne said. "Won't that be dangerous? And why the mafia? Why deal with those criminals?"

"I need them," Mark replied, offering nothing further. A plan was forming in his mind.

"I don't like this one bit," his grandmother added firmly. "Why don't you and Paige just drop all of this and concentrate on getting the children back. Then the four of you can get away . . . disappear for a while! We'll hide you where no one will ever find you for as long as it takes. Leave others in the FBI to search for those lunatics."

"That would be nice, Grandma," Mark said. "But it's not that easy. For one thing, I'm deputy leader of the FBI team searching for those extremists. Yes, our top priority is getting the children back safely. For the moment we have to leave that with the experts. Meanwhile, I'm going to need Prescott Enterprises and Continental Del Rio to help with a plan I'm working on. It's one of the reasons I'm here. Mr. Caprionni also figures in that plan.

"Here's what I have in mind."

Earlier, Mark told Warren about a decidedly unconventional plan taking shape in his mind, one he was hoping would appeal not only to the enlightened self-interest of those in the mafia he intended to approach, but also to their sense of honor.

Mark knew it was a gamble. But Warren had been intrigued. He'd authorized Mark to approach his grandparents about enlisting the massive resources of Prescott Enterprises and Continental Del Rio, with its vast coast-to-coast retail operations and employee network. Together they would form the core of a powerful alliance Mark thought would be quite unique. He was right, mostly.

Chapter 5

New York City

After a five-day visit with his grandparents, Mark and Paige flew back to New York with his grandfather. Mark's stress over the dinner with his parents had turned out to be a non-event. They had enjoyed a pleasant dinner alone just with Catherine, Mark's mom. His father's executive jet had been grounded in Wichita, KS after developing problems with its navigation system. Mark was not disappointed.

After landing at LaGuardia, Mark's grandfather Paul went straight to the house on Candlewood Lake to oversee repair work.

Warren had called Mark to a high-level meeting at FBI regional headquarters in New York. There would be senior representatives of key national security and intelligence agencies, civilian and military. Warren promised Mark to expand on the startling news he'd shared just prior to Mark's departure for Kansas City.

More than a dozen departments and agencies were represented at the meeting, including Homeland Security, National Security Agency, CIA, Defense Intelligence Agency, DEA, the FBI and the State Department's Coordinator for Counterterrorism.

"Most of you are aware," Warren told the gathering, "the FBI has assigned a special task force to track down a network of ISIS-trained terrorists here in America. We've managed to place an undercover agent close to that group. He tells us the ISIS network is commanded by a man called Abdul Rhamir.

"We have also learned this group is planning a series of attacks on major cities across the country. We are convinced these reports are accurate and that the attacks could be imminent. What we do not know at this time is how many attacks are being planned or where."

"Yeah, we've been briefed on this," interrupted Douglas Hernandez, a senior executive with the CIA. "Frankly, Warren, I think your evidence concerning these so-called terrorists is awfully thin . . . would never stand up before a grand jury, much less in court."

"More recently," Warren said, ignoring the interruption, "we received confirmation from our undercover agent that Rhamir also has a team somewhere here in America assigned to detonate a small nuclear device, if there is such a thing. Yes, that is correct . . . a nuclear device.

"I can see from the surprise on some faces here that this comes as news to you. Well, we believe the nuclear attack could come as soon as the next few weeks. However, we've not learned yet where that might be or when. That's why you're here."

The room fell silent.

"Our agent overheard conversations indicating the device is a small compact version," Warren said. "Around two megatons. Small, yes, but it would wipe out the downtown core of any American city. And it would render a huge area radioactive and uninhabitable for decades. The device may be one of those reported missing when the old Soviet Union disintegrated. More than 100 of these so-called suitcase nuclear bombs disappeared. All of us know the CIA has learned that some are being sold on the black market."

"Listen Warren," said Arnold Tewkesbury, assistant deputy undersecretary for Homeland Security. "I respect what you and your folks are trying to do for America, but frankly we have received not one shred of acceptable evidence to corroborate what you're telling us. If this got out, there would be widespread panic. Besides, this is a matter of national security policy and that's our job. You're messing around with it. We can't have that!"

"Arnold, all of this surfaced in the course of our investigation," Warren said. "We've not gone out of our way on this. Can't you see? We've tapped into what could be an extremely vital intelligence bonanza, and we're offering it to you. In return, we need your support and cooperation."

"Let me be clear about this," Tewkesbury said. "I am telling you to stay out of this. After I leave here, I'm going to have a chat with the FBI director. You and your guys need to concentrate on tracking down those troublemakers you call jihadists. Leave this nuclear thing to us in Homeland Security. We're better equipped to deal with things like this. And besides, this gets into a matter of policy, like I've said."

He stood. It was the signal the meeting was over.

"Good God!" Mark exploded. His outburst stopped everyone, commanding their attention.

"What the hell is the matter with you people?" he said. "There is a serious and imminent threat to the lives of innocent Americans, possibly thousands maybe even millions. And it's also a serious threat to this country's economic wellbeing. And you cast legitimate intelligence aside like it's some minor inconvenience.

"Don't you get it? This is no time to be playing cover-your-ass politics or one-upmanship. Our task force has every right to expect support from all of you . . . your active assistance. That's why Warren invited you. Instead, here you are sitting on your thumbs, ready to shove your heads up where the sun doesn't shine. I'm appalled at what I've been hearing. You need to be ashamed of yourselves!"

"Listen here, young man!" Tewkesbury said. His voice was almost a shout as he said: "You're way out of line, and far out beyond your depth! What you observed here is a matter of national security policy. You would be well advised to stick with those operational matters within your limited scope of responsibility. Do *you* understand?"

"Never in my life," Mark exclaimed, "have I been witness to such abject stupidity . . . and dangerously abject stupidity at that!"

"Watch your mouth, young man!" Tewksbury shouted angrily, posturing like the top executive he wanted everyone to see. He turned and stalked out of the room.

Mark and Warren stayed behind after the others left.

"What a bunch of assholes!" Mark said.

"Easy now, Mark," Warren said. "I know how you feel, but it's very clear now that our task force is on its own, at least for now. Meanwhile, try to remember, they may be assholes but they happen to be assholes that're on our side."

They shared a chuckle, and then got back to work.

*

Candlewood Lake

In their short time away, repairs to Mark and Paige's house had advanced remarkably. Being from a rich and influential family helped. Having Mark's grandfather involved helped even more.

Work crews were toiling away in all parts of the house thanks to the resources and influence of Prescott Enterprises. The couple noticed the patio doors and the two-stories of great room windows had been replaced. A pile of new furniture matching exactly their 'old' furniture was still packaged from shipping and waiting in a corner of the spacious great room. One team of workers was finishing repairs to the bar counter, another was installing new mirrors and glass shelving behind the bar. A third crew was installing new cabinets in the kitchen. And a large clean-up crew was busy sweeping, vacuuming and dusting. Still others were working on outside repairs and on grounds clean-up.

Soon after arriving, Paige made it clear she was reluctant to spend the night. She was traumatized over the kidnapping of her children, by Anashi's murder, and by the attack on their home. In the end, she finally agreed to stay only because Mark's grandfather had asked her to. Despite his influence with the repairs, his prime focus had been on helping to recover the children. Paul insisted on staying in the house. He was certain that being on site would help Paige confront the heavy load of stress she was dealing with. Her professional training helped her see the merit of that, if somewhat reluctantly.

That evening, with the workers gone for the day and the bodyguards watching an NBA game on TV, Paul sat at the dining room table with Mark, Paige and Douglas to consider their next steps.

"I've learned a little bit about organized crime over the years," Paul said, "but I have no experience at all with ISIS, al-Qaeda or other terrorists . . . can't help you there. You know more about them than any of us, Mark. Is there anything else you can tell us about this group in New York or what they're up to?"

"Well, yes, Grandpa," Mark replied. "As far as we know, it began when ISIS got a few jihad fighters into America a few years ago. They were originally al-Qaeda and trained at a camp in North Waziristan, Pakistan. Some got into the country on student and visitor visas, others by simply flying here as tourists or on business and then disappearing.

"Their job is to recruit and train American-born young men to become jihadists. They've also sent a few hundred to fight with ISIS in Syria and Iraq. Those who've come back joined Rhamir's group.

"They've had the most success recruiting misfits and disillusioned offspring from low-income families. Many of those trained have been sent across the country to be ready when called upon. Evidently, that time has come."

"Why doesn't Homeland Security know about this?" Paul said.

"Oh, they do, and so do the others," Mark said. "It's a sore point for Warren and me and our task force, let me tell you. They're telling us we don't have enough evidence for them to act, so we can't get the resources. As one small example, thanks to the interference of Homeland Security, the FBI higher-ups won't provide our task force with enough money even to operate wiretaps, much less extensive surveillance. Warren's credibility is the only thing keeping them at bay. And he tells me many senior people now won't return his calls.

"Anyway, right now, we've got to focus on getting Edward and Caylyn back," Mark said.

Douglas briefed them on the FBI's plans being set in motion to protect Mark while he pretended to be a suicide bomber to recover the children.

Chapter 6

Caprionni Mansion, Staten Island

"Mark, Mark, Mark!"

Joe Caprionni began shouting at him as soon as he entered the old man's den. It caught Mark off guard. The godfather's tone was a mixture of extreme anger tempered with a hint of sadness.

"With respect, Godfather, may I ask what this is all about?" Mark said with enforced calm, struggling to focus, to think through his confusion and shock. Anger was the last thing he expected from Caprionni. The fury on the aged mafia don's face deepened the furrows more than usual.

"What am I to do with you?" he snarled, ignoring Mark. "I give you my trust, my respect. And you . . . you . . . this is how you honor that trust . . . how you show me respect? I treated you like a son, Trimonti. And this is how you repay me?"

They stood on opposite sides of an antique oak desk in the den of Caprionni's three-story red brick mansion on Staten Island. Mark had kept his commitment to meet after returning from Kansas City. He had never seen Caprionni so angry. He'd expected a warm greeting. At least that's what Vinny had told him. This reaction was disturbing. Mark was already on emotional overload, grieving Anashi's death and agonizing over Edward and Caylyn's safety.

Another surprise was meeting with Caprionni one-on-one. It had never happened. Other members of the mafia family had always been there, at the very least Vinny, who insisted on being at every meeting. Not this time.

"Did I do something wrong?" Mark insisted.

"Do not insult me, Trimonti!" Caprionni shouted back. "Vincenza told me all about what you've been doing behind my back . . . with the Maniero's. Don't you lie to me! I give you a very important job for the family and you betray me! You betray me, Trimonti! How could you? Vincenza told me you've been making deals with the Maniero's. You have no respect. I am saddened. I am disappointed in you. Now get out! I should not be wasting my time on you. Get out!"

"That's not true!" Mark protested as forcefully as he dared. "I have done nothing of the kind, Godfather. What you have heard are lies! Pure lies! You must believe me."

"I said, get out!" the elder Caprionni shouted, almost screaming. His steel-grey eyes held a fury that sent chills through combat-hardened Mark's psyche. The tall and distinguished-looking mob boss stood abruptly from his big desk, turned his back on Mark, and walked briskly out through the back door of the den.

Mark stood. He was confused and frightened. This was the last thing he needed. And he'd been denied being able to tell Caprionni what was really happening.

He was relieved that he'd got Paige moved in with his Uncle Doug and Aunt Jennifer at their well-guarded home in Danbury, CT, before coming to meet Caprionni. She'd agreed to spend last night at Candlewood Lake, but Mark could see the strain had taken a heavy toll. They agreed both of them would rest better at his aunt and uncle's home.

So this is how Vinny plans to get even, Mark thought. *What lousy damned timing. Just because I provoked that little shit a couple of times. Well, he deserved it, the prick. But, Christ, this could get me killed!*

He would come close to being right.

As Mark walked out of the den, two of Caprionni's armed soldiers converged. Their faces showed no emotion. Their hands were tucked inside their jackets.

"You need to come with us, Mr. Mark," said Arnie Ravelo, nodding toward the back door of the house. "Please keep your hands where we can see them."

Arnie was a trusted 'made man', one of Caprionni's top lieutenants. He'd always treated Mark with respect, even deference, calling him Mr. Mark, never just Mark or Mr. Trimonti.

But today, Arnie apparently had a different role: enforcer. It was an unwelcome change in their relationship, evidently for both. The mafia lieutenant clearly was in charge, reluctantly. He gestured for Mark to raise his arms. He patted Mark down to be sure he wasn't armed. Arnie found Mark's iPhone, shrugged and returned it to the shirt pocket where Mark had put it before meeting Caprionni. Arnie forgot, or deliberately did not check Mark for an ankle holster.

Mark had told his bodyguards to wait in the FBI office. He didn't want to explain them to Caprionni, just yet. He'd always been confident and self-reliant, but now he was feeling vulnerable.

The other mafia soldier was Vito Silva. Mark hardly knew him. Vito had the classic look of someone who'd grown up on the streets of a tough neighborhood. The short, overweight Vito led them outside to a car parked in the driveway beside the house, screened by dense bushes. Another Caprionni soldier was waiting behind the steering wheel. He didn't recognize him.

Mark realized the .22 caliber backup weapon in his ankle holster would be no match for three veteran mafia enforcers, all experienced shooters packing .357 Magnums or the like. Arnie opened the left rear door and motioned Mark to get in. As he sat down, Arnie followed. Vito got in the other side, squashing him in the middle between the two big burly men.

This is not promising! Mark told himself, making a weak solo attempt at dark humor.

The car started down the driveway when Vinny suddenly appeared in front.

The driver hit the brakes. "Damn that kid!" he said. He cursed again quietly under his breath.

At first, Mark hoped that Vinny's father might have had a change of heart. Instead, Vinny slipped into the front passenger seat. He turned and grinned menacingly. Mark understood. Vinny didn't want to miss the fun . . . watching him being murdered.

As the car turned onto the street, Mark turned his head to Arnie and motioned he needed to blow his nose. Arnie nodded. He reached into his shirt pocket.

This was going to be a long shot. Mark hoped that he remembered the location of the app for the emergency feature. He swiped it 'on', grateful he'd muted it before meeting with Caprionni. Using his index finger, he quickly pushed the 911 app. At the same time, he willed his other fingers to extract his handkerchief. He blew his nose unnecessarily and returned the handkerchief and the phone.

"Arnie, did Mr. Caprionni order you to 'whack ' me?" Mark asked. The question was intended as a distraction. "Or was it Vinny here?"

"Mr. Mark," Arnie replied respectfully in his thick Sicilian accent, his eyes focused out the side window. Mark caught a look of sadness on his face. "Please, this is not a good question to ask."

"Shut up Arnie!" Vinny ordered over his shoulder from the front seat. Mark could feel Arnie's arm and leg stiffen at Vinny's order. Arnie disliked Vinny even more than he did.

Mark knew his chances of surviving this day were not good.

"We're going down to the warehouse, right?" Mark said, turning his head and looking directly at Arnie, hoping his mobile was transmitting. The Mafioso kept looking intently out the window, saying nothing. His ruddy face betrayed sorrow and his brown eyes a trace of anger.

The warehouse owned by Caprionni was on the Hudson River waterfront. Mark knew that's where bodies were dropped through a trapdoor. They landed in a waiting speedboat equipped with an oversized engine box. The bodies would be taken out to sea. Cement blocks chained to the legs made sure the bodies were never seen again. Mark had been forced to witness the execution of a mafia soldier from a Miami crime family trying to push its way into New York. He'd watched as the man was shot twice behind the ear and his body dumped through the trapdoor. Mark didn't relish the prospect of the same fate.

"Yeah, Mr. Mark," Arnie finally said heavily, ignoring Vinny's order. "You could say we're gonna take a little ride that way."

"Arnie!" Vinny shouted. "I told you to shut the fuck up!"

Mark knew the Caprionni mansion was under visual surveillance by the task force. His backup hope was that the team, located in a rented house on a hill overlooking the property, would see their car leaving and shadow them. He wasn't sure. Budget cuts had made surveillance erratic.

The long black Lincoln Town Car arrived at the docks and turned right, down a wide aging wharf. A huge warehouse door facing the river was open. The car slowed, and turned into the warehouse. It stopped. The driver got out. He walked back and pushed a button to close the big door. Then he drove the car across the vast empty warehouse to within a few feet of where Mark remembered the trapdoor was located.

Mark watched as the driver got out again. He stepped back from the car, pulling a gun from a shoulder holster. Vito opened the rear door on the right side. He got out, opened the trunk and pulled out an Uzi. He stepped back from the car, standing guard.

Yup! Mark thought. *These guys mean business. Awe, shit!*

Memories of Paige and the kids raced through his mind along with sadness and regrets for all of the experiences that now they were going to miss together.

Vinny got out of the front passenger side. He pulled his handgun and walked around the rear of the car to Arnie's side.

That little prick wants a good view seeing me murdered, Mark thought grimly.

Then Arnie got out. He waved his gun, motioning Mark to get out. Arnie again avoided eye contact.

Mark stepped from the car and pretended to stumble forwards. He slipped the gun from his ankle holster then lunged upward and sideways, grabbing Vinny from behind. Mark held Vinny around the neck in a one-arm chokehold, slamming his gun down on Vinny's arm. Vinny's gun hit the cement floor and spun under the car. The driver swung around, aiming his gun toward them. Mark fired twice, opening two holes in the white turtleneck jersey covering his chest. The driver went down. Arnie swung his gun toward Mark. Vinny and the car were partly shielding him from Vito's Uzi.

"Hold it! I don't want to shoot you, Arnie!" Mark ordered firmly. His gun was pointed directly at Arnie's forehead, less than six feet away. "You know I won't miss, my friend. Please drop your gun right now!"

Arnie's gun hit the cement floor just as Mark heard a short burst from the Uzi. He felt a bullet graze his right shoulder. Mark spun his human shield around at the same time as he heard multiple rifle shots ring out. Vito's face flashed a surprised look, and then pain as his body jumped back and forth, almost dancing. Bullets from automatic weapons were riddling his body from multiple hidden directions, throwing him side to side. The Uzi fell from Vito's limp hands. He stumbled backwards and then crumpled heavily in a heap.

It was over.

Before Mark could react, Arnie stepped forward quickly and landed his huge fist into Vinny's midsection. Vinny went down heavily on all four.

"Jeez," Vinny said, gasping for air. "What the fuck was that all about?"

Arnie stepped back then swung a hard kick into Vinny's ribs, sending him writhing on the floor in pain.

Vinny slowly pulled himself to one knee. Mark and Arnie exchanged faint smiles. Vinny was whimpering and shaking like a baby as members of the FBI task force and the NYPD ran over. They checked on Vito and the driver. Both were dead. They retrieved their weapons.

Mark turned Vinny over to members of the SWAT team. Arnie and Vinny were spread-eagled and frisked, then handcuffed. Mark could see from behind that Vinny had wet his pants. It amused him that the godfather's useless son wore the new $4,500 hand-stitched Caraceni silk suit he'd bragged about to Mark just over a week earlier.

"Thank you, thank you," Mark said to Warren. "Boy, I sure am glad you got my message."

Mark didn't know the task force had put other projects on hold so they could provide surveillance 24/7 on the Caprionni mansion. Warren and the others were not as trusting of Caprionni as Mark had been.

"Oh, we've been monitoring your phone conversations, including your call a few minutes ago," Warren said. "While you and Arnie were talking in the car, the task force and the NYPD SWAT team were en route to the warehouse. Luckily, we arrived before you, in time to set up video surveillance. Caught the whole thing on video.

"We've more than enough to prosecute this bunch. Anyway, it looks like you damned near had this under control all by yourself, hotshot. Oh, and by the way, congratulations!"

"Thank you," Mark said. "I got lucky this time, thanks to you."

"No, not this," Warren laughed, looking around. "For the last few months you've been acting as my deputy commander, unofficially. Well, the appointment's official now."

"Well, I'll be darned!" Mark said.

"Hey, those things happen to rising stars," Warren chuckled. "I've seen what you can do. And this organization desperately needs people with brains and guts and principles, just like you. So, get used to it. My boss stuck his neck out and approved your appointment. We're to phone him as soon as we get back to the office."

"Speaking about phone calls," Mark said. "I've got to make a call right away. Give me a minute, okay?"

Warren nodded.

Mark speed dialed Joe Caprionni's direct line.

"Yeah? What's this? That you, Trimonti?"

"Yes it is, Mr. Caprionni," Mark said.

"What the hell's goin' on?" Caprionni demanded. "You still with us? Just whad'ya think you're doin'?"

Caprionni had seen Mark's name on his phone's Caller ID.

"I'm holding Vinny and Arnie," Mark said firmly. His voice was laden with menace. "Vito and the other guy, the driver . . . they're both dead. You and me, Caprionni, we're gonna talk! And that'll be right away, or I'm gonna shoot Vinny in the head! Do you hear me?"

Mark was certain Caprionni could hear Vinny whimpering in the background. The elder Caprionni was silent. He feared for his son, and was taken aback by Mark's disrespectful manner. Nobody talked to the godfather like that and got away with it. But his only son, he and his wife's only child, was being held and threatened with death. He didn't want to explain to his strong-willed Sicilian-American wife why or how their son had been killed. He decided to listen, to find out what Mark was up to and to find a way to get Vincenza back. Then he would deal with Mark.

"Yeah, yeah, Trimonti, okay," Caprionni replied. "So how ya wanna to do this?"

"I'm coming to your home, Caprionni," Mark said bluntly. "Tell your soldiers I'm coming in. Vinny and Arnie will be staying with my friends until after we talk. When I leave safely, Vinny and Arnie get to come home. You got that? If something happens to me, they die. Is that clear? Or maybe they'll special deliver Vinny's head to your wife. Understood?"

"You would do such a thing, Trimonti?" the mafia boss asked, surprised and angry. "Who do you think you are? Who are these friends you speak about? The Maniero's, right? Yeah, see, I was right about you. You disappoint me, you traitor! You're a nothing . . . a lowlife! I shoulda whacked you weeks ago."

"Now you listen to me, Caprionni!" Mark shouted back sharply. "You're dead wrong! Do you hear me? Dead wrong! You don't trust the Maniero's . . . I don't trust them. We are going to talk about this when I get there. And this time, you're gonna damned well listen to me!"

"Yeah, yeah," Caprionni said, furious and exasperated. "So when you wanna meet?" His mind was on full alert now, plotting to get his son back . . . and to get revenge.

"In 90 minutes. I will be at your home in 90 minutes!" he replied. Mark pronounced the words distinctly and forcefully. He hung up on the godfather.

Chapter 7

East Harlem, New York City

"Today is a special occasion," said Abdul Rhamir, rising to his full six-foot height. "Today we congratulate our latest recruits to our holy war! Allah be praised."

"Allahu Akbar! (God is great)," the crowd responded, and then applauded.

Rhamir sat between his two deputies, Frank Larigani and Ali-Mumar Shahid. Arrayed in front of them was a group of jihadists, trainers, the newly trained and some recruits. They were in a back room of a mosque where Rhamir was a part time Imam. It was six blocks from the rent-controlled high-rise apartment in Harlem that Rhamir shared with his elderly mother. Gatherings like this were rare. Normally, to avoid attracting attention they met only in pairs and small groups, and in scattered locations.

"We owe much to our Islamic State friends who provided our fighters with priceless training in combat to share with you who have joined us. We will express our gratitude to them by being hugely successful in our holy war against the American infidels!"

"Allahu Akbar!" the crowd shouted.

"Allahu Akbar!" he replied.

"Some of you," Rhamir continued, "will join our headquarters to prepare our first offensives. Others will become trainers at a camp we will be opening soon. The rest of you will join cells across the country to help recruit and train more jihadists!"

"Allahu Akbar!" they said enthusiastically.

"Allahu Akbar!" he replied.

He did not tell the group that among them was a secret team of fighters trained to detonate a nuclear device. It was to be smuggled into America from North Korea in the coming weeks.

"We can be proud of the progress we have made," Rhamir said. "It is less than six months since we received orders from ISIS to 'go live'. We are busy building our network of sleeper cells across America. With your help we will prepare them to fight in the coming jihad and to take control of many associations and agencies across this country. This will prepare the way for our new Islamic State of America!"

The group applauded wildly.

Rhamir was exaggerating what was in motion, in order to whip up enthusiasm. He understood that in the aftermath of the nuclear explosion nothing else would matter to the media or the authorities for weeks. It would camouflage the takeovers of agencies and associations he was planning.

Today, his task was to build the morale of the 24 fighters and recruits crowded into a semi-circle on the floor in the small, sparsely furnished meeting room and to welcome the additional 15 new jihadists back from fighting with ISIS.

"I want to congratulate our fighters," Rhamir said. "And I want to welcome you home. I know your arduous journey took many weeks. It was necessary to stagger your journeys among ports of entry and routes to avoid raising suspicions. Today, we will share with you more details of the attacks we are planning."

Rhamir had hoped for more fighters. But the 39 he now had, himself included, would have to do, along with the still untrained recruits here and the ones being identified across the country. He had picked the best of his experienced jihadists to become trainers at the new camp he had established near Chapman, NY.

The group buzzed with excitement for what they imagined lay ahead.

"Allahu Akbar!" the powerfully built Rhamir shouted, his dark brown eyes sparkling with excitement. Rhamir's hawk-like face created a well-deserved sinister appearance.

"Allahu Akbar!" came back the boisterous response from his expanded team of fighters.

"Those of you who have been trained, are now soldiers of Islam!" Rhamir continued. "Remember always, you are soldiers of Allah . . . jihadists who will join in our great holy war against the imperialistic Americans!"

Thirty-eight other voices rose in a united roar of approval.

"Today," Rhamir continued, "Today, right here, you become fighters in a new army, a great army. We call it, The Islamic Army of America!"

Another roar went up from his followers.

"Today we officially declare war on the infidels!" he shouted. "Today we begin to plan our holy war in detail.

"We will test new ideas and new techniques . . . we have some wonderful new assault systems to test out!"

"Our first three attacks will be with bombs . . . car bombs . . . truck bombs, and some completely new concepts: parcel bombs, aerial bombs and briefcase bombs. The new ones are clever, wonderful ideas, but they must be tested for future phases of our glorious war. The bombs are easy to make and will use a military-grade explosive, PETN. We will show you how.

"The parcel bomb is very clever," Rhamir continued. "We will use it to attack post offices and other government offices across America. Here's how it works. We pack a box with two pounds of PETN, a detonator and a modified cell phone. We put an address label and a return address on it. And then we write, 'Return to Sender' on it, with an arrow to a phony return address. One of our fighters leaves the parcel on the hood of a car as if forgotten, or beside an outside mailbox. The parcel will be too big to go into a street mailbox.

"An infidel Good Samaritan will see it and take it inside for us. Our fighter will be in position a few blocks away, and detonate the bomb by dialing the cell phone wired to the charge. We will test this system on a smaller post office first. A bomb like that should be able to level a five-story office building. During our glorious war, we will use it to kill many, many more infidels in dozens of post offices and other places all across America!

"It will be glorious!"

Rhamir's team applauded vigorously. They laughed and talked excitedly about this clever way of creating havoc in America's well-ordered way of life. It would kill hundreds and terrorize millions!

"The second delivery system is just as exciting but it must also be tested," Rhamir said. "Even a small amount of PETN will deliver all the explosive capacity we need to create disaster and widespread panic at many sites. We must give thanks to Allah and to our brave fellow jihadist here, Alfred Naughton, who Allah has inspired and brought to our great holy war. Alfred will tell you more about his glorious invention."

Alfred stood.

"The beauty of this weapon is that we have control until the last second," Naughton began. His ebony skin, round glasses framed in white, and geeky appearance caused muffled snickers among the crowd.

"We pack half a pound of PETN into a big radio controlled model airplane. We attach an impact detonator to the front of the explosive. No one will suspect model aircraft hobbyists are jihadist fighters. It will get us very close to our targets. By the way, that much PETN will seriously damage a walk-up apartment building."

The jihadists grew silent with respect for Naughton's ingenuity. He continued:

"Teams of our brave fighters will attack targets across America. I am very proud that Rhamir has decided to include this technique among his attack plans. The results will be magnificent! We can also attack domestic water supply reservoirs. We simply pack concentrated toxins as we do PETN for the other attacks. But for these we include just a few ounces of PETN, enough to spread the poison widely in the reservoirs."

As Naughton was speaking, Rhamir realized to his dismay he should have thought about using the model aircraft bomb to attack Mark Trimonti's house. Naughton's invention got him thinking.

"Why not use drones?" said a voice from among the jihadists.

"Good question," Naughton said. "It is true that model drones are cheap now, readily available and easy to use. However, we will be employing impact detonators. I have experimented with both. I feel the large type of model airplane I have in mind will provide more reliable detonation and will serve our needs much better."

When Naughton was finished, Rhamir described the briefcase bombs. He said large briefcases full of PETN would be fitted with spring-loaded detonators. The bombs would arm themselves when they were set down on their spines. The explosives would be triggered when the briefcases were lifted or knocked over. An explosion of that much PETN placed strategically in a lower floor could seriously damage, even topple a high-rise office building.

Rhamir then described opportunities for their 'army's' very first suicide bombers to become martyrs.

"We all must remember," he said, "the Quran promises all martyrs eternity in Paradise and the favors of 72 virgins."

He was under pressure from Islamic State to find and train suicide bombers. That's why he'd kidnapped Mark Trimonti's kids. Trimonti would blow himself up while trying to recover them safely, setting an example to encourage other fighters. Mark didn't know Rhamir planned to kill the children and throw their bodies in a dumpster after Trimonti exploded the car bomb. He was keeping the kids alive for a last minute phone call. They would speak to Mark and Paige ahead of time, giving him instructions where to find them. It would be a lie. An ambush would be waiting, and the children killed.

Rhamir's fighters would never know their first suicide bomber was an infidel. He relished the irony. Meanwhile, his aging mother was guarding the two Trimonti 'brats' in the back bedroom of their rent-controlled apartment in Harlem.

In addition to the first attacks, Rhamir had compiled a list of a dozen other high priority targets for attack, known only to him, to be hit after the first four. He hadn't decided when. At the top of his list was New York City. He had two targets in mind. Lincoln Center would be attacked during a major event. He favored attacking Times Square with the nuclear bomb on New Year's Eve when a million people would be gathered to celebrate. But there still was no word yet from ISIS on how or when the nuclear device would arrive. He was growing impatient.

Rhamir had made a mental list of other intended targets. Within months of the first four, they would proceed to attack other cities. These would begin the all-out holy war he craved against America.

Chapter 8

Rhamir's Apartment, East Harlem

"I want my Mommy," four-year-old Caylyn Tremblay told her big brother, Edward. He was a mature 6½. "I want my Mommy," she repeated. Big tears rolled down the perfect skin of her tiny cheeks.

"I know, Caylyn," Edward said, determined to be strong and trying again to comfort his little sister. "I want Mom and Dad, too. I'm sure they'll be here soon."

Consoling his little sister had become a full time job for Edward. Looking after her was helping him cope. Caylyn's crying spells had repeated many times in the five days since they'd been kidnapped.

The two children were in the back bedroom of Abdul Rhamir's shabby two-bedroom apartment in Harlem. Edward understood they had been kidnapped. He sensed what that meant. Caylyn was confused. She just wanted her mother, Paige.

Edward didn't tell his little sister, but he sensed they could be in danger of being killed if things went wrong.

Meanwhile, their only distractions were a television set turned on constantly during the day, and an assortment of dog-eared books and magazines. Most contained strange writing and illustrations that didn't look like anything they had at home.

Luckily, there was a stack of old National Geographic magazines. Edward tried to keep Caylyn busy explaining the colorful pictures, when they weren't watching kids' shows on TV. Regardless, he still had trouble occupying his blond-haired little sister, her cute pigtails in disarray despite the occasional kindly attention from the old woman who stayed with them. Edward understood she was there to guard them, and that she was not happy about it.

"When're Mommy and Daddy coming to get us?" Caylyn kept asking Edward through tears, time after time. "Where's Anashi?"

"I don't know," Edward would reply each time as calmly as he could manage. They hadn't seen their nanny since a group of rough-looking men grabbed them in their driveway from Anashi's car.

Most of the time, the old woman sat in one corner of the room by the window. She was dressed mostly in black, a scarf over her head. She spent most of the day rocking in her chair and knitting. When she spoke to them, which wasn't often, it was in a kind manner. The woman used words Edward and Caylyn didn't understand. She sat near the only window; they weren't to go near it. An old-fashioned blind was pulled down.

Six-year-old Edward Tremblay was tall and mature for his age. His teachers were convinced their unusually bright and observant student was gifted. And he had an insatiable curiosity. It would be a good thing for him and his little sister.

While being held captive, a lack of things to do gave Edward an abundance of time to observe. From the first day, he'd noticed that a tall heavy dark-skinned man that others called Abdul Rhamir was in charge. He lived there with the old woman.

Other people came and went from time to time. Occasionally there were meetings in the living room, sometimes with just a few people and once with a large number. The big meeting had been noisy. He and Caylyn were ordered to stay in the bedroom with the old woman. Once a lady had a sleepover with the man called Rhamir, but Edward knew she didn't live there.

Another evening, Rhamir left with some visitors and was still gone the next morning. They'd brought along a young man named Farouk, who they left behind as a guard. Edward also noticed the old woman stayed awake all day but often yawned a lot and looked tired by afternoon. At night, she slept soundly on a cot in their room, snoring softly. She didn't wake one time when Edward stumbled over his shoes on the way to the bathroom, falling flat on the floor. She stirred, but didn't wake.

Edward had an idea.

A few nights later, around 8 p.m., Rhamir went out with two men who'd come for supper. The young man called Farouk stayed behind. A plan was forming in Edward's fertile young mind. But he hadn't yet figured out what to do about Farouk. So, after Caylyn and the old woman fell asleep, Edward kept peeking out of the bedroom door.

Farouk was sitting on a reclining chair in the living room watching television. His back was to Edward, smoking cigarettes and drinking coffee. Edward watched as Farouk crushed an empty cigarette package and threw it in a corner. The slim, ruddy skinned youth muttered something in a language Edward didn't understand. The tone sounded like a curse. Farouk stood up. Edward hastily closed the bedroom door quietly. He listened carefully and then heard the front door close. He slipped out of their room and carefully checked the apartment. No one else was there.

Edward quickly went back to their room and over to Caylyn's bed. Putting a hand lightly over her mouth, he woke her gently.

"We're getting away from here," he whispered. Then he helped her dress and put on her coat. "We're going to go look for Mom and Dad." Caylyn nodded happily, anticipating that soon she would see her mommy.

The two children glanced at the old woman sound asleep, then tiptoed quietly to the front door. Edward listened, and then cautiously opened it. He stuck out his head, looking both ways. The dimly lit hallway was filled with cooking odors and trash, but no one. He grabbed Caylyn's hand and closed the door quietly.

"We're gonna use the stairs," he whispered. Edward knew he couldn't risk the elevator. The doors could open with Farouk standing right there, waiting. They'd be trapped.

As quietly as he could manage, Edward closed the steel fire door behind them. They ran down three flights of stairs in their socks. Edward and Caylyn stopped at the bottom to put on their shoes, then slipped out into the alley.

"Okay," Edward said. "Here, hold my hand. This will take us to a street. Maybe we can find someone to help us, maybe even a policeman."

They walked half a block to where the alley reached the street. Just as they stepped out onto the sidewalk, they heard a loud voice.

"Hey! Where the hell do you think you're going? Come back here you little shits!"

It was Farouk!

"Quick Caylyn! Run!" Edward said, grabbing his little sister's hand. They turned and ran back down to the end of the alley, across another street and around a corner, pausing to catch their breath behind a row of stinking dumpsters.

"There," Edward said. "Squeeze through that fence. Quickly! That man is too big. He won't get through."

It was a narrow opening between an eight-foot chain link fence and a dirty brown brick building. Caylyn slipped through the opening easily. Edward was barely able to squeeze through.

Farouk turned the corner just in time to catch a glimpse of them at the end of the alley.

"Stop! Damn you!" Farouk shouted. As he ran after them, he fired a silenced. 38-caliber Bersa Thunder at Edward. He missed. Farouk fired three more shots, missing. By the time Farouk got to the fence, he couldn't see the kids. He tried and failed to squeeze through the opening. It took time to climb the fence and get to the street. By then, the kids were nowhere in sight. He continued a frantic search farther and farther from the apartment. Meanwhile, all he could think of was the anger that he surely would face from Rhamir.

Edward and Caylyn had run as fast as they could.

"C'mon Caylyn," Edward said, urging her on. "We can't slow down now. Hurry, Caylyn!"

They turned corners, doubled back, ran again and slipped through more narrow openings in fences. What they didn't realize is their frantic running had taken them in a big circle route back to within two blocks of the apartment where they'd been held.

Chapter 9

Caprionni Mansion, Staten Island

Mark stopped his car on the wide curved cement driveway of Caprionni's red brick mansion on Staten Island. Two mafia soldiers, Uzi's pointing up, met him in the covered entryway. The soldiers escorted him through the front door.

"Aren't you going to frisk me?" Mark asked, thinking about a precaution he'd taken.

"No," one mumbled. "Mr. Caprionni's orders."

Mark relaxed as they crossed the two-story foyer clad in almond-colored marble. The three walked down a picture-lined hall to the godfather's den. Framed photographs of Joe Caprionni, arm-in-arm with celebrities and politicians lined both sides of the 'rogues gallery' as Mark thought of it. The Mafioso in front knocked on the door. Mark heard a muffled "Come". The thug opened the door and stepped aside. Mark went in. He heard the door close firmly behind him.

"Well?" Caprionni said. "Get on with it!"

Caprionni was behind his large desk, rolling a Cuban cigar with the fingers of his left hand, ready to light it with a wood match in his right hand. Mark crossed the room and sat facing the mafia boss across the desk. He knew Caprionni kept a .32 caliber handgun in the drawer in front of him. The drawer was closed. Mark hoped the godfather was too concerned about his son to do anything rash. He took comfort from his own precaution: a loaded .22 caliber handgun in his ankle holster.

"We have much to get caught up on, Mr. Caprionni," Mark said, his voice firm but respectful.

"Yeah, yeah!" Caprionni said sharply, his voice rising. He threw the burning match into a crystal ashtray without lighting his cigar. "What do you think you're doing? You kidnap my son Vincenza and my man Arnie! And you are disrespectful to me on the phone. What am I to think? Just what the hell are you trying to pull off here, Trimonti?"

"Now just one minute!" Mark said. He raised his voice and spoke sharply. "You ordered your goons to kill me! Remember? They screwed up. Now, we have things to settle, and we're going to settle them right here, and right now!"

They stared menacingly at each other, and then accepted the other's resolve. Mark willed himself to calm down. He continued:

"First, Mr. Caprionni, let me apologize for my language and manner of speaking to you just now and on the phone," Mark said, willing himself to use a respectful tone. He didn't want to blow this . . . he had plans that needed Caprionni's cooperation. "And I regret kidnapping Vinny and Arnie. But it is for a very good reason – for you and for me. I will explain."

"What is this?" the mafia godfather interrupted. "You are one of my men but you don't call me godfather anymore?"

"With respect, you are mistaken this time," Mark replied. "As a matter of fact, I don't work for you.

And if I may say so, sir, I most certainly dislike the way you planned to terminate my employment."

The mafia godfather ignored Mark's dark humor. He waited for Mark to continue, still absently fingering the cigar in his left hand. With his right, he stroked a grey Clark Gable moustache, a throwback to the past.

"To be quite honest," Mark continued, "I never did work for you."

Caprionni opened his mouth to speak. Mark held up his hand.

"Hear me out. Regardless what you thought, and appearances, I never worked for you. The fact is I am an FBI special agent. Yes, that is true. I've been working undercover. My real name is Mark Tremblay."

Caprionni's body snapped back sharply in his chair, his eyes wide with shock and disbelief. The expensive Cuban cigar fell to the floor, forgotten.

"That's right,' Mark continued calmly. "I am assigned to an FBI anti-drug task force. My job was to infiltrate your family and to gather information the FBI and DEA can use to arrest all of you and take down your organization. We have enough right now to do just that."

While Mark was speaking, the mafia godfather stared at him, his mouth opening and closing in disbelief. The expressions on his face shifted between anger, surprise, bewilderment, and back to anger. Mark kept a close watch in case Caprionni's hands moved toward his desk drawer.

"I should whack you right here, right now!" Caprionni shouted, slamming his hand flat on the desk. "Who the hell do you think you are, coming in here and spying on us?"

The slap on the desk sounded like a gunshot. A split-second later Mark heard the door open behind him. He wasn't surprised. He quietly crossed his left leg on his right knee, placing his right hand on his ankle next to the .22-caliber Beretta concealed beneath his pant leg.

"You okay, Mr. Caprionni?" a gruff, worried voice asked.

"Yeah, yeah," the mafia chief growled, waving his right hand. "It's all right. You can go! Shut the door!"

Turning to Mark, he said, "Okay, okay! Where do we go from here? So, you've arrested my son and Arnie! Are you going to hold them? Where are they? How do I get my son back? When are you going to arrest all of us?"

"Hold on, sir. Hear me out," Mark said, holding up his hand again. "What I'm about to tell you will answer most of your questions.

"First of all, I should tell you we'd prefer to avoid arrests and grand juries if possible, at least for now. They will create a media circus that both we, and you I'm sure, want to avoid. You'll understand in a minute, there's a very good reason.

"I've been authorized to offer you a deal. I must tell you it's a take-it-or-leave-it deal. There will be no negotiating."

"What are you talking about?" Caprionni growled impatiently. "What kind of a deal? Are you telling me the FBI is offering a deal to me, for Christ's sake? How come they're willing to make a deal? What's goin' on, kid? What the hell are they up to?"

Mark had searched records for previous collaborations between law enforcement and organized crime. He found only one. He'd learned a piece of history about the mafia he wondered whether even Caprionni knew about. In April 1961, a Chicago mafia family with lucrative illegal interests in Havana was invited by the CIA to help with the infamous Bay of Pigs invasion of Cuba. That precedent was enough for Warren; he authorized Mark to make Caprionni an unusual proposition. It was one that both hoped would appeal to Caprionni's sense of honor and win the support of senior FBI authorities.

"First, Mr. Caprionni, you should know I have not been trying to make any deals whatsoever with the Maniero family."

Mark waited for his firm emphasis on "not" to register.

Caprionni stared back stone faced, not sure whether to believe him. Caprionni's information had come from his own son, Vincenza.

"Why the hell would I?" Mark said. "I know a bunch of goons made the hit on my home. I'm damned sure the Maniero's had something to do with that. They were trying to kill my wife and I.

"Tell me, why would they do that if I was cozying up with them? And those thugs or someone working with them kidnapped our two children and savagely murdered their nanny, just before I went out of town. That's the other reason I'm here . . . the main reason, I guess. This is going to sound strange, but I'm here to ask for your help. I need your organization's network on the street to help find our two children and get them back safely."

Caprionni sat quietly, contemplating what he'd just heard.

"I'll come back to the children in a moment, Mr. Caprionni," Mark continued. "But first, I will take you into my trust. I'm about to share with you some highly secret information. It's about those who I think were involved in the hit. Our intelligence tells us the Maniero's hired the hitmen. But they probably don't know those hitmen were from a group of terrorists trained by ISIS in the Middle East, and are now located right here in New York."

"Are you serious?" Caprionni said, his eyes growing bigger. "Terrorists living right here under our noses, and we don't know about it?"

"Yeah," Mark said. "But what they're planning is what's got us worried. Let me back up a bit. Several months ago, just like you asked, Vinny and I put word out on the street that the Caprionni family was looking to expand its legitimate business interests. You were looking for investments. Right?"

Caprionni nodded with a mixture of curiosity and impatience.

"Well, we began contacting people and others approached us," Mark continued. "We checked them all out and I prepared a short list. I thought the list was going to you. But Vinny narrowed the list down to one. He insisted on doing this by himself ... said he was acting with your approval."

"First time I heard of it," Caprionni said. "I was wondering what was taking you two so long."

"At first," Mark continued, "Everything seemed on the up and up. But after a few meetings, it was obvious these people had no legitimate businesses to sell. I became suspicious their sights were set on your drug business. I tried to tell Vinny but he wouldn't listen. I threatened to go to you on my own unless he discussed it with you.

"Anyway, long story short, those lunatics wanted me to spy on you and to help them take over your drug operations. I refused. It turns out they were from that terrorist cell I told you about.

"Yes, that's right," Mark said, seeing the surprise in Caprionni's eyes.

"I think they've either teamed up with the Maniero's or are just using them. I'm not sure which. The FBI is convinced both the Maniero's and the terrorists want your drug operation.

"I don't have to tell you that if the Maniero's had control of your large drug business, and with their share of the market, they would control most of the drug business in New York and the east coast. On the other hand, the terrorists desperately need drug money to finance attacks they are planning on America."

"What the hell's going on?" Caprionni said, sitting upright. It was the first time Mark had seen the mafia don looking confused and even apprehensive.

Then remembering his deeply imbedded manners, Caprionni abruptly switched gears and said:

"I'm sorry about your children," he said. His tone was subdued and earnest. "And I am very sorry about the loss of your children's nanny. Of course, we will put the word on the street to find the children. This is a terrible thing these animals have done to your family."

Then Caprionni's demeanor abruptly changed again. It was obvious another thought had come to him. His eyes became bright with anger . . . and much harder:

"How come you know all of this? Where did you get that information? Is it any good? Maybe you just made it all up. Huh? Maybe you got it from the Maniero's! Maybe you're just trying to bullshit me . . . to get me to do things I don't want to do?"

Caprionni was on a rant.

"All right!" Mark shouted back, losing his patience, his anger returning. "What's it going to take for you to believe me . . . for you to believe that when I say something I mean it? Maybe you need some proof that I'm holding Vinny and Arnie. Will that do it? Will that prove to you I mean what I say?

"I'll get you proof, goddamnit! One call and I'll have a finger, or maybe one of Vinny's ears, delivered right here to you . . . or maybe delivered to his mother. Yeah, to his mother! One call!"

Caprionni glared at him, bluntly dismissive, obviously skeptical.

"You . . . you're not up to doing such things," the mafia don shot back, his tone derisive.

Mark pulled out his iPhone and dialed his disconnected home phone at Candlewood Lake. A recorded male voice came on the line. It said the line was no longer in service. But all that Caprionni could hear was the indistinct sound of a male voice in the background.

"What is this, Trimonti . . . uh . . . Tremblay?" Caprionni asked. "What are you doing?"

"Yeah, this is Mark," he said, ignoring Caprionni, turning slightly away, beginning his bluff.

"Look, Mr. Caprionni needs proof we're holding Vinny. How about you cut off his little finger and send it over? Yeah, really, that's just what I said. Yeah, I mean it, seriously . . . cut the damned thing off and right away. Yes, I'm serious, for Christ sake! Do it! From his left hand. Bolt cutters will take it off easy, no problem! Stuff a gag in his mouth so the neighbors can't hear him scream. Yeah, yeah, do it . . . do it now, damn it!"

Mark paused as if listening to someone on the other end. He watched out of the corner of his eye as Caprionni's expressions changed from contempt to concern, and then to alarm.

"Let me speak with Vincenza!" Caprionni demanded. "Give me proof. I will speak with my son."

"No you won't!" Mark replied calmly. "That's not going to happen. Vinny will try to tell you where he is."

He held the phone to his chest, anger flashing in his eyes. Mark lifted the smartphone back to his ear, and pretended to answer someone on the other end of the phone.

"Yeah, yeah, okay," he said. "Fair enough. Okay, just take half the finger. Throw in that stupid pinky ring of his too. Yeah, for proof."

Mark laughed darkly.

"I don't give a fuck about that," Mark said. "Look, if the little shithead bleeds he bleeds. Just wrap the stub in some rags.

"Oh, and have the finger delivered to his mother. Address a package to her and send it by courier, right? Yeah, okay, get on with it! And send the pinky ring too. I'll stay here with the old man. I'll keep him in his den. Call me when the delivery's been made. Yeah, sure . . . I'll be waiting."

Mark knew he was taking a big gamble with his charade

"Jesus Christ, kid!" Caprionni shouted, jumping to his feet, almost screaming. "Stop! Stop! Don't do it! Don't do that, to my son . . . to my wife . . . to his mother! Please! Don't do it! Hold on! Let's talk."

"Just a minute," Mark said into the dead phone then held it back to his chest again.

He turned to the ashen-faced mafia boss.

"You say you need some proof . . . proof that when I say something I mean it. Right?" Mark said coolly. "Well, I'll have the proof within the hour."

"Never mind that," Caprionni said urgently, now contrite. "I believe you! I believe you, young man. Christ almighty, I believe you. Don't hurt my son. Not like that, for Christ's sake. Not like that! Promise me!"

"Okay," Mark said into the iPhone. "Listen, about the finger. Hold off . . . for now, anyway. Yeah, maybe there's a change of plans. Listen, I'll call you back if we need to go ahead. Yeah, that's right. Don't do anything until you hear from me. Okay?"

He hung up.

"Jeez," the mafia godfather said. "I thought I could be a hard ass. Christ almighty, Mark, you can be one miserable goddamned son of a bitch!"

"Thank you," Mark replied coldly, suppressing a smile.

"Is this . . . this thing you were going to do to Vincenza? Is it okay with the FBI?" Caprionni asked. "Do they approve of you doing such things like this? Do they approve of torture?"

"What they don't know, they don't know!" Mark said. "So what? You tell them, I'll deny it. Who're they going to believe, you or me? But never mind. You want to hear my proposal or not?"

"Maybe I can trust you, maybe I cannot" Caprionni replied. "We'll see. Just get on with it. Tell me about this deal you've cooked up. Then we will see."

"All right," Mark began. "I'm going to let you in on a few more things that maybe I shouldn't. But I'm going to trust you! Understand?"

Caprionni sat impassively, looking Mark straight in the eye. He couldn't tell whether the old man was fuming mad or just waiting to listen. He decided to take a chance.

"What I've told you comes from undercover surveillance of the Maniero family. Yeah, we have someone working undercover there too, just like I was here." Mark watched Caprionni try to stifle a flinch, and fail.

"I tell you this because I know you don't trust the Maniero's anymore than I do. So, you're not going to tell them. Our undercover guy confirmed the Maniero's hired three thugs to hit my home. Two spoke with slight Middle Eastern accents. No mystery who they are.

"And you'd better understand something else. Although my wife and I were targeted the other day, we're just a small piece of what they're up to. I have all the proof I need that your family is a prime target, too. Like I said, they want the money from your drug business and probably others, to finance their plans. They don't care about anyone who gets in their way."

Until he was confident about Caprionni's support and cooperation, Mark decided not to tell the mafia don about another undercover agent . . . one who'd recently made his way into the terrorists' headquarters cell.

"No damned way," Caprionni said, sitting back in his luxurious high back chair. "There's no way that scum is getting their hands on my drug business! No damned way! They had better not even try. Not even when we're ready to go fully legitimate. I'm gonna shut it down. Nobody gets it! Period! Not them . . . not anybody!

"So what about this deal of yours, Mark?" Caprionni asked, refocusing on their conversation. "What're you saying? What're you talking about here, anyway?"

"We need your help here too, Mr. Caprionni," Mark said. "We need your family to help us go after these fanatics. I wouldn't ask this of you without making a personal commitment first. My family is in this, too. My parents are the major shareholders of Continental Oil and Gas, and my grandparents own Prescott Enterprises. They have pledged to bring all of the resources of the two companies to help in this fight."

Mark could see that Caprionni recognized both names and was impressed.

"Tell me," Caprionni demanded. "Tell me, why are you doing this. You've gotta be a rich kid, for Christ's sake. Good Lord young man, you've got it made. Your family's hugely wealthy. What the hell are you doing working for the FBI?

"You must be insane," Caprionni added. But he couldn't hide the look of respect for Mark on his face.

"Yes, I'm damned lucky," he added. "And I'm grateful my family has provided for me generously. I didn't earn it, but it has allowed me to do other things, worthwhile things.

"In that sense, Mr. Caprionni, that's why I'm here. I'm asking you and your organization to step forward for your country, for America. From what the FBI has learned, these terrorists are the most serious threat our country has ever faced on American soil since the Civil War. I'm sure you understand that helping us will also be in the best interests of your family and the others in The Commission.

"The war is here, now, sir. We have to stop these lunatics before they do something terrible, and hurt innocent people. Look what they've done in other countries to innocent civilians – women, children, old people. Now, they're determined to commit those same atrocities here in America.

"What I'm about to tell you is top secret, but you need to know. The FBI has learned that among other attacks, a team of these terrorists intends to explode a nuclear device somewhere in America, and sometime soon."

"Mother of God!" Caprionni said, jumping to his feet. "A nuclear bomb? Are you sure? How could they get such a thing? Where?"

"Sadly, there are enough rogue nations out there willing to sell almost anything for the right price," Mark said. "That means the stakes could suddenly become very damn high here in America."

"You're telling me you want my family to cooperate with the FBI?" Caprionni said, visibly shaken. "Are you crazy? You want my family to make a deal with the cops? Sure, I'll do what I can to help get your children back . . . but about this, you can't be serious?"

"Oh yeah," Mark replied. "I'm deadly serious. I couldn't be more serious. We desperately need eyes and ears that an organization like yours and your colleagues can provide, not just in New York City but also across the country. Your mafia families have people doing business in places where the terrorists are recruiting, in ghettos and other low-income neighborhoods. We need the help of your organization's contacts in those areas. We sure could use some good intelligence from those places.

"What I'm proposing is an unusual . . . call it an extreme . . . alliance if you like, between your family, the FBI and other law enforcement, and civilian businesses. We might bring others into this as well, perhaps even the military. It won't be long before the military is involved, anyway. To be quite frank with you, sir, I never thought I'd say this, but we could end up working on the same side."

Mark chuckled.

Then to his surprise, Caprionni glared back at him. The old man's mood clearly had turned again . . . it was brooding and menacing once again.

What's up with him, now? Mark thought, taken aback.

"Well," Caprionni said angrily. "The hell with your FBI thing. Maybe later. But first things first. Right now, I'm gonna whack those fucking Maniero's before they and their crazy friends come after us. I can't afford to wait. I'm gonna teach them a fuckin' lesson they won't ever forget. You hear me? Those Maniero's . . . they're goddamned traitors. They're helping a bunch of terrorists who want to destroy this great country of ours! What's this world coming to, anyway?"

"Hold on, hold on, Mr. Caprionni!" Mark said, his voice louder than he intended. "Hold on just a minute, damn it! I can't tel! you what to do, or what not to do. But you'd better understand two things. First, you would not know any of this if I hadn't told you. Right? Sure, you can go ahead and hit the Maniero's. I can't stop you, now. That's no big deal compared with what's at stake here.

"But if you go to war with the Maniero's it'll open a whole new can of worms. I guarantee you it'll kill any deal between us, and it will cost you big time! The FBI will go after your family and all the other families with a vengeance. And you can trust me on that! You'll be shut down in hours. I mean it. And remember, Mr. Caprionni, to get the Maniero's and those terrorists off your back for good, you need me, and the FBI. You need the FBI to tell you the 'who's', and the 'when's' and the 'where's' of what they're up to. On the other hand, you help us with your connections and we will help you and your family. I'm offering you a good deal.

"Mr. Caprionni," Mark added, "if you are willing to help us, the Maniero's will have a very, very long time in jail to reflect on what they've done."

"What about my family and my people?" Caprionni asked. "You gonna send us all to jail, too, like the Maniero's, when this is all over? How do I know you won't do that? Huh?"

"I can tell you this, sir," Mark replied. "The New York attorney-general has signed off on an offer, and the governor is backing him all the way.

"Here's the deal: the attorney-general has agreed to overlook almost everything regarding your family except murders where they've enough evidence to prosecute, or are too high profile to ignore. You know investigations are underway. He won't stop those involving murders. But he's willing to put a stay on the others. He understands there are much bigger stakes here and it's all about saving innocent lives, possibly thousands of lives, maybe even millions. In short, partial immunity is the best I can promise."

They looked at each other a long time. Mark saw Caprionni slowly relax as he processed what Mark had just told him. He guessed Caprionni had made a decision, but was going to think about it for a while.

While waiting, Mark shared details of Anashi's short life and the brutality of her vicious beating and murder. He explained that Paige had given Anashi her first job. She'd earned a university degree in early childhood education and was the daughter of an Iranian refugee couple who'd escaped many years ago from the repression of their native country.

Caprionni could relate. He'd come here as an infant with his immigrant parents years earlier. Mark wanted Caprionni to be reminded that most immigrants, including people of Middle Eastern origin living in America, were patriotic and productive people, grateful to be here. Anashi's parents had been like that. They'd built successful careers. Her father was a college science teacher and her mother an elementary school teacher. They'd died on board American Airlines Flight 77 when it crashed into the Pentagon on Sept. 11, 2001. Anashi was in her early teens at the time.

"This is disgraceful!" Caprionni exclaimed, his eyes glistening. "That's savage! Inhuman!"

Mark had not seen this emotional side of the powerful old mafia don before.

"This is barbaric!" Caprionni raged on angrily, slamming his fist on his desk. He glanced at the door in case one of his soldiers felt they needed to check on him again. The door remained closed.

"These are not human beings. Even wild animals behave in more civilized ways. We must destroy them before they can hurt more people!"

He stopped suddenly. He'd surprised himself by using the word 'we' so pointedly and emphatically.

At that moment, Caprionni realized he'd made a commitment instinctively to work with the FBI. He could see Mark had picked up on it. Caprionni was too proud to backtrack. He looked at Mark, smiled slightly and then nodded his head. He sat down and uttered a long sigh.

"Well, okay, maybe," he said, looking up at Mark. "This is strange . . . very strange indeed. Ah . . . lemme think about it a bit more . . . okay?"

Mark nodded back. But they knew they'd reached an understanding.

"All right, now," the godfather said. "Tell me, how can my people help you get your little ones back?"

Chapter 10

East Harlem

"I'm tired!" Caylyn said. Tears were streaming down her cherubic little cheeks. Between sobs she told her brother she couldn't run any farther.

"Okay," Edward said. He gave his little sister an affectionate hug.

"We can rest here for a little while. Sit on the curb. I'll keep watch. Maybe someone will come along who can help us."

While the children were catching their breath, Edward looked up and down the street. None of the buildings looked friendly or inviting. Then he spotted a policeman leaning against a fence a block away. The children ran over and explained what had happened. The cop was startled at first, then crouched down and listened. He told them he knew where they could get a soda and some chips while he called their parents.

The cop took each of them by the hand and walked to a diner four blocks away. It was almost 9:15 p.m. Edward and Caylyn were tired, thirsty and hungry. Their clothes were dirty and rumpled. The cop bought them a soda each and an extra large order of fries to share.

*

NYPD Officer Nancy Gardner told her partner, "Let's grab a coffee . . . shift's about done. Besides, I need to pee."

"Yeah," replied Officer Dominic Parfeniuk, "I could use a break before we check in."

It had been an unusually quiet evening for the pair patrolling in Harlem. A few shoplifting calls, one vagrant, three calls about drug deals in progress and a call they worried about most, a domestic dispute. It was 9:30 p.m., and soon they'd be heading back to the precinct.

Dominic was driving.

"Hold it, Dom!" Nancy said. "Stop! Quick! Pull over!"

Const. Parfeniuk was startled but did what his partner asked.

"What's up, Nance?" he said. "You see something?"

"Yeah," she replied. "That diner back there."

"Yeah, I know," Dominic said. "I'd've stopped but there's no place to park. I know another . . ."

"No, no, not that," Nancy replied excitedly, looking back over her shoulder towards the diner. "In the window . . . I mean through the window. I think I saw those two missing kids. You know, that APB we got a few days ago. Remember? Those kids who were grabbed out in the country, in Connecticut. Their name was Truesdale or Thompson, or something like that. It could be them in the restaurant! Sure looked like them."

"C'mon, Nance," Dominic said. "You're telling me you saw them? Here? In the middle of Harlem?"

"Yeah, I think so!" Nancy replied. "Looked like they were with a cop, just sitting there. I think they were having a soda. Odd. Maybe he's called it in . . . waiting for social services. I don't remember hearing anything on the radio. Do you?"

"Naw," Dominic said. "Nothing like that. Maybe a different channel?"

"I dunno," Nancy said. "Dominic, I got a feeling. I wanna go back there."

They were half a block past the diner. Dominic had pulled the squad car into a bus stop and turned on the four-way flashers. Something told him leave the roof lights off. As they walked back toward the diner, he saw Nancy loosen her weapon. Her athletic body was on alert. Dominic had learned to respect his partner's instincts. On more than one occasion those instincts had saved him from injury or possibly worse in the two years they'd been partners, and vice versa. He checked his weapon.

"Dom, I'm going in the front door and see what's going on. Okay?" she said. "Can you take the rear door? Just in case I need backup?"

"Sure, Nance," Dominic replied. "You're being pretty skittish. You sure you don't want me to go in with you? D'ya know something I don't?"

"No," Nancy said reassuringly. Her face had an uneasy grin. "Just a feeling; just being cautious, partner."

They separated at the corner of the diner. Dominic disappeared down the alley. Nancy waited a few seconds then headed for the front door.

"Hey, man." Nancy approached the seated cop. He was facing her. He looked up, startled. She didn't recognize him. He was in her precinct so she should have known him. Odd. That was a red flag. The two small children with him had their backs to her. They looked dirty and disheveled. Nancy's instincts were silently shouting at her. She caught him glancing at the loosened gun holster on her belt as she said, "I see you've got some company tonight. Your kids?"

"Hey," the beat cop replied uneasily. He wore no badge, which was against regulations. That was a huge red flag. Now she was on full alert. "Naw, not mine; found these two wandering the streets a few minutes ago. Tried to get a phone number or address from them. They don't seem to know."

"Call this in yet?" Nancy said.

"Nope, not yet," the cop replied. "Just got here."

"You want me to?" she asked as she took a step forward, glancing down.

The cute little blue-eyed girl was fussing with a bent straw. The boy seemed nervous and awkward. She took another step forward so she could see the children's faces better. The cop stiffened when she took the second step, sitting up straighter. Another red flag! She glanced down at the boy. She guessed he was six or maybe seven. His head shook ever so slightly side-to-side, signaling a 'no'. Her peripheral vision picked up Dominic entering through the kitchen, behind the cop.

"I'll call this in, if you like?" she repeated as Dominic in his socks quietly closed the distance to within 10 feet of the cop.

"In a minute," the beat cop replied. "The kids were real thirsty . . . wanted a drink. And hungry. Got them some fries."

The children had empty soda glasses in front of them. The ice had melted into a trace of colored water at the bottom of their paper cups. A large plate in front of them was empty except for scraps and leftover ketchup. It was obvious they'd been here a while. Another red flag.

Nancy reached for her radio. The cop jumped into the aisle. He pulled his service weapon, evidently thinking she'd gone for hers. It felt like slow motion to her, as he raised his weapon and pointed it at her. Instinctively, Nancy leaped toward the cop, swatting at his weapon while quickly stepping to her right to shield the children with her body. She heard a shot and glanced at the cop. A bullet from his gun pierced the flesh of her right forearm. Immediately, two more shots followed. A look of surprise appeared on the cop's face. Then a third shot. The cop coughed. A trickle of blood escaped the left corner of his mouth. His weapon dropped, his knees buckled. He fell toward her. Nancy kicked his weapon away. She rolled him over. His eyes were open. She bent down and checked for a pulse. There was none.

Dominic stepped forward quickly and crouched over the fallen rogue cop, service weapon in hand, being careful to block the terrified children's view of the body. He threw his uniform jacket over the dead man's head and shoulders.

"Thanks," Nancy said as she gathered up the frightened children. "Nice shooting."

He stepped forward to examine Nancy's arm.

"Just a scratch," she said as Dominic tied his handkerchief over the wound to slow the bleeding
"Partners," he said, smiling.
"Partners," Nancy replied softly.
Nancy took the children to a booth in a far corner of the diner. She sat them down, speaking quietly to calm them. Dominic called for backup.
The boy identified himself and his sister as Edward and Caylyn Tremblay. He told Nancy they'd been kidnapped. Edward described their escape from the apartment. He told her the beat cop found them two blocks from the apartment and had walked them to the diner. The cop had made a call on his cell phone while they were drinking their sodas and eating their fries.
"The policeman told us he called Mom and Dad," Edward said. "He said they would be picking us up soon, but I know that's not true. He doesn't know our phone number. Well, we didn't give it to him."
"We're trying to figure out what he was up to," Nancy said. "Anyway, I'm going to call your Mom and Dad right now. You can speak with them. Then we'll take you home as soon as we can."
Edward gave her the number of his Dad's cell phone.
Nancy suspected the dead cop's call was to the kidnappers, and that he was an off-duty patrolman taking kickbacks to act as a lookout. When Dominic searched the cop's pockets for ID, he found $500 in fresh fifty-dollar bills. That signaled a payoff.
Nancy and the children hid in the kitchen with the staff, in case the kidnappers arrived before their backup. Dominic put on a cook's cap and gown to

stand guard. Soon, three patrol cars arrived on the scene, lights flashing and sirens wailing.

Two hours later, Paige Tremblay's face was awash with tears of joy as she came running down the sidewalk to greet Edward and Caylyn.

The children had arrived in a police cruiser at their Uncle Douglas and Aunt Jennifer's house in Danbury. Dominic had driven, after a confrontation with social services about who would return the children to their parents. It was against NYPD regulations, but Nancy and Dominic took the children and left, challenging the imperious social services workers to stop them.

On the way to Danbury, Edward sat in the front seat beside Dominic. They were ignoring more NYPD rules. But that was the only way Edward could reach the controls for the flashing blue, red and white roof lights and for the siren. Nancy and Caylyn were content to sit in the back seat during the long journey, watching the boys play. Caylyn was in a car seat reluctantly provided by social services. Edward's booster seat was empty.

Later that evening, as the reunited family relaxed in front of the TV, Mark sat on the sofa with his right arm around Paige's shoulders. The two children were curled up on their parents' laps sound asleep. They'd all had a big day.

"I guess that training of yours is going to come in handy now," Mark said, relieved at how relaxed and happy his young wife looked now that the children were back with her.

"What do you mean, Hon?" Paige asked. Her head was nestled on his wide muscular chest.

"It could be a challenge for them, trying to feel safe again, after what they've been through," Mark said. "With your training, you can help them through that. What a gift for them."

"I guess you're right," Paige replied, looking down at the children with a gentle smile, her hand on Caylyn's sleeping head. "I sure didn't expect this would be how I'd use my degree for the first time."

Paige had completed most of her doctoral studies in child psychology, trying to keep busy while her first husband was away in Afghanistan. Only the defense of her doctoral thesis had been outstanding when he died. After they met, Mark encouraged her to complete her studies. Paige received her degree just weeks before they'd moved to Candlewood Lake.

The next day, when Edward returned to school, he had quite a story to tell his first grade class. Caylyn thought she ought to have a good story, too, to tell at her play school class. But she wasn't exactly sure what had happened. What she did know was that she was very happy to be back home with her Mommy and Daddy.

Chapter 11

Candlewood Lake

Rhamir was obsessed with revenge. He had failed the first time he tried to kill Mark, for refusing to help him take over Joe Caprionni's drug operations. Then, he became angry when his own men, his best fighters, had botched the hit. Now, he was even more furious after learning that not only was Mark an FBI agent and a former Navy SEAL, but the children had escaped.

Years earlier while a Navy SEAL Mark had participated in attacks on Taliban and al-Qaeda hideouts in Afghanistan and neighboring Pakistan. Members of Rhamir's family had been killed. Then, members of Mark's former elite commando unit had killed Osama bin Laden. And now, US and allied warplanes were killing ISIS fighters in Syria and Iraq.

By the will of Allah, this is not the end of it! Rhamir vowed.

His focus had turned to Mark's newly repaired home on Candlewood Lake. Two fighters were assigned to stake it out and watch for indications that Mark and his family were moving back. Rhamir planned to attack when it was confirmed that Mark, Paige and their two children had settled in. The thought of wiping out the entire family pleased him. His burning thirst for revenge was fueling a plan taking shape in his mind.

A few weeks earlier, with repairs almost finished, Mark had asked Paige when she thought they should plan to move back. He wanted to make arrangements for the move.

"Never!" she replied vehemently. "I've thought hard about it, Mark. I know how much you love that house, but I have to be honest. There's absolutely no way I'm ever going to live there again. Not ever!"

The discussion had continued off and on for a few days. Mark wanted to be sure she wouldn't change her mind later. Finally, he was convinced Paige was adamant. The next day, he arranged to list the house with the local Re/Max real estate agency.

Within days, agent Hillary Bixby got a call.

"We're at a home you have listed on Candlewood Lake," Tim Hornby said. "Are you free to do a showing right now?"

"Sorry but I'm tied up," Hillary said. "I can be available tomorrow afternoon. Will that work for you?"

Tim agreed.

"See you then," Hillary said.

Tim and Joanne Hornby and their two children had been driving through the area and spotted the newly installed 'For Sale' sign. No one was home, so they walked around the property anyway. On the huge deck at the back, they peered in through two-story windows overlooking Candlewood Lake. The setting and the view were overwhelming.

"It's perfect! It's absolutely magnificent!" Joanne had said. "Let's call for a showing right away. What do you think?" She wanted to make an offer before anyone else.

At 1 p.m. the following afternoon, the Hornby family met Hillary for a showing. Joanne couldn't understand why anyone would give up the tastefully decorated home. It looked like a show home out of an architectural magazine. Both Tim and Joanne loved the open concept living room/dining room/kitchen with its cathedral ceiling. They sat down with Hillary at what looked like a brand new dining room table to prepare an offer.

Meanwhile, across a bay on the opposite shore, movements at the Tremblay house were being watched through binoculars from a private aircraft hangar.

"They're back!" said Ismail El-Merhebi. "That traitor Trimonti and his family! They've moved back in. They did that fast. We were here just two days ago. We'd better tell Rhamir right away."

The observers had assumed, correctly, that the owners of the hangar where they were hiding had gone away for the summer. As a result, El-Merhebi and Rashid Sharif Sayfildin had been coming and going freely. Their movements attracted a few curious looks from neighbors. None had challenged the strange men to explain what they were doing there.

The two observers had found the job boring. For two weeks they'd been watching the house across the bay. Until now, they'd observed only tradesmen coming and going. Finally, the repairs appeared completed. Then no one had showed up for a few days, until today. They phoned Rhamir, who'd been on his way there anyway to check up on his fighters.

He was suspicious about their reports of no sightings. He didn't trust anyone.

The trespassers' excitement was running high as Rhamir arrived in the hangar 10 minutes later.

"See," Sayfildin said. He handed a pair of binoculars to Rhamir and pointed to activity across the lake.

All three agreed the people they could see thorugh the windows of the house must be Mark and Paige and her two children, walking around checking out the repairs. Apparently they had a guest or maybe a new nanny.

"Wonderful," Rhamir said, peering through the binoculars. "One more infidel will be a bonus for what we have in mind for you!"

Rhamir looked on as Sayfildin filled the tiny gas tank in the model aircraft they'd brought when they'd begun surveillance. Its 70-inch wingspan was unusually large for a radio-controlled aircraft. But a plane that size could carry the half-pound payload of PETN explosive they'd fitted into the fuselage. It was enough to severely damage a small office building. Sayfildin turned on the radio control consol. El-Merhebi started the motor of the Kadet LT-40 aircraft. Sayfildin left the RC console and took hold of the model's tail assembly to control it for take-off. A nod from El-Merhebi, whose back was to the lake, would signal Sayfildin to release the model aircraft's tail.

"Stop! Stop!" Sayfildin shouted over the whine of the model's engine, waving his right hand wildly. "Hold on!" Sayfildin's left hand still held the plane's tail. He gestured wildly toward the lake. El-Merhebi turned off the motor. He and Rhamir looked in the direction Sayfildin was pointing.

"What the fuck!" Rhamir said. A float-equipped Cessna circled low, leveled off and made a smooth landing on the lake. It stopped 500 yards away. As they watched, the plane paused briefly, turned and then accelerated loudly toward the hangar where they stood.

"Quick," Rhamir shouted to the others as the plane headed for the ramp leading up to the hangar. "Over there!"

The three scrambled behind a half-wall and huddled in the shadows. They were in a makeshift office equipped with a desk, a chair, some bookshelves and a phone attached to the cement block hangar wall.

El-Merhebi struggled to fit the big model in with them without damaging a wing or the tail. That would have ended their mission. The trespassers heard the throaty roar of the floatplane's powerful engine draw closer then diminish for a few moments. Suddenly the engine thundered loudly. To their surprise, peering over the half-wall, the floatplane came surging up the shallow ramp, the engine at a deafening roar. The floats had wheels mounted under them, making the plane amphibious. Once in the hangar, the plane's engine died.

"Careful with that step beside the fuselage," a man's voice was heard through an open cockpit window. "It gets slippery."

An athletic man in his late 40s climbed down. He scrambled across behind the idle prop from the port side pontoon to the starboard side facing the hiding place.

"Here Love, let me help," he said to a shapely woman slightly younger than him. He held her hand as she climbed down.

They both reached up to assist a boy, about 14, and a girl, about 12, scramble down to the cement floor.

"Stay out of sight," Rhamir whispered to the other two men, motioning them to crouch down further . He stood and stepped around the chest high partition, pulling a Beretta 92FS machine pistol from his belt behind his back. He inserted a 15-round clip and checked on a second clip in his jacket pocket.

"Hello folks," he said as he walked from the shadows over to the startled family. Rhamir held the Beretta behind his right thigh. The family was obviously the owner of the property. The expressions on their faces made it clear they were annoyed at the intruder, and apprehensive.

Without another word, Rhamir raised the machine pistol and began firing. The man lunged toward the woman, trying to protect her. Bullets got him first. He fell backwards, landing on his back beneath the aircraft. The woman tried to scream as bullets ripped into her throat and chest. She fell backward on top of him. The startled boy tripped and fell forward, landing face down on the cement floor. Rhamir took four quick steps forward as the boy began to raise himself trying not to cry, his mouth bleeding. A shower of bullets ripped into his blond head and back. Rhamir turned and fired a short burst at the terrified girl, frozen in fear. She crumpled where she stood. Rhamir changed clips and fired more bursts into all four bodies. The hangar fell silent. Smoke and the smell of burnt gunpowder hung heavily in the air.

"Ismail, Rashid!" Rhamir shouted. "Get out here, now! Hurry!

"Take your plane and the controls, and get under the floatplane," he said.

The two men crawled under. They repeated their start-up sequence. El-Merhebi was at the controls. Sayfildin again held the tail of the model aircraft, its wheels on the cement floor, nose pointing toward the lake. El-Merhebi revved the motor and then nodded to Sayfildin. He released the big model airplane.

The heavily laden plane moved forward slowly at first on the rough cement floor. El-Merhebi pushed the throttle all the way. The small engine roared and the plane gained speed as it started down the short ramp. Half way to the water, it became airborne. All three men let out a sigh of relief. The model airplane gained altitude slowly as it flew across the bay on its way to the target, a quarter mile away.

Sayfildin watched the plane's progress through binoculars. He relayed guidance to El-Merhebi, hoping next time he'd get to operate the controls. Their leader, Abdul Rhamir, hands shielding his eyes from the bright sunlight, watched with smug satisfaction as the model plane grew smaller and smaller, getting closer and closer to the two-story windows of the house across the bay.

Hillary Bixby and her clients, the Hornby family, were in the great room of the house. They'd enjoyed watching the neighbor's floatplane come in for a landing on the lake. Still admiring the spectacular view, they were discussing the prospects of their offer when the model airplane crashed through a second-story section of the great room windows. The model airplane's wings and landing gear were sheared off. An impact detonator exploded the PETN a split second later.

An enormous fiery explosion leveled the home and two-car garage within seconds. Scattered bits of debris carried on huge clouds of flame were spread over a radius of more than 50 yards. A power transformer 10 yards from the house partly melted, and then exploded. Mark and Paige's dream home had been turned into a pile of charred rubble by the ball of flame and fire that followed. Little remained but twisted beams, shattered timbers and charred pieces of building materials. Bodies were scattered in and around the blast site. The coroner's office painstakingly recovered as many body parts as they could find.

Connecticut State Police investigators were curious about the long sheets of hardened steel left standing where an otherwise destroyed bar had been. They were even more curious about the trap door, underground vault and tunnel leading under the garage to an adjacent grove of trees.

When Emile Bilodeaux of Global Security International had arrived at the scene, he located the supervisor of the investigation team.

"Before reporting any of this," Emile had told him, "you need to check with Lt. Sanchez and the FBI. I can tell you this was the home of an FBI undercover agent. I expect the FBI will assure you this investigation is to be treated as highly classified."

The CSI supervisor phoned Sanchez and an FBI contact to confirm Emile's story. The investigators were briefed and their reports sanitized.

When news stories flashed across local television screens, it became obvious to Rhamir that Mark, Paige and their family were not among those killed in the explosion.

Rhamir's initial delight over their 'drone' attack turned again to fury.

"You let me down again!" Rhamir shouted at Sayfildin and El-Merhebi. Once more he'd failed to kill Mark and his family; his lust for revenge was left unrequited again. Rhamir promised himself that he would not rest until Mark and his whole family and everyone else connected with them had been wiped out.

A few news reporters speculated the blast might have been caused by a natural gas leak possibly associated with the recent renovations. Authorities did not confirm nor contradict them. The truth, made public, would serve no useful purpose.

*

East Harlem

Despite being in a rage for days over his failure to 'get' Mark and his family, Rhamir finally realized there were more pressing matters needing his attention: final preparations for the start of his holy war.

He called his followers to the back room of a mosque in Harlem.

"Our attacks in the three cities will demoralize those infidel Americans," he said. "And we will also leave a signature they cannot possibly misunderstand. At the very same time as those three glorious attacks, we will also choose an infidel at random in Washington and behead him on the steps of the Lincoln Memorial, and then post it on YouTube."

"Allahu Akbar!" his followers shouted.

"Allahu Akbar," he replied.

"All of this will demonstrate that our glorious Islamic Army of America is at war with America . . . it will prove that we can wage our holy war in their homeland whenever we want and wherever we please!"

He reasoned that the attacks, and then the nuclear explosion, would showcase the superiority of his version of Islam. However, he'd still heard nothing from ISIS about progress on shipping the nuclear device they'd promised. He was growing concerned.

Regardless, he was determined to proceed with the first four attacks. September 11 was drawing closer. Rhamir looked upon the attacks on the World Trade Center and the Pentagon and the crash of Flight 93 in Shanksville, PA, not as the tragedy the American news media had made it out to be, but as a magnificent achievement by the 'great holy warrior martyr' Osama bin Laden.

Rhamir believed his initial attacks would rival 9/11, but would occur *before* that anniversary. He'd decided all of the attacks would be on Saturday, August 20, almost three weeks before the 9/11 anniversary. He believed the scheduling would catch law enforcement by surprise. They would be focused on security plans for the anniversary of 9/11 and would not have begun to go on alert by then. Once more, he congratulated himself on the brilliant strategist he had convinced himself that he had become.

Rhamir had gathered his jihadists for a pep talk before dispersing them to make final arrangements for their attacks. The mosque he chose was far away from the previous mosque and old apartment he'd abandoned after the Tremblay children escaped.

"You must remember," he began, "the infidels do not understand things like we do ... they are no longer agile in their ways of thinking as we are. Their society has become too fat and too lazy. They are complacent. They have no fight left in them any more.

"Look how they failed in Vietnam . . . and they failed in Somalia . . . they failed in Iraq . . . they failed in Afghanistan . . . and they failed in Syria. The imperialists have failed everywhere they've tried to defeat men of purpose and especially the fighters of Islam like us. Why? They are infidels that's why! It is we, who are the chosen ones. It is we, who wage holy war in the name of Allah! It is we, who will show them that Islam and Sharia Law are the only way!"

As he spoke, his fighters accompanied his words with more shouts of "Allahu Akbar!" and cries of joy. They were excited that soon they would be fighting the American imperialists. The terrorist leader was proud of being head of his self-styled 'Islamic Army'.

Like most of his jihad fighters, Rhamir had grown up in America. He was born a year after his parents immigrated to New York from Iran 32 years earlier. Sturdily built and unusually tall for his culture, as a youth Rhamir had been the classic schoolyard bully. He was a bright child but his outspoken nature and disrespect for basic rules of behavior marked him as an outcast at a young age. His mother doted on her only child and chose to overlook his behavior. She learned little English and was a subservient wife. Her husband, an IT expert, handled all matters outside the home. Rhamir was 20 when his father was killed in a subway accident. He dropped out of MIT and took over the role as head of the household. He and his mother lived off the proceeds from his father's modest life insurance policy and meager spousal company pension. Rhamir had much time on his hands and became immersed in his Muslim religion. He joined an Islamic fundamentalist group that taught him to hate the culture and institutions of his country. Rhamir spent much of the family's limited spare income preparing for the holy jihad he envisioned one day.

Rhamir shouted to his adoring followers:

"Our jihad is the beginning of the end of American imperialism. Why? The corrupt capitalists cannot see beyond their own selfishness. They do not recognize that their insatiable greed for money and power are destroying their country. What fools they are! Their criminal ways caused the world's economies to collapse in 2008. That is continuing today and it is crippling all western capitalist economies. You will have the honor of helping to hasten their collapse.

"To make their situation even worse, over the years they have sent jobs to other countries. Stupid! Look how that has backfired. Those were the very jobs, the very earning power, those companies needed here for people to buy their goods . . . goods they are making elsewhere. Now there is no money in this country to buy those goods. They've destroyed their own economy! How dumb is that? Pure greed! This is why their society is crumbling. One day, we will replace it with our own glorious regime, the People's Islamic Republic of America!"

Again, Rhamir was interrupted with cheers and shouts of "Allahu Akbar!"

"We will attack across America . . . with parcel bombs, with car bombs, with briefcase bombs, with aerial bombs, and with truck and car bombs!

"You are the soldiers, the fighters of the Islamic Army of America!" Rhamir shouted, prompting more loud cheers of excitement.

"In some attacks, our brave fighters will be given the privilege of becoming martyrs to Allah, for our new Islamic Army. They will earn their eternal places in Paradise."

Cheers and shouts of "Allahu Akbar" interrupted Rhamir once more.

Later that day, he sent Larigani and four other trained fighters to begin setting up the training camp and bomb factory. It would be on a rented acreage near Chapman, NY. Soon, the camp would be training more and more recruits, and manufacturing the many PETN bombs they would be using soon.

Chapter 12

Tempe, AZ

Located some 2,400 miles southwest of East Harlem is the picturesque desert city of Tempe, AZ.

"You're pretty young to be so henpecked," chided one of Michael Shapiro's fellow students. "Man, you need to hang out more with us guys. Get a refresher on what freedom was like. Bet ya don't even remember!"

In a campus bistro, the fourth-year engineering student was having coffee with a group of fellow students attending Arizona State University. They'd just finished a Saturday morning seminar. It was August 20. The group chatted about a course project. As they talked, Michael grew restless. The tall, athletic student couldn't wait to leave so he could be with Anne Marie and their two pre-school children.

On his way home, Michael would run an errand. It would be the last act of his young life.

Michael took a lot of ribbing from friends and fellow students over the affection he had no hesitation about showing for his high school sweetheart. They'd married four years earlier. He knew his colleagues were envious; he understood few men had the courage to express their affection openly.

Michael and Anne Marie had grown up a few blocks from each other. They were children of affluent families in Sedona, a tourist town 120 miles north of Phoenix. The two were inseparable during high school, much to the concern of their parents. A few months after graduation, both were 'lost' when his family insisted that Michael come with them on an extended trip.

"We need you to crew," his father had said.

Much against his wishes, Michael was taken on a four-month cruise through the Hawaiian Islands aboard his parent's 46-foot sailboat, *The Blue Teal*.

"It's our way of congratulating you for being accepted into engineering at ASU," his mother had said. "We're so proud of you!"

Michael didn't see it that way. The trip meant a long separation from Anne Marie. Both sets of parents thought it a good idea for the two youngsters to cool their ardor for a while. Michael's mother, his older sister, and he served as crew. His father was captain. Six months after his return, he and Anne Marie became engaged. Their parents worried about that, too. The couple married a year later, causing their parents even more apprehension. The newlyweds were just 21 years old.

Their first home was in a small townhouse near ASU. Michael had encouraged Anne Marie to enroll in the fine arts program at ASU. She'd dreamed of becoming an artist since elementary school. Her art had won top awards at several juried exhibitions, drawing the attention of the art community. Twice she'd been invited to present private showings at prominent art galleries, one in downtown Phoenix, the other at a large gallery in Scottsdale's prestigious artists' district.

"Come on!" Michael had said. "Enroll with me. We'll be attending school together. How great is that?"

Their plans changed when she became pregnant unexpectedly with Janice. She was finishing her second year in fine arts. Her pregnancy was a surprise but certainly not a disappointment. Anne Marie yearned to become a mother. Fourteen months after Janice was born, they became pregnant with Darrin. Anne Marie was deliriously happy and devoted her life to being a full time mom and wife. She was still determined to complete her degree some day but decided that could wait until both their children were out of diapers. After watching the contented young family, all four parents happily shifted their focus to becoming doting grandparents.

"It's time, Sweetie," Anne Marie said to 25-month-old Janice. "We're going to start you on potty training."

It was early for most children, but she sensed Janice was ready. Anne Marie also choose this day to begin exploring the ASU website about returning to her studies. She remembered affectionately her earlier experiences at the Herberger Institute for Design and The Arts.

She couldn't wait to share her thoughts with Michael. She looked at her watch. He'd be on his way home now. A thrill coursed through her trim body. Then she remembered asking Michael to mail her grandmother's birthday card. The card was late so she'd asked him to send it by priority mail, which meant stopping at the post office.

The delay disappointed her, having to wait those precious few extra minutes until she would be in his arms again. The thought gave her goose bumps.

Chapter 13

Near Raleigh, NC

Stan Tassel was proud of being Cherokee. His hobby was studying early Native American culture, especially Cherokee history. What he learned often made him unhappy. His temper would rise when he thought about how Native Americans had been cruelly mistreated by European settlers almost 200 years ago. His ancestors were among tens of thousands who'd suffered. Many died from the barbaric treatment.

He was especially proud of one thing. In the late 1830's, his forbearers had left their prosperous farms and fled into the Smokey Mountains of North Carolina to escape forced relocation. Others of the Cherokee Nation and of four more Native American communities had been moved against their will onto reservations 2,200 miles away in Oklahoma. They'd lost their fight to stop tribal lands from being stolen by European immigrant land speculators and then sold to builders of cotton and tobacco plantations.

Stories were scrolling though Stan's mind on that fateful August 20 as he sat parked out front of IBM's headquarters in Research Triangle Park, near Raleigh, NC. He was waiting for Josephine, his wife of almost 30 years, wondering what might have become of his ancestors had they not escaped from the infamous "Trail of Tears" of 1838. But that was then, and today he and Josephine were preparing for a special celebration.

It was Saturday and the couple was going to run some last minute errands. They were flying off early Sunday morning for a much-anticipated two weeks in Dominican Republic. It was their gift to themselves for their 30th wedding anniversary they'd celebrate while there.

Thirty years earlier in Durham, NC, their marriage had been considered the most improbable union of the century. Her friends and his friends – they shared few back then – had made bets on how quickly the marriage would fail. A swarthy and raven-haired Stan, at the time sporting a pair of long braids, had just graduated from Kansas State University as a wildlife biologist and been hired by the North Carolina natural resources department. Josephine was the first black woman to graduate from prestigious Duke University with a doctorate degree in mathematics. She was now a senior project leader at IBM's huge research and development center in the state's famous Research Triangle Park, America's largest research center. IBM's complex alone employed more than 11,000 people, almost a quarter of all those who worked at the sprawling RTP campus.

You're a gorgeous woman still! he said to himself, admiring Josephine's appearance through the passenger side mirror of their car as she walked toward him. He was going to tell her that right after she got into the car. He loved her slim figure, appreciating that it was no small achievement for a mother of two in her mid-50s. Their daughter Allison was also a mother of her own two small preschoolers and lived in nearby Raleigh. Their son, Will, was in his final year of law at Josephine's alma mater, Duke University.

As she neared the car, Stan's attention was distracted when a white panel truck jumped the curb, drove through a row of manicured shrubs and headed up the wide sidewalk toward the front entrance. It was peculiar behavior for any service vehicle, especially Progress Energy, a respected local electrical utility.

The panel truck's unusual action was also noticed from Josephine's third floor office window. Mary Gillespie had watched her boss's progress with a touch of envy. Mary was Josephine's executive assistant and a divorced single mother. She adored Josephine and thought her the best boss anyone could possibly have. Mary willingly agreed to work this Saturday. Besides, she needed the overtime to pay off some overdue bills.

In just a few seconds, their lives and those of nearby fellow workers would end . . . and the lives of thousands of family, friends and colleagues, and the rest of America, would forever carry the pain of the tragedy about to unfold.

Chapter 14

East Harlem

Rhamir had chosen Houston as one of his first three targets. For years, he'd dreamed of attacking the American space program. While much of the program had been cancelled, he remained obsessed with destroying something about this symbol of American intellectual achievement. Rhamir knew secure areas at the Johnson Space Center, especially around the Mission control complex, were impenetrable. Here, as at other NASA sites across America, world-leading research was continuing despite the curtailed space program.

Rhamir had options. Houston was also a key US port and a major American oil production and refining center. Even more important, the metropolitan population of almost six million meant huge crowds would be drawn to sporting events. That gave him an idea.

He would attack the 72,000-seat Reliant Stadium while filled with fans during an NFL home game. Many of the Houston Texans' ardent fans would be NASA workers. A pre-season game was scheduled for August 20th.

It's good enough! Rhamir thought.

Rhamir saw the coincidence of dates as a sign from Allah. Texans would be hosting the New Orleans Saints. The stadium would be sold out. It always was. At that time of year, fans were eager. It amused him to think: *Those fans will be dying for action, and so they shall.* A plan formed in his deranged mind.

We can use multiple attack methods here! he thought. *The stadium will be perfect for one of our model airplane 'drones', and for car bombs, briefcase bombs and backpack bombs.*

Rhamir became excited as he thought how the attack scenario would unfold. A model airplane that exploded during the half-time show would create enough panic that crowds would flee toward the four main exits. Explosions by briefcase bombs would follow. They'd be given beforehand to workers in concession stands, and asked to hold them while they went to the rest room. The workers would be given generous tips.

The panic created by the initial explosions would cause many of the bombs to be knocked over and triggered. The ruse would elude security patrols. Timed to go off simultaneously would be backpack bombs, dropped earlier in trash bins. Panicked fans would also flee into the parking lots where they would stumble into cars, setting off bombs wired to security alarms. The car bombs would kill hundreds more people, maybe even thousands. He smiled to himself as he thought about how much deadly shrapnel he could pack into these cars – construction screws, nails, ball bearings, fencing staples, bolts, washers and nuts, and razor wire to rip people's throats and shred their skin.

It will be glorious! he thought.

Rhamir estimated he would need 12 to 15 jihadists. That would put a strain on their resources. He briefed a delighted Shahid and put him in charge of the attack, authorizing a core of experienced jihadists. "I want you to start immediately on planning the logistics," Rhamir said.

Finally, I'm to be given the responsibilities of a real deputy, Shahid thought with excitement.

Rhamir described to him in detail how the bombs were to be prepared and deployed for the attack. He'd downloaded a stadium seating chart and a diagram of the eight parking lots around Reliant Stadium. He gave Shahid copies.

"You will need to choose a lieutenant for this assignment," Rhamir said.

"I'm going to appoint Khaled Mahmoud," Shahid said. "He received high praise during his training. He is a very promising jihadist."

He liked 26-year-old Khaled from their first meeting. He was bright, had recently returned from training and fighting with ISIS in Iraq, and had displayed a keen interest in their holy jihad.

Shahid phoned and arranged to meet Khaled in the three-bedroom East Harlem apartment that Khaled shared with eight other jihadists. There, he gave Khaled a description of their new assignment, without providing details.

Rhamir, Shahid and the rest of the terrorists were unaware that Khaled was an FBI undercover agent. Mark Tremblay had instructed him to report on the terrorists whenever he could without risking his cover. Both understood the assignment was risky. Khaled would try to get close to Rhamir's inner circle. It would be an intelligence bonanza.

Khaled was motivated to bring the terrorists to justice.

He was the second child of Aban and Malika Mahmoud. He, his sister Malala and their parents had immigrated to America from their native Pakistan. Khaled had just turned four at the time. He was 15 when his father, a rising star in a Wall Street investment firm, was in the wrong place at the wrong time the day al-Qaeda-trained fanatics destroyed the World Trade Center. Eighteen-year-old Malala was visiting her father at the time. His mother never got over the deaths of her daughter and husband. Two years later, she committed suicide. The family who took Khaled in, and other family friends understood that his mother's suicide was the result of her broken heart. Although fluent in Urdu, Pakistan's most common language, Khaled spoke perfect English. His friends assumed he'd been born in America.

The deaths of his parents and sister, and the global spread of savagery by ISIS, the Taliban, Boko Haram and others turned Khaled into a sworn enemy of religious extremists. The day after graduating from college with a degree in criminology, Khaled called the FBI's counterterrorism hotline. He explained his parents' deaths. Khaled was interviewed. His story was checked out thoroughly. Three months after his call to the FBI, Khaled told his adoptive family and friends he was leaving to backpack around the world. He dropped from sight. A day later, Khaled was in Quantico. He completed the 20-week basic training and then was accepted for intelligence training. He focused on counterterrorism. Less than a year after graduating Khaled had worked his way into a group of rebellious youths in Harlem attached to Rhamir's sleeper cell of jihadists. Khaled knew he'd been accepted when he was sent to Iraq to train and then fight with ISIS.

"Our friends in Iraq were impressed by how well you did at the training camp," Shahid said to him in Urdu. "And they say you speak Urdu fluently. Where did you learn it?"

"I was born in Damadola, in the North-West Frontier Province," Khaled said truthfully in fluent Urdu. "My parents brought me to America when I was four."

"Where's your family now?" Shahid persisted, shifting back to English.

"Dead," Khaled answered without giving details. "I have no other family here. They're all back home."

Shahid liked what he was hearing.

"Do you know who the holy warrior martyr Anwar al-Awlaki is?" Shahid continued.

Khaled's instructors at Quantico had told him about this lieutenant of Osama bin Laden. But try as he might he couldn't remember anyone in his group of wannabe jihadists or the leaders ever mentioning the name. He decided to be cautious.

"Uh . . . I think so, but I'm not sure," he answered.

"Well, you should!" Shahid said exuberantly. "Someone in ISIS must have contacted al-Qaeda and told him about you. I'm told, al-Awklai was very impressed and asked your name. That is very good! Al-Awklai was carrying on the work of Osama bin

Laden. Then, those imperialist American swine murdered him in Pakistan with one of their drones.

"Did you know al-Awaklai was an American?" Shahid continued. "Yes! His parents were from Yemen but he was born in this country . . . in Las Cruses, New Mexico! He led many successful attacks on the infidels, and trained many glorious fighters for the jihad."

As he spoke, Shahid was finding much pleasure in his newly self-appointed role as mentor of promising young jihadi like Khaled.

Three days later, Shahid was back at the apartment. He told Khaled they would be traveling soon. Five days after that, they were on I-75 heading south near Chattanooga, TN when Shahid finally told him their destination was Houston.

Shahid said Khaled was now his deputy and the two of them would lead a team of fighters in an attack on 72,000-seat Reliant Stadium. It would be on August 20 during a pre-season home game. Even the parking lots would be filled with fans taking part in tailgating parties.

Khaled began a desperate search for an opportunity to call Mark.

*

Houston, Texas

The day after arriving in Houston, Shahid took Khaled shopping. At a thrift shop, they bought a pile of second-hand uniform coveralls, used backpacks and well-worn briefcases. Wearing the coveralls, and carrying hand tools in toolboxes from a pawnshop, Shahid and Khaled talked their way past security posing as maintenance personnel arriving to do repairs.

"We're going to tour the stadium," Shahid said. "I want to make some sketches and draw maps while we're there. Here, take this camera. Get some pictures of the seating, the scoreboards and center field. Then we will go through the tunnels under the stands so I can make more sketches. I want you to take pictures also of the stairways, locations of restrooms, concession booths and the four main gates."

*

Meanwhile, in a low-income suburb called South Houston, Jammal Garvey was celebrating his 19th birthday. He would not see his 20th.

Jammal lived in a tiny apartment with his mother Ladonna and little sister Roshona. He was finishing a special summer course for gifted students at University of Houston and would soon be starting his sophomore year in computer science. He'd waited until the morning of his birthday to tell his mother and sister he'd been approved for membership in the University's prestigious Honors College. Ladonna was overjoyed and proud of her son. Just a few years earlier, he'd seemed lost, or so she'd feared.

Jammal had survived a close call with drugs and gangs. But now his prime interests were maintaining his honors level grades, scholarships, and being a fan of the Houston Texans NFL team. He wasn't just any old fan . . . but a fiercely loyal one. So, for her son's 19th birthday, Ladonna managed to wrangle two seats for the game on August 20. They were in the coveted Section 107, almost at center field and only eight rows back from the Texans' bench. Ladonna was convinced of Divine intervention when the Texans' Ticket Exchange Office called offering two tickets for the August 20 game. It was a pre-season game, but Ladonna felt lucky to get any tickets at all.

Ladonna had planned far ahead in order to pull off this treat for her son. Her request to the ticket office had gone in almost a year earlier. And money was tight. To pay for the tickets, at the shocking $355 each demanded by the owner, she'd worked extra shifts and scrimped on expenses since Jammal's 18th birthday. Earlier, unexpected medical expenses had left Ladonna feeling guilty that she'd been unable to afford much for his 18th, an important milestone birthday. So, she decided to splurge for his 19th.

The family was experiencing rough times. Three years earlier, just before Jammal turned 16, his father was fired as a foreman at Odland Construction Ltd. and went to jail. Tyrone Garvey, a 12-year employee, had been running his own construction company on the side, building cement sidewalks and patios. The trouble was, all of the materials were stolen from Odland warehouses. Six other Odland employees were involved and were fired. Tyrone was the ringleader and held a position of trust in the company. A no-nonsense judge sent him to jail for four years. The others had received suspended sentences.

The family lost the four-bedroom, 2½-bath rancher Ladonna and Tyrone had scrimped for years to buy in the Williamsburg Settlement, a middle class suburb of Katy, in greater Houston. With no income, Ladonna couldn't meet the mortgage payments. And there was little equity left after Tyrone's legal expenses, property taxes and real estate fees when she sold the house. Ladonna moved with her two children into a two-bedroom one-bath 'economy' apartment on Broadway Street in South Houston. With no education past high school, she felt lucky to find work as a clerk at a nearby Chevron Food Mart.

Shortly after they moved to South Houston, Jammal began hanging out with a group of teenaged big-spenders attached to the infamous Houstones gang. Before going to jail, his father always had money when Jammal needed it. With his dad in jail, the money had stopped. Soon, 16-year-old Jammal started running drugs for the Houstones. One day, he skipped classes at Milby High School, a common occurrence. Jammal decided to do some heisting at the 99-Cent Store on Broadway for stuff he'd fence or trade later. Then he went to meet his Houstones drug contacts at Luciano's Pizza, farther down the street.

Jammal didn't notice that a Milby High guidance counselor, Victor Morenz, was there, having a quick pizza lunch.

"Hey, that 99-Cent Store's a pushover," Jammal boasted to his friends, showing them his proceeds of shoplifting.

Morenz overheard him. He recognized Jammal as one of the gifted kids at Milby. He'd come to the attention of counselors as a promising student during the transfer of his records from Katy. Victor and other teachers were concerned about the direction that Jammal's life was taking.

Back at Milby High, Victor phoned a not-for-profit agency called Youth Horizons Unlimited, a national non-profit organization. Its role was to intervene when promising juveniles appeared headed for trouble. The agency's prime funding came from the Prescott Foundation, financed personally by Anne and Paul Winston. Youth Horizons never took action without parental approval and support. They contacted Ladonna. She eagerly approved sending him to a prestigious private school. Within a few months, Jammal's insatiable thirst for knowledge and the close caring support he received began chasing away the emotional demons he'd been accumulating since his father's imprisonment.

Jammal graduated high school and won a scholarship to study computer science at University of Houston. Ladonna wanted him to live at home while attending university. So did he. That meant more than an hour on the bus each way every day. He understood it would be much quicker for him to drive to the campus. A car would take only 15 minutes, tops. And there was plenty of cheap parking off Wheeler Street, a reasonable walk for young legs to his classes in Philip G. Hoffman Hall. There was just one problem . . . no car.

Three weeks after his freshman classes began Jammal went to collect their mail in the lobby.

Among the mail was a padded 6 x 9 inch envelope addressed to him. It had no return address.

"Do either of you have any idea what this is all about?" he said, suspecting his mother or sister might be up to something for his birthday.

"Not me," his mother said. His sister shrugged her shoulder, looking curious.

Jammal tore open the end of the brown envelope.

Out fell a set of car keys. Included in the envelope were the ownership, registration and insurance documents made out in his name for a two-year-old off-lease Impreza sedan. Enclosed also were a typed note with directions where to find the car, a parking tag for the University lot near Hofmann Hall, and 50 crisp new twenty-dollar bills. Jammal later assumed correctly the cash was for gas and maintenance. The note was not signed.

Jamal found the car parked in front of Luciano's Pizza. The location was no accident. He got the message.

No one else except Anne Winston would ever know about a secret trip to and from Houston two days earlier taken by Paul Winston.

Chapter 15

Atlanta, GA

With his teams of fighters deployed for the four attacks, Rhamir attended a gathering of the Muslim Brotherhood of America (MBA) in Atlanta, GA. He belonged to the secretive MBA but was inwardly scornful of their moderate ways. Rhamir's plan was to become known among MBA leaders in advance of the day when he would lead the Islamic Army of America to victory and assume the leadership of the new People's Islamic Government of America that he would create.

Rhamir had another reason for being there: meeting with his nuclear attack team.

"It's on its way!" Rhamir told his three fighters. "The device was shipped last week."

The nuclear team had checked into the Days Inn College Park near Hartsfield-Jackson International Airport. Rhamir had skipped some MBA sessions to meet with Mohamed Shokar, Lakhbir Barehi and Anwar Chegini in their economy motel rooms. They had much to discuss.

Rhamir explained ISIS had obtained the "suitcase nuke" – as they were called – from North Korea. When the former Soviet Union dissolved, about 100 of the portable two-kiloton nuclear bombs had gone missing. Even the Russian successor to the former Soviet KGB secret service was unable to track them down. North Korea's 'supreme leader' Kim Jong-un had given ISIS the nuclear device as a gesture of good will and solidarity in their mutual fight against America and other western 'imperialist' countries. Aware the device would require devious smuggling to get it into the country, Rhamir was pleased with ISIS's clever strategy.

"Allah be praised!" an enthusiastic Rhamir said. "The message I received was that our nuclear package is arriving in a container labeled as machinery parts. It will be made to look like its being shipped from South Korean. The container will arrive in a few weeks. I'll let you know. Meanwhile, I want you to round up a truck with a flatbed trailer capable of hauling the container, and an empty trailer to unload the other contents. I'll tell you later where to take it."

"What else is in the container?" Barehi asked.

"Junk machinery parts as camouflage . . . and PETN for the next phase of our war," Rhamir said. A malicious grin played at the corners of his mouth. "We're going to show those American infidels what a modern war is like, and we will do it in their own country, for a change. They'll see how they like it!"

Rhamir already knew where the suitcase nuke would arrive. It was on board a tramp steamer bound for a remote abandoned dock north of the Port of Miami. Like Rhamir had said, the container was labeled 'machinery parts'. It also contained almost a ton of PETN.

His nuclear jihadists were well qualified to check and prepare the bomb, and would deliver it to Times Square. Barehi was in charge of logistics. He'd been trained in guerilla tactics by al-Qaeda in Pakistan and then had gone underground while earning a master's degree in civil engineering from MIT. That's where Rhamir had met him. Egypt-born Shokar was the technical brains, with a doctorate in atomic physics from Princeton University. He was in America on an expired student visa and in charge of getting the device ready. Chegini had been trained as a heavy equipment mechanic before coming to America from Algeria on a student visa ostensibly to study mechanical engineering at UCLA. His assignment was to install the nuclear device and set the timer.

That evening, Rhamir met separately with the rest of his elite jihadists at the conference. They would organize a shadow standby Sharia government structure ready for their successful revolution. The leader of the team was Fahim Tahir, a doctoral graduate in economics from Stanford. Tahir was a contradiction. He was a brilliant economist with a promising future. But secretly he was also a fanatical Islamist, who saw himself as succeeding Rhamir one day. He was aware of Larigani's position as chief lieutenant and of Shahid's ambitious nature. His abundant ego didn't allow him to consider either a threat to his goal. Besides, Tahir was as close to being a confidant to Rhamir as anyone, including Larigani and Shahid. He was also Rhamir's primary authority on a key strategy in their North American Islamic war and revolution – to destabilize the American economy. Tahir knew how to do it.

Tahir had joined the Muslim Brotherhood five years earlier. Having kept his radical beliefs secret, he was on the MBA's board and also president of the

Islamic Council of America, the most influential of the Brotherhood's front organizations. The ICA's public stand advocating peaceful coexistence among all peoples and faiths was a ruse but had drawn attention in Washington. As a result, Tahir had been appointed by the White House to a senior position on the influential National Commission on Race and Cultural Relations. Only Rhamir knew of Tahir's true sentiments, not even Tahir's wife.

At just 34, Tahir was the 'golden boy' of Rhamir's revolution strategy. Not only did Tahir have a respected reputation nationally, his name had been mentioned as a potential Republican candidate for Congress from his home state of California.

"Our glorious jihad needs your help and influence more directly now," Rhamir told him when the two met privately. "As you will see very soon, all of our work will start bringing results at last."

"I am at your service, Rhamir," the fashionably dressed Tahir told his leader. He envied Rhamir, for his imposing stature and position of leadership.

"I have an urgent job for you," Rhamir said. "I need you to meet as soon as possible with each of our key jihadists gathering intelligence in schools, mosques, special interest organizations, government agencies and the military reserves," Rhamir said. "They must be put on alert to monitor everyone around them when our war begins. That will be on August 20. It's imperative this intelligence is coordinated with our fighters before the next phases of our glorious war. We must deal promptly and firmly with doubters and detractors. You are now in command of our intelligence forces."

"I'm honored," Tahir replied with genuine excitement. It was the next step toward his ambition, he thought. "I will not let you down. I will clear my schedule and do as you require."

Chapter 16

East Harlem

August 20 had finally arrived. It was time!
Rhamir's excitement mounted as he paced the
floor in his latest Harlem apartment. He struggled to
concentrate. The four teams of fighters were poised
to synchronize their attacks. Rhamir glanced again
and again at the clock. The minutes ticked toward
the top of the hour.

His eyes kept switching between the clock and his
television set, waiting impatiently. Soon would come
the first 'Breaking News' reports of the attacks.

*

Tempe, AZ

Michael Shapiro was driving home from the
University of Arizona slightly impatient that his
lovely young wife Anne Marie had asked him to
stop at the post office. She wanted him to mail a
birthday card to her Oma (grandmother) Colleen
Mayer in Winter Springs, Florida. Time was short.
Anne Marie was adamant it had to be on time. That
meant standing in line for counter service and paying
for Priority Mail. At a stoplight, he took the
envelope out of his briefcase. It was beside him on
the front seat of the six-year-old BMW 328i sedan
he'd restored and prized so highly.

"Shit!" he said out loud, as he came too quickly upon the left turn he needed to slip into the parking lot at the Tempe post office. Finally, there was a break in the traffic. Michael gunned his BMW into the lot. He was pleasantly surprised to find a vacant spot just a few stalls from the front door. His heart sank as he noticed through the windows a sea of people milling about in the lobby. The post office was busy. No chance for a quick in-and-out.

Michael headed for the front door. A package on the sidewalk caught his attention. It was propped against the wall, and appeared abandoned. Instinctively, he picked it up. The package was heavy, maybe a couple of pounds. It was wrapped in brown paper. An arrow in black marker through the address label pointed to the return address. Written awkwardly were the words, "Return to Sender". Michael thought the package might have slipped off a postal worker's cart or someone couldn't fit it into a mailbox and left it, not wanting to wait in line. He took the package inside and tried the mailbox. It wouldn't fit. Michael took it to a clerk serving another customer. The customer gave him a sharp disapproving look. He left the package, and smiled to the customer. He wished her a nice day, and meant it.

Be patient, he reminded himself.

He went back to the end of the agonizingly long line that snaked back and forth several times across the lobby. About a dozen other people were hanging around the lobby, presumably waiting for someone in the lineup.

Michael kept struggling to remain calm while waiting his turn in the single-story post office. He was eager to get home to Anne Marie and to play with their two children. His heart burst with pride every time he thought of their young family. Michael and Anne Marie had all sorts of plans. They'd even opened savings accounts for the children's college education.

Meanwhile, two blocks from the post office, Ahmed Gamma, a baby when his parents came to America from Egypt 19 years earlier, sat in a car on South College Avenue. He punched into the cell phone balanced on his knee a number written on a piece of paper. As he watched the small screen display the numbers, he thought what a pity it was to discard the stolen phone in a dumpster after the attack. But those were his orders. And he was a soldier. Now, the numbers were set. All he had to do was wait for the call on his real phone and push the 'Send' button.

His excitement grew as the last few seconds ticked by. Then he got the call.

"Now!" Gamma said out loud and pushed, 'Send'.

Chapter 17

South Houston, TX

Enthusiasm was running high as the Garvey family woke on game day. It was hard to tell who was more excited – Ladonna, Roshona or Jammal. He was finishing up a summer course at University of Houston and getting ready for the first semester of his sophomore year. Ladonna was delighted with Jammal's marks. He was quietly proud of his grades, too.

"Hey Roshona," Jammal said as he left for the university. "See you on campus for lunch. Call me when you get there. Don't be late!"

He was teasing Roshona. Jammal knew his little sister was a stickler for punctuality.

Jammal was looking forward to attending the game with Roshona. She was a huge Texans fan too. He was fond of his little sister, with her penchant for brightly colored clothes and beaded braids. He especially enjoyed Roshona's sharp wit and mischievous nature. He took pride in setting a good example for her, thanks to his mother's intervention three years earlier.

Roshona was in her senior year at Milby High and earning honor's grades. She'd already received advanced acceptance for nurses training when she graduated next spring. Roshona was well aware their mother would have become a nurse except she'd got pregnant in her teens, and now was struggling to support herself and her two children. Roshona's mission in life was to see that her mother's dream came true, through her, and to eventually earn enough to give her mother an easier life.

Jammal had gone early to the university to finish an assignment. He'd been there only two hours when his cell phone rang.

"Hi, Jammy!" his sister said, using her affectionate nickname for him. "I'm downstairs in the lobby."

He was surprised. They weren't due to leave for the game at Reliant Stadium for at least two hours. Jammal had planned to get in more study time.

"What's up sis?" he asked. "How come you're so early?"

"I was sitting at home and had an idea, Jammal," she replied.

"Oh, oh!" Jammal replied in a teasing tone. "Did it hurt much?"

"C'mon Jammy," Roshona chuckled. "Momma got those great tickets for you and me. I want to do something for her. To say 'thank you' for everything she does for us, you know. I thought maybe we could go shopping before the game. I've an idea."

"Good for you, little sister," Jammal said. He was impressed and pleased Roshona had thought to do something nice for their Mom.

"Look, why don't we go over to Moody Towers and grab something to eat?" Jammal said. "It's not far from my car. We can take care of your shopping on our way to the stadium. Okay?"

"Our shopping," she corrected him.

Over lunch, Roshona said she'd overheard their mother telling a friend that someday she wanted to treat herself to a spa, a whole day of it, just as soon as she got a few dollars ahead. A wonderful package being advertised by Etheria Salon was just what she dreamed about. It was on for half price. Roshona knew those 'few extra dollars' would be a long time coming. Their mother always spent extra dollars on her children, rarely on herself.

"What will that set us back?" Jammal asked.

"Well, I've saved $200 from babysitting," Roshona said with a smile, her dark brown eyes lighting up her pretty face.

"So that'll about cover it, right?" her brother said with a teasing look.

"'Fraid not, big brother," she replied, her eyes smiling as brightly as the red lipstick she wore. She added: "You're in for at least half. Hey, with your scholarships and student loans, you outta be coughing up the whole thing!"

"So, just how much is the whole thing?" he asked.

"Regularly only $445 plus taxes, say $500 even," came the answer.

"Good Lord!" Jammal said, gasping with genuine surprise. "We're not trading her in on a new Mom, you know!"

"Of course not," Roshona giggled. "That's the fee for the Spa's 'Heavenly Day'. Mom will get seven hours of being thoroughly pampered. She'll get a body scrub, a cocoon, a Vichy shower, lunch, a deep cleansing facial, a manicure and pedicure, a blow dry and hair styling, and a makeup application, and . . ."

She'd lost Jammal.

His attention went AWOL somewhere between 'body scrub' and 'cocoon'.

"Look, Jammal," Roshona said, "I called them and explained what was up with us and our tight budget. They said their 50-percent-off sale ended yesterday, but they agreed to extend the sale for us. The Spa will give us the whole package for $300 cash, taxes in . . . one heck of a deal and it's for Mom. If you cough up $175, I'll put in $125. You good with that, oh rich big brother of mine?"

"Okay, okay," Jammal conceded. "You know what Mom likes better than me. Guess this is it. Tell you what, you do $100 and I'll do $200."

"The lady said they have a gift certificate," Roshona said. "I looked it up on their website. It's really nice. And we've got time to stop and pick up the gift certificate. We'll surprise Mom when we get home. What do you think?"

"That's a go," Jammal said. They stood to leave. He gave her a one-armed big brother hug. "Good for you! I'm really proud of you, little sister."

Chapter 18

August 20

At the top of the hour, near the South College Avenue Post office in Tempe, AZ, Ahmed got a call and pressed the 'Send" button on the stolen cell phone. At that same moment in Houston, on a signal from Shahid, a radio controlled model aircraft loaded with half a pound of PETN explosive was sent on its murderous flight by Lakhbir Sajiadi and Mohamed Medhi Royan. The model plane went careening toward center field at half time in Reliant Stadium, setting off a massive chain reaction.

Farther east, four panel trucks were at their destinations in RTP near Raleigh, NC. Those drivers received calls from Shahid and promptly detonated the bombs in their vehicles, looking forward to their promised rewards as martyrs in Paradise.

News reports flashed around the world that huge explosions in three cities had claimed unknown thousands of innocent lives. Injuries were expected to be in the tens of thousands. News coverage of each of the three disasters commanded top priority on local, national and international media around the world.

Competing with those breaking news reports was another report from Washington, DC. News footage on TV was showing yellow crime scene tape and a tarp covering an unidentified man on a park bench.

Police said the young man had been beheaded minutes earlier on the steps of the Lincoln Memorial.

Someone identifying himself only as the leader of the Islamic Army of America, phoned Associated Press, Reuters and the major television networks, claiming responsibility for the explosions and the beheading. He said his army was establishing an ISIS fundamentalist state in America. No one had ever heard of the Islamic Army of America.

TV news anchors and commentators dropped all pretense of journalistic objectivity. They demanded to know why no one had anticipated these attacks and murders, much less been prepared. Several claimed falsely that they had inside knowledge, saying there had been more than enough reports of threats and warnings.

To no one's surprise, TV reporters desperate for audience ratings began to out-speculate one another in a feeding frenzy of blame and accusations over the supposed failure to prevent the blatant attacks and barbaric murders. The President's office, the FBI and Homeland Security not surprisingly topped the news media's lists of candidates for villain-of-the-month.

Chapter 19

Danbury, CT

Mark and Paige watched in horror the television reports of simultaneous bombings in Tempe, Houston and Research Triangle Park, and the senseless beheading in Washington. The couple was in the den of their new home in Danbury, CT. They had fully equipped offices duplicating their official offices.

"Oh, my God, Mark," Paige said, her face creased with distress. "Our worst fears! It's happened. Oh, my God! What do we do?"

Tears welled up in her eyes, as she pulled closer to Mark for comfort.

"Good God!" Mark gasped. "There must be thousands of innocent people involved, hurt and murdered for absolutely no reason. Bloody barbarians! Those bastards are worse than I thought. We've got to stop them, and right now!

"We expected they'd try something," Mark added, struggling to stay calm. "But we had no idea . . . those stupid goddamned budget cuts. Just maybe, those dunderheads in Washington got the message. Surely they understand now, the war is here."

He wondered, with dread, about undercover reports the radicals had a nuclear device. What he saw on TV left no doubt they would use it, if they had one.

"I sure as hell hope this removes any doubts where Caprionni will stand," he said, half to himself.

Mark had barely uttered the words when his iPhone rang. He wasn't surprised to see the caller was the mafia godfather himself.

"Mark!" Caprionni shouted over the phone. "Are you watching television? My God, man! Did you see what those savages have done to us, to our great country? It's outrageous! You were right about those bastards! You were right, son! All those poor people killed and hurt. We've got to stop them and right now!"

"Yes, Mr. Caprionni," Mark managed to say. He was surprised to hear Caprionni use his first name, and taken aback even more when Caprionni called him, 'son'. Mark took these as good signs.

"As I mentioned, sir, we need your help, very much so."

"Yes, yes!" Caprionni replied impatiently. "Okay, okay. You got it. Look, maybe I can do something. You leave that with me. I will get back to you very soon."

Caprionni abruptly hung up without saying goodbye . . . as usual.

The call from Caprionni left Mark worried about what might be going through the mind of the influential crime boss. Caprionni was still angry with the Maniero family and wanted them whacked. Mark realized there wasn't much more he could do to prevent that. And now he had much bigger problems.

His iPhone rang again.

"Hi Uncle Doug," he said. "Yeah, we've been watching the news. It's horrible, but maybe now we'll get the support we need, that everyone needs. They've got to be stopped right now! We need an all out offensive."

Amid reports of the mindless slaughters came announcements that Homeland Security had raised the National Terrorism Advisory System (NTAS) level to 'Imminent Threat Alert', the highest level, and that all law enforcement and security agencies had been placed on full alert. The Pentagon also ordered the armed forces placed on DEFCON Two, its second highest alert level.

"I've got some ideas I want to run past you," Mark told his uncle. "Can you get Prescott and Continental to go on the offence right away? It's abundantly obvious now that we need much more than passive observation. Oh, I should tell you, Paige wants to help. She has some really good ideas. What do you think?"

"An enthusiastic 'of course' to both your questions," his uncle replied. "I'll set up a meeting with our planning group. Ask Paige to join us; she'll be a great asset!

"And you're right, Mark. We've got to go after those bastards all out. I'll ask the folks at Prescott and Continental to enlist other large companies they deal with as well. And I personally will contact folks I know in the American Chamber of Commerce to bring other companies on board. I guess it's up to us. Hell, those Homeland Security bureaucrats have dropped the ball on this one, big time. Goddamn it! Their dithering has allowed those sons of bitches to attack not just those poor victims and their families, but all of us . . . all of us . . . each and every one of us!

"What in hell's gone wrong with the damned security and law enforcement in this country?" Douglas continued, getting angrier as he spoke. "Those idiots have got to climb out of their cushy silos or we're going to be in even deeper trouble. Shit, if we don't fight back, and right now, we're as good as giving those bastards license to attack us again and again.

"Just let me know what you need . . . what we can do. Okay? And ask Paige to give me a call on my direct line," he added, struggling to calm down. "I'd like to put her in charge of a combined Ops Center we're setting up, if you're okay with that. I have a feeling she'll be great at coordinating the work of both companies. I know the folks will be just delighted to have her on board."

"Yes, indeed," Mark replied, encouraged by his normally reserved uncle's forceful reaction. "I'll be in touch very soon with some ideas how Prescott and Continental could expand their support. I need some approvals, then I'll call you."

Prescott Enterprises was a large international merchant bank and holding company with a reputation for astute strategies and smart investing. It had turned around scores of small companies facing bankruptcy and made them profitable again. Paul and Anne had built Prescott into a multi-national corporation with assets exceeding $125 billion. Their personal net worth was over $3.2 billion. Continental Del Rio Oil and Gas had been an early investment by Prescott that had paid off handsomely. Today, Continental was a highly successful integrated exploration and development company with substantial investments in exploration, refining, pipelines and retail travel centers across the country. Its net asset value alone was more than $48 billion.

Mark's strategy was to bring into his alliance the impressive human networks and considerable talents represented by the large Continental and Prescott organizations and their associated companies. His boss and mentor, Warren Mitchell, was enthusiastic about Mark's idea of bringing together an alliance of highly principled civilian organizations. He had encouraged Mark to run with it.

"Do your best," he had told Mark. "I've got your back." It summed up Warren's leadership style: giving people opportunities to generate ideas, take responsibility and grow professionally.

Now, Mark wanted to ramp that up, getting the two big companies to become more proactive. His next challenge would be to team them up with organized crime. He knew it would be a monumental challenge, from both sides.

Chapter 20

East Harlem

More and more details of the terrorist attacks in the four cities continued to emerge over the next several hours. Rhamir and his army of jihadists rejoiced with each new revelation on the news media.

"Allahu Akbar!" Rhamir said to the small group of headquarters jihadists gathered in his East Harlem apartment.

"Allahu Akbar!" they replied.

"I have sent messages of congratulations to all of our brave fighters for this glorious victory," he told them. He'd sent coded emails to each team from a public library, reminding them the beheading and attacks were just the opening salvos in a much larger holy war their Islamic Army had launched to convert America into an extremist Islamic state.

"I told them also about the congratulations and encouragement we have received from our glorious ISIS leaders in Syria and Iraq, and from al-Qaeda in Pakistan and Afghanistan, and even from Yemen, Iran and Somalia! They are delighted, and maybe even a bit envious of our triumph!"

The sentiments he'd received impressed Rhamir. He knew the efforts each leader must have gone through to evade surveillance in order to send their messages. The messages would have been prepared on their computers, put on flash drives, and transported by a trusted courier to random locations. There, the messages would be transferred to another computer and then transmitted in coded messages on the Internet.

Elsewhere across America, the savage attacks were anything but cause for rejoicing among the families and the friends of the dead and injured. The numbers were staggering and growing, as more and more confirmed reports came in. The news media, beginning to grasp the seriousness of the attacks on American soil, were now showing a semblance of rational reporting.

They would soon turn their attention to follow-up stories like these:

Washington, DC

"Well, I know you don't see black single dads every day," Trayvon Jefferson had told the woman behind the desk. Receptionist Kati Watson relayed this story to investigators and a TV interviewer:

"I am black as you can see, and my daughter Alicia needs daycare", Trayvon had told her. "I just got a job doing security at the Lincoln Memorial. It starts at 8 o'clock tomorrow morning. I'd arranged for a neighbor to look after her, but her husband had a heart attack. Can't now. I've no one to look after her while I'm at work."

"You're right, Mr. Jefferson," the receptionist said she had told Trayvon. "Single fathers are not common, and single black fathers like yourself are rare. That's why I'm telling you we have to make background checks. It's just routine. But it takes time to confirm that you are who you say you are."

Kati told Trayvon she would put Alicia in a temporary slot, but just for a week. That's the best she could do, and it should be enough time for the paperwork.

She said Trayvon was all smiles when he told her: "Oh, thank you, Miss! Thank you so much!" She could see his world had immediately become much brighter. He'd added: "You're a gem!"

"Let's go Love," Trayvon had said to his five-year-old daughter.

Kati said Trayvon had wanted to celebrate and had offered to buy his daughter an ice cream cone. She overheard Alicia say her favorite was strawberry. Trayvon had replied his favorite was butterscotch. The last she'd seen them, the father and daughter were heading for an ice cream stand near the Lincoln Memorial.

Fifteen minutes later, Trayvon and Alicia were carrying ice cream cones. They'd sat on a bench beside the walk leading to the Reflecting Pool. Trayvon was proud of his new job. He would be guarding one of the nation's most important monuments.

The TV reporter reconstructed what happened next from Kati's remarks and the observations of witnesses on the scene:

"Can I go run around here a bit?" Alicia had asked her Daddy.

"Sure," Trayvon had replied. "But be sure you stay on the walk, beside the Reflecting Pool. Okay?"

"Okay, Daddy." And away she went to burn of off a bit more of her abundant energy.

Trayvon stood to stretch and watch Alicia. Her back was to him. She was running at top speed up the Reflecting Pool. He worried about her falling and skinning her knees. His unfinished ice cream was in his hand.

A hand grabbed his hair and pulled his body back across the bench. Half standing, leaning backward, Trayvon saw from the corner of his right eye a brown hand with a long shiny knife. He felt a sharp pain at the base of his throat. It was the last sensation Trayvon Jefferson ever experienced.

A woman screamed. A crowd gathered. Police sirens wailed.

The headless body of a black male about 32 years old lay sprawled across a park bench, arms over the back of the bench. A pool of blood had formed in the grass behind the bench. A man's head lay six feet away, its eyes open and sightless.

A little girl ran up and made her way through the assembled crowd to the bench where she and her Daddy had been sitting minutes earlier. There were traces of pink ice cream on her lips and cheeks.

Alicia looked, and started screaming hysterically: "Daddy! Daddy! Daddy!" over and over and over.

A woman stepped from the crowd of terrified onlookers, picked up Alicia and wrapped her tight in her arms, turning so Alicia faced away from the gruesome scene. Police checked the dead man's ID and made the connection between him and Alicia. The city's child protective service was called.

People on the scene interviewed by police investigators gave conflicting reports of the attackers. There was one visual everyone agreed about: both attackers wore black jumpsuits and black balaclavas covering their heads and faces. One man had a blood-splattered knife in his right hand. The other carried a compact video camera and recorded the savage event. Both had disappeared immediately. The jumpsuits and balaclavas along with a blood streaked knife were found discarded in a nearby dumpster.

*

Tempe, AZ

Anne Marie and Janice were watching a children's show on television. She'd just finished changing Darrin's diaper. He was lying on his pad in the middle of their tiny living room floor. The children's show was interrupted by a breaking news bulletin:

"We have received preliminary reports of a large explosion moments ago at a post office in downtown Tempe," the news anchor said. "The USPS office is near the campus of Arizona State University. Early reports from witnesses indicate the post office was heavily damaged."

The investigation later revealed most of the customers and staff inside could not have survived the intense explosion. A crater three feet deep had been created where the lobby and part of the parking lot had once been.

Anne Marie froze as news bulletin updates flashed across the TV screen. She kept telling herself Michael was not there, that he could have gone to any one of three other post offices near the ASU campus. The delusion wasn't working.

Four hours later, Michael was still not home. Despite repeated frantic calls, Anne Marie had been unable to reach Michael's cell phone, or her parents or Michael's parents. She knew that her parents had gone on a daylong hike into the Superstition Mountains, as they did every Saturday. They didn't like mobile phones. Michael's parents were shopping somewhere in Phoenix. They usually had one or both of their mobile phones with them, but often didn't remember to turn them on.

Anne Marie had somehow managed to feed both children their supper. The three then sat on the living room sofa. She held both children close to her, paralyzed with fear and fighting to push away what her instincts kept screaming at her.

Still glued to the TV, the sound turned low, a now-panicky Anne Marie caught a glimpse through their living room window of an Arizona State University police cruiser pulling up out front. Anne Marie was almost hysterical and barely able to stand when she finally opened the front door. Two uniformed campus police officers stood there. Darrin, restless and fighting sleep, was perched on her left hip. A visibly nervous and sleepy Janice clung to her mother's right leg.

Anne Marie glanced at the somber looks on the two police officers faces and understood. She swayed as her knees began to buckle. The female police officer leapt forward, grabbing her around the waist with one hand and Janice with the other. A male officer stepped quickly through the door and around them, catching Darrin as he began to slip from his stricken mother's arm.

Anne Marie screamed repeatedly, "No! Oh, No! Oh, God, Noooooo!" while Const. Betsy Watson half carried her, and a screaming Janice to their living room sofa.

Const. Stan Valenzuela cradled Darrin in his arms, trying to calm him. He headed for the kitchen to shield the bewildered little boy from his uncontrollably grieving mother and wailing sister. Eventually, Const. Watson was able to inform Anne Marie that Michael had been one of the first casualties to be identified.

First responders had recovered Michael's ASU student card and driver's license. Watson did not explain that a wallet with his ID had been recovered from the right rear jeans pocket of a corpse with a mangled head found in the parking lot and assumed to be that of Michael Shapiro.

Michael had been fifth from the counter when the two-pound package of PETN beneath it exploded. The fiery blast threw him and 17 others almost 40 feet out the front plate glass windows into the parking lot. Chunks of cement of all sizes torn from the building were thrown 30 feet in the air. Heavy pieces rained down on injured and unconscious people. They'd been thrown like rag dolls onto the hoods of cars and trucks, between vehicles and scattered around the parking lot.

The falling chunks of cement killed many who'd miraculously survived the initial explosion. Michael was one of them. After the initial blast, he was barely conscious in the parking lot as he instinctively struggled to stand. His hand and half of his right forearm were missing. Michael had landed face down. He struggled to get up using his left arm and the stump of his right, blood gushing all around him. Michael was almost to his knees when a 28-pound chunk of cement with a three-foot length of rebar through it landed at the base of his skull. His head was turned into an unrecognizable bloody mass of brain, tissue and bone. The rebar pierced his back, pinning his body to the parking lot.

Inside a pile of rubble where the post office had been, 32 bodies were scattered around the lobby and behind the counter. A split second after the massive blast what remained of the roof had come tumbling into the lobby and mail sorting area in the back. A metal utilities post, turned into a spear by the force of the enormous blast, had impaled a man working on a sorting machine in the back shop. His limb body hung suspended inches from the floor, pinned to a cement block wall. Cement pillars holding the ceiling and roof were reduced to dust and gravel. A woman employee's body was cut almost in half by the metal fin from a circular conveyor ripped to shreds. Parts of the conveyor had been scattered like deadly Frisbees in all directions. Across the street, homes and small businesses were heavily damaged. Inside, first responders and volunteers found residents, and employees and customers either dead or seriously injured under collapsed homes and buildings.

*

Michael's parents, Beth and Joe Shapiro, first caught news of an explosion near ASU on their car radio while driving north on Interstate 17 toward their home in Sedona. They'd spent a long day shopping in Phoenix. Beth was driving and had waited for Joe to wake from a nap before turning on the radio.

"Joe," Beth said anxiously, glancing over at her still-sleepy husband in the passenger seat. "Did you hear on the radio there's been a terrible explosion in Tempe near ASU? We need to phone Michael and Anne Marie right away . . . to make sure they and the kids are all right. Okay? Will you call them please?"

Joe nodded, still groggy. He turned on his iPhone. He speed-dialed their home number. There was no answer. He called Michael's iPhone. No answer. He waited 10 minutes. Beth was growing more impatient by the minute. Joe called their home again. A male voice answered. It wasn't Michael.

"I'm calling for Michael or Anne Marie Shapiro," Joe said. "Do I have the correct number?"

"Who's calling please?" the voice asked.

"This is Joe Shapiro," he answered. "I'm Michael Shapiro's father. Who am I speaking to?"

"Sir, you have the correct number," the authoritative-sounding voice said. There was a long pause.

"My name is Const. Stan Valenzuela. I'm with the Arizona State University Police Department. Before we continue, sir, may I ask you something? Are you driving a vehicle? I can hear sounds of a vehicle in the background."

Joe assured the constable he was a passenger in a car driven by his wife.

"I'm afraid I have some terrible news for you, sir. I regret very much having to tell you this over the phone, but we're going to need your help here. Your son Michael was in an explosion at a post office here in Tempe. I'm very sorry to have to tell you this, Mr. Shapiro, but your son has been identified among those deceased. My partner and I are here with Mrs. Shapiro . . . with Anne Marie . . . and her children. I'm very, very sorry, sir."

Joe suppressed the urge to question . . . to challenge this horrible news. He was concerned about Beth. His hand holding the iPhone fell to his lap, the phone forgotten in the shock. He stared blankly out the windshield, trying desperately to maintain his composure and make sense of what he'd just heard. Joe glanced from the corner of his eye toward his slim, elegant wife. She'd been watching with rising alarm the changes of expression on his face.

"You'd better pull over, Beth," he said, his voice barely audible. The iPhone was abandoned on his lap. He lifted his hands partially up in a gesture of helplessness. Both hands were shaking uncontrollably.

"Sir, sir, can you hear me?" Const. Valenzuela shouted into the phone. "Are you all right, sir? Can you hear me?"

Joe finally heard the voice. He put the iPhone back to his ear as Beth quickly pulled their Lexus RX 350

SUV onto the far shoulder of the highway and braked hard. Gravel and dust flew as the car came to an awkward, skidding stop.

"Are you nearby, sir?" the constable asked.

"Ah, no constable, we're not," Joe said, struggling to focus. His voice was flat and expressionless. "We've . . . ah . . . we're just about to turn off I-17 onto Highway 179. We . . . we're 20 minutes from Sedona." With a huge force of will he added, "We'd better go on to Sedona, and then come right there. Anne Marie's parents live in Sedona, too. They're friends. We better tell them . . . in person . . . and, ah, bring them back there with us. Thank you, constable. Good bye."

Joe got out of the car quickly and leaned back against the rear door, his body and knees trembling, his eyes filling. Later, Joe couldn't remember having leapt absentmindedly from the car. Beth came running around the front of the car to Joe's side, crying with fear over what little she'd heard. Beth knew the news would be devastating. Joe held her close as he told her, as gently as he could that their only son was dead. Beth screamed, "No!" "No!" "No!" again and again. She screamed louder and louder, as if her desperate cries could somehow cancel what she'd just heard. They stood beside their car at the interchange of I-17 and Highway 179 holding each other tight, in shock . . . overwhelmed with grief.

A northbound Arizona Highway Patrol car slowed down and pulled over onto the shoulder behind their car. The blue, red and amber flashing roof lights went on as the cruiser came to a stop. The officer, at first thinking they might be having car trouble, quickly recognized they were distressed. Joe left Beth and walked, shaking, supporting himself on the back of their car to the driver's side, as the officer stepped out of the patrol car. Leaning both hands on the hood of the cruiser to steady himself Joe struggled to maintain his composure as he explained what the ASU police constable had just told him on the phone. When he finished, he glanced back toward their car. Beth was nowhere to be seen.

"Beth!" he shouted. "Beth!" In a panic, he ran back to the passenger side. He found Beth, collapsed down on her haunches, her head and shoulders turned toward the car door, uncontrollable sobs tumbling out in convulsions of grief.

Officer Juan Crowe followed, saw Joe tending to Beth and returned to his cruiser. He got on his radio and was patched through to Michael's phone number that Joe had managed through his grief to give him. Officer Crowe spoke with Const. Valenzuela and then with his own supervisor. He was told to accompany the Shapiro's to Sedona. Then he was to escort both sets of parents back to Tempe so they could be with Anne Marie and their grandchildren. Joe sped behind the state police cruiser, its roof lights flashing, to Anne Marie's parent's home. Throughout the short drive, Beth sat beside Joe, crying inconsolably, refusing to release his right arm clasped tightly in both of her hands, her head on his shoulder.

Don and Carol McAndrews had returned hungry from their hike and were ready to sit down to an early supper. They were delighted to see Shapiro's

166

car pull unexpectedly into their driveway. The two couples had become friends after their offspring began dating at Sedona Red Rock High School. The McAndrews couldn't see the AHP cruiser stopped in front of their neighbors' home, its roof lights off. Don and Carol scurried around, happily anticipating the unexpected visit, quickly setting two more places on the dining room table.

The happy smiles lighting Don and Carol's faces as they answered the door together would not be seen again for a very long time.

Chapter 21

Research Triangle Park, NC

Back in early August, eight of Rhamir's fighters had arrived in Morrisville, NC, an exquisitely groomed historic town between Raleigh and Research Triangle Park. The jihadists were in four white second hand panel trucks and two white used cars. Rhamir believed the color gave the impression of official. To reinforce this subterfuge, the men had used a laptop to create homemade decals resembling those on the vehicles of Progress Energy, an electric utility company that served the area.

En route to Morrisville, the panel trucks had met a transport at a rest stop near Interstates 10 and 295, west of Jeffersonville, FL. There, in the middle of the night, Rhamir's jihadists had unloaded cartons of PETN explosive from the transport. They would be used to attack the IBM campus at Research Triangle Park. During the next few days, each of the panel trucks was rigged with 550 pounds of PETN, detonator caps, wiring and switches to set off massive explosions in four locations around the sprawling IBM research facility.

And then August 20 had arrived.

The vehicles drove in convoy along Interstate 40 to Davis Drive and the East Cornwallis Road entrance to RTP. There, they split into two shorter convoys of one car followed by two panel trucks. Jihadists in the cars were to eliminate security, thereby allowing the trucks to get onto the IBM property. The car drivers coordinated their mini-convoys with walkie-talkies. Both drivers were armed with Uzi submachine guns fitted with silencers. Their partners in the passenger seats had AK-47 assault rifles, also fitted with silencers, lying on the floor behind the front seat.

As the first convoy approached its checkpoint, an overweight security guard eased himself up out of a chair and waddled from the booth, looking annoyed at the inconvenience.

"Your authorization?" the indifferent guard demanded, holding out his hand. He glanced casually into the car and then back at the two white panel trucks that had pulled up behind. They looked harmless enough. Besides, all three vehicles had Progress Energy logos on the doors. The second guard remained in the booth absorbed in a copy of Playboy and a box of cold fries.

The car driver, Arthur Sheikh Tanir, reached his right hand down below the car seat, under his legs. His fingers closed around the Uzi lying there. At the same moment, Randy Ghahramanlou slipped out of the passenger seat of the two-door car, pulling as he went the AK-47 behind the seat. Both jihadists opened fire at the same time. The two guards died instantly from multiple bullet wounds to the head and upper body. A similar violent scenario unfolded simultaneously at the other security booth. The two guardhouses were more than 200 yards from the nearest building – far enough that no one heard the silenced gunshots. The fighters drove the cars through the gates and pulled into parking spots behind the guard booths. This allowed the panel trucks carrying the PETN to pass and the drivers, soon to be martyrs, to proceed to their assigned detonation points and await their calls.

After the trucks passed, the two cars carrying the four jihadists pulled U-turns at the guard booths and headed back to I-40. Minutes later, they were turning off the Interstate into Raleigh-Durham International Airport.

Meanwhile, outside IBM's headquarters building, Stan Tassel was affectionately watching in the rear view mirror as his wife of 30 years, Josephine neared their car. Even after all these years, his heart warmed every time he saw her. He knew she felt the same way about him.

As Stan looked through the passenger side rear view mirror, a bright flash in the cab of the panel truck behind him distracted his attention. The truck disappeared. For a nanosecond, Stan caught a fleeting glimpse of Josephine and the look of surprise and horror on her face. Then her body flew past their car and beyond his field of vision. Before he could move his head, their car was flying through the air. It landed 30 yards away in a parking lot and rolled repeatedly for another 15 yards until what little remained of it slammed against the cement base of a light standard. Except for the portion of the passenger compartment with Stan's lifeless body, much of the Ford Expedition was missing. Parts of Josephine's body would never be recovered.

In the headquarters building, single mom Mary Gillespie had just waved to Josephine from their second floor office when she caught a glimpse of the explosion out of the corner of her left eye. Parts of the double-pane plate glass window she was looking through slammed into her body, carrying her across the office and against the inner office wall, ripping it from its moorings. The force of the huge blast carried the 'human sandwich' that had been Mary Gillespie almost 200 feet into the interior of the building. More than 120 people were killed and at least 260 others injured, some critically, at that location alone.

After leaving RTP, the four jihadists drove to the Raleigh-Durham airport, parked the two cars, removed the coveralls concealing their business suits, cleared security and were at separate check-in counters. They now appeared as young professionals. The jihadi boarded two different flights in pairs, one of them just minutes after the multiple blasts.

Delta Airlines Flight 1184, bound for Phoenix, AZ, took off from Raleigh-Durham International Airport over a deep ravine beyond Runway 5 L. Passengers on board included Arthur Sheikh Tanir and Randy Ghahramanlou, both immaculately dressed in American-style suits and ties.

"Allahu Akbar!" Ghahramanlou and Tanir whispered quietly to each other as the plane climbed for altitude circling over Research Triangle Park. Passengers on the right side of the aircraft could see four columns of black smoke rising from RTP. On I-40 below them, a seemingly uncoordinated profusion of police, fire and ambulance vehicles was heading at high speed from both directions toward the IBM campus, lights and sirens blazing.

After landing in Phoenix, and after making certain they were not followed, the two jihadist fighters would make their way to a second training camp that Rhamir was building in the mountains southeast of Albuquerque, NM. Tanir and Ghahramanlou were the first of two teams to leave the Raleigh-Durham airport that day.

The other two-man team boarded Delta flight 1908, for Tucson, AZ, via Atlanta. They would also take a circuitous route to their destination. All four were looking forward to helping finish the new camp. There, they would join with other members of the Islamic Army to celebrate the martyrdom of the four fighters who'd driven the truck bombs in Research Triangle Park, and gone to Paradise.

Chapter 22

Durham, NC

It was late afternoon on August 20 by the time the three-man team had located William (Will) Tassel in the Goodson Law Library at Duke University. The university's police chief Jack Holbestad, Chaplain Robert Stillman and North Carolina State Trooper Donald Mendez found Will reading academic law reviews in Journals Alcove #1 on Level 4 of the library. Most of Will's fellow summer session law students had gone for the weekend.

"Will?" Chief Holbestad asked. "William Tassel?"

"Yes, sir," a startled Will said looking up to find two police uniforms and a clerical suit gathered at the entrance to his study alcove. "What can I do for you?"

Will's surprise was followed by a flash of insight, and then by a wave of foreboding. Something was terribly wrong. Chief Holbestad pulled over a chair from another alcove and sat down facing Will.

"Are you related to Stanley and Josephine Tassel?" the chief asked. He knew the answer but was obliged officially to obtain confirmation.

"Yes, I am," Will nodded, his apprehension now turned to fear. "What's the matter? What's going on?"

"I'm very sorry Will, but we have some very bad news for you," he said. "Just over two hours ago there were a number of terrible explosions at the IBM complex in RTP. Did you not hear about it?"

"No sir," Will replied. "I've been studying, trying to finish up some research here. What's wrong?"

"Well, son, I regret very much having to inform you that your parents, Stanley and Josephine Tassel, were victims of those blasts. It is my unpleasant duty to advise you that both of your parents are deceased."

Will recoiled in shock as if hit in the chest by a baseball bat. The youthful chaplain stepped forward and knelt on one knee in front of Will, taking the young man's right hand in both of his. He began performing the rituals of comfort he'd been taught at the seminary while a student.

*

Raleigh, NC

Two hours earlier, in Raleigh, Allison el-Masri (nee Tassel) had just put one-year-old Joseph Stanley down for an afternoon nap at their home on Turner Glen Drive. Allison and her three-year-old daughter, Jessie, were watching Jessie's favorite TV program, Dinosaur Train, when a news bulletin appeared.

Allison stared in disbelief at the news coverage describing the four massive simultaneous explosions on the IBM campus at RTP. After watching transfixed for almost 15 minutes, the phone rang. It was her husband, Joey, owner of a successful construction company. He'd gone to his office to catch up on paperwork.

"Have you been watching TV?" Joey asked. He was on his iPhone walking toward his car in the almost empty company parking lot.

"Yes," Allison replied, her throat tense. As she spoke, the station cut into regular programming again, this time for live coverage from its news helicopter over the IBM headquarters building. Close-up visuals began appearing on the screen.

"Oh, my God, Joey!" Allison screamed. "That's Dad's car! That's Mom and Dad's car! I see their car! What the hell's going on? It's on its side in the parking lot. I know it's their car. Oh, my God! Dad was picking Mom up. Their car's in pieces, Joey. Oh my God! What's happened? What's going on? Are they all right?"

"I'm on my way, Allison," Joey said, forcing himself to stay calm. He'd watched initial coverage on his office TV after a friend called to alert him.

As she hung up the phone, Allison's eyes filled. Grieving sounds began to emerge from deep within her soul as she collapsed on the living room sofa, holding her bewildered daughter tight to her body.

On his way home, Joey called his parents on the hands-free Bluetooth in his car. Now retired, they'd immigrated many years earlier to Raleigh from Egypt as a newly married couple before he was born. They were no strangers to irrational violence, or to the importance of family support at such times. Joey's next call was to his best friend, a senior manager in the RTP security department.

"What's going on, Hal," he said. Joey could hear pandemonium in the background. As soon as his friend could make out who was calling he hurriedly confirmed Joey's worst fears.

"I'm really sorry, Joey," Hal said. "One of our guys on the scene has recovered some ID's. One of those, I'm sorry to say, was from Stan's body. They found him in a Chev Suburban. We also found a purse with Josephine's ID. I shouldn't tell you this, Joey, but the purse strap was tangled on the dismembered arm of a female a few yards from the Suburban. I hate to say this, but it probably is Josephine's. We've not found the rest of her body yet."

Allison was looking out their living room window when she saw Joey's Range Rover come to a hurried stop in the driveway. She recoiled at the look in his eyes as he rushed through the door.

"No! No! No!" Allison screamed, shaking her head. Tears began flowing freely despite her struggle to remain calm in front of their daughter. It was just too much. Suddenly her emotions erupted into uncontrollable grief. She was barely aware of Joey's parents arriving moments later. Joey wrapped his arms around Allison as a storm of emotions overtook her. He half-carried his grieving wife to their bedroom.

Eventually, Joey was able to tell Allison he would notify her widowed grandmother, Anita Tassel. He went into their den and dialed the number. Joey dreaded the message he'd promised to deliver. The loss of her son would devastate Allison's kind-hearted grandmother, still raw with grief from losing her husband of 53 years just 10 months earlier.

Who could do such a horrible thing? Joey kept asking himself. *What kind of depraved barbaric monsters could do such a thing?*

Later, police would confirm explosions had occurred simultaneously at four locations on the IBM campus. All four evidently had involved panel trucks. Investigators concluded suicide bombers had driven the vehicles. The panel trucks had jumped curbs and in some cases crossed lawns and parking lots, ending up against the walls of buildings just before detonation.

An RTP public affairs spokesperson told an impromptu news conference preliminary estimates by police placed the death toll in the explosions at close to 480 and the number of injured at more than 1,240, including dozens in critical condition. Both numbers were expected to increase.

Chapter 23

Houston

Shahid was feeling smug about how they'd snuck the radio controlled model aircraft into Reliant Stadium and hid it in a construction locker.

In minutes, the big model airplane would be used to initiate the attack. He knew little about American professional sports, but his jihadists told him that for this pre-season game a popular band would provide half-time entertainment at mid-field. One of the band's multiple six-foot sound speakers would be a perfect target for the model aircraft, filled with PETN and fitted with an impact detonator.

In the weeks leading up to the game, Shahid and his fighters had dressed as maintenance workers each day. They'd used fake identification to convince security personnel of their legitimacy. After a few days, they were recognized and accepted. During that time, Shahid had made a point of making friends with Jorge Villanueva, a security supervisor at Reliant Stadium. It helped their cover story to be greeted each day by a senior guard on duty at the stadium. Shahid had learned Villanueva was divorced, born in Puerto Rico and lived alone a few blocks from the stadium. He was a fiercely loyal Texans fan and had lived in New York before moving to Houston four years ago. That gave Shahid an idea.

A year earlier in New York, he'd recruited Monroe Ayala, a hoodlum of Puerto Rican descent, living in Brooklyn's tough Bushwick neighborhood. Ayala was on the run from charges involving an armed robbery. It would be his third armed robbery charge. If convicted he'd be looking at a very long time behind bars. Ayala was already on parole from his second armed robbery conviction after serving four years. While hiding in Shahid's apartment in New York, Ayala admitted to committing more than a dozen other crimes, most of them violent, although he was never charged. It was quite a history for someone not yet 28 years old. Shahid had flown Ayala to Houston. He introduced Ayala to Villanueva. The two hit it off, chatting away in their shared Hispanic dialect. Ayala kept his past a secret. Soon, the older Villanueva and young Ayala were frequenting bars after hours and chasing women together. Ayala was sharp enough to know Shahid was up to something.

"Okay," Ayala had said to Shahid one evening. The others were outside the rundown townhouses they'd rented. "What the fuck's going on . . . you hooking me up with Villanueva? Got somethun to do with the job here, right?"

"Yes it does," Shahid told him. "He doesn't know it yet, but Villanueva's going to supply us with some of his uniforms on the day of the attack. You're gonna get them from him the night before. Kill him and take the uniforms, okay? Whatever else you find in his place is yours."

Ayala glared at Shahid long and hard, and then looked away smiling inwardly. He knew Villanueva kept a large amount of cash in a cheap portable safe under his bed. He saw him go into it one night when both became too drunk to go anywhere. They'd ordered more booze and a pizza delivered. He also knew Villanueva had a Rolex watch given to him by his grandfather, a retired New York City watchmaker. A few other things belonging to Villanueva interested Ayala as well. He looked forward to having them. Ayala's weapon of choice was a switchblade, which he'd make sure was very sharp.

Shahid's ramshackle townhouse in the Meadows Place suburb of Houston served as headquarters for the attack. The other jihadists were housed in adjacent townhouses. The fighters used his basement to mix the PETN and make the shaped charges for the three kinds of bombs – the 'drone' bomb, the briefcase bombs and the backpack bombs. They would be assembled at the stadium. The car bombs were assembled one by one in Shahid's tumble down garage. The fighters had packed 350 pounds of PETN into each car. The explosives were wired to detonate when the car security alarm went off. A toggle switch would put the alarm circuits onto live standby once the cars were in the stadium parking lots. Much of the remaining space in the back seat and trunk of each car was packed with bolts, washers, ball bearings, fencing staples, nails and loose coils of razor wire.

Shahid chose two fighters to steal tow trucks and bring them into the parking lots just before game time. They would gain entry through a service gate staffed by a jihadi fighter wearing one of

Villanueva's uniforms. The regular guard would be sent elsewhere by a fighter dressed in another of the dead supervisor's uniforms, unlikely to be challenged. During the first half of the game, each tow truck driver would remove two vehicles near the assigned gates. The hang-passes in those four cars would be removed from the rearview mirrors and distributed to four drivers to enter the parking lots with the car bombs.

Shahid, his RC model aircraft crew and the teams of fighters assigned to place the backpack and briefcase bombs had all dressed as usual in the maintenance company coveralls with fake identification tags. Two fighters were sent to each of the four gates. At an agreed time, one from each team was to drop the backpack bombs into trashcans near the restroom doors on the lower level after setting the timers. The other members of the teams were to give concession workers near the four exits large tips to keep the briefcase bombs while they claimed to use the restroom. There, in the panic after the model aircraft exploded, the briefcase bombs would be knocked over and detonated. The backpack bombs had a double purpose. Shahid expected them to be detonated when the briefcase bombs exploded. If any failed, the timers would detonate them.

And now, the hour had arrived at last!

Shahid re-checked his wristwatch. The car bombs would be in the parking lots by now with the alarm systems enabled.

"We're in place and ready to go," said Nick Estahani over their walkie-talkies. Fighters at other gates also reported that the briefcase and backpack bombs were in place.

"Get ready," Shahid said over the radio. "Watch for the model plane."

Shahid and his model aircraft crew, Mohamed Medhi Royan and Lakhbir Sajiadi, were high up in the stadium, above the Comcast Gate, in the last row of seats. Their departure would have to wait until the panic and confusion had settled down. Shahid nodded at Royan and Sajiadi.

"Proceed," he said.

Royan started the motor while Sajiadi held the aircraft. Royan revved the motor and worked the controls to confirm everything was operating properly. It was noisy. Nearby fans looked at them curiously but concluded they must be part of the halftime show. Royan looked over Sajiadi's shoulder at a security guard jogging up the stairs toward them drawn by the noise, dodging fans leaving early for restrooms and the concessions. He gunned the engine and nodded. Sajiadi held up the heavily laden model aircraft and its deadly cargo. Then he sent it off with a firm but gentle push, not wanting to jostle the impact detonator. Royan had gunned the motor to full throttle.

The airplane swooped sharply downward skimming over the heads of startled fans. The plane finally picked up speed. It headed down toward one of the huge black audio speakers at center field. Shahid reached for the silenced gun tucked in the back of his belt as the security guard arrived. The guard was the first to die there that day, but not the only one.

Minutes earlier in the parking lot, undercover agent Khaled was sweating more than usual in the August sun as he raised the hood of the car he'd driven to the northwest corner of Section 18 in the South Kirby Lot. He located the wires to the security alarm and the backup timer. Using diagonal pliers, Khaled carefully cut sections out of both sets of wires. Khaled threw away the pieces of wire and pliers, and gently closed the hood.

He ran toward the stadium hoping to find a payphone. Somehow, he had to alert the police or security, or try to reach Mark. He was deeply stressed; he'd been kept from getting away on his own to call Mark. Since they'd arrived, Shahid had kept Khaled with him, day and night. Now, he was desperately hoping he could get word out soon enough to intercept a few of the bombers, and possibly evacuate at least some fans from the stadium in time to reduce the loss of life and injuries.

Khaled frantically asked the attendant at the Amegy Bank Gate to let him through to use a payphone in the stadium.

"Where's your ticket?" the gate attendant said. When he tried to explain the urgency, the attendant signaled for a security guard.

"You can't go in there without a ticket, sir," the guard said, standing in front of him. Khaled's coveralls with the maintenance logo and nametag made no difference with the game underway. When he tried to explain that bombs were set to go off in the stadium and he needed to call 911 urgently to prevent a disaster, the guard told him:

"Look fella, I've seen all sorts of lame attempts to get in without a ticket but I'll grant you, this is a new one. Now move along unless you have a ticket."

"Then, can I at least use your radio?" Khaled pleaded, pointing toward the guard's belt. "It's critically important that I contact the police or someone in the FBI."

"No!" the guard shot back, "Don't be stupid! You can't use my radio. It's for official use only. Now, if you don't get the hell out of here right now, I'm going to have you arrested. Go on! Get lost. Now!"

Khaled turned and ran from the parking lot to their arranged meeting place in the Metrolink station. He hoped to find a payphone and make a call where the others wouldn't overhear. Shahid had confiscated all of their mobile phones after they'd arrived in Houston, for security reasons he claimed. Khaled knew Shahid didn't trust his fighters. He had that in common with Rhamir.

When Khaled arrived, many of the other fighters were already there. He had no choice but join with them. Khaled nonetheless scoured the walls of the station for a payphone. No luck. Mobile phones had all but made traditional payphones obsolete. And it was Khaled's bad luck, the train they were taking to Shahid's townhouse, showed up within minutes.

*

In the stands, Jammal left his choice seat at mid-field beside his little sister Roshona just before half time. Texans were leading 10-3.

"I'll get ahead of the crowd," he said. "What would you like?"

"A smoky," she said. "Fully loaded. And a Diet Dr. Pepper."

At the concession, he noticed a large briefcase on the floor at the back of the booth. It seemed out of place. Jammal was curious but headed back. He was anxious to get to his seat before the half time rush, and he didn't want to miss the show. Jammal arrived back with their food as Space Junk, one of the hottest current rock-hop groups, was loudly moving into the sound track for its popular new music video. It would be its last performance.

Only a few fans heard the throaty whine of the model airplane motor over the music booming from the speakers. Sight of the little aircraft puzzled some in the mid-field crowd. They watched as it made a sweeping turn over the Texans' mid-field logo and then slam into the side of a large speaker. Half a pound of PETN exploded. The singers, the musicians, football players and coaches for the Texans, and another 23 people, were killed immediately. Rescue crews later found the bodies and the IDs of fans seated at mid-field. The bodies included Jammal and Roshona. Another 450 mid-field fans suffered injuries ranging from minor cuts and bruises to broken limbs and severe internal injuries.

Eight other blasts in rapid succession rocked the stadium. All were massive, destroying nearby restrooms and stairwells. Stands and support structures collapsed onto panicked fans, sweeping away seats, as well as walkways and dozens of dying spectators. Other terrified fans fought to get out of the four main exits after the midfield blast, when more explosions at each gate destroyed large sections of the surrounding cement structures, raining down chunks of cement and seats, as well as more dead and dying fans on top of those in the exits. Fans who had managed to get out ahead of the explosions at the gates were met with enormous blasts in parking lots just outside three of the four main entrance gates. Three car bombs had done their horrific work.

Authorities later reported at least 2,380 people in the stadium had died in the numerous explosions – at mid-field, in and around the restrooms and concession stands, and around three of the four exits. More than 7,580 others were injured, many critically. Police estimated the three car bombs killed another 450 in the parking lots and injured at least 1,100. They conceded the toll of dead and injured would likely climb much higher.

The explosions in the parking lots left craters six feet deep and 80 feet in diameter. Three entrances to the stadium had disappeared. The skeleton of the structure was damaged so severely it was later ruled unstable and condemned. Some vehicles near the car bombs were found as much as 30 yards away on top of other vehicles. Police were surprised to find in the parking lot near the Amegy Bank Gate a car bomb with a large unexploded load of PETN and shrapnel inside. They did not announce why the car bomb hadn't exploded but shared that information with the FBI's counterterrorism experts.

*

South Houston

Ladonna Garvey was behind the counter at the Chevron Food Mart when a Houston Police cruiser pulled up out front. She didn't give it a thought. Houston cops stopped there all the time to get coffee, use the restrooms or leave photos of people they were looking for. Ladonna had been busy that afternoon helping restock shelves between her shifts at the counter. She guessed it would be just after half time at the football game.

Thoughts of her two children enjoying the game brought a warm smile to her gentle countenance. She was immensely proud of them. It pleased her how much they enjoyed each other's company. Nothing was more important to her than the happiness of the two people she loved beyond life itself.

Ladonna hardly noticed when two cops walked in and spoke with her supervisor. But her attention focused quickly when he looked her way and his right hand sprang to his mouth. Alarm spread through her body when he pointed directly at her. The tense looks on the three faces frightened her. Hair on the back of her neck stood up. She walked unsteadily to them, feeling her heart constricted by the apprehension coursing through her body.

"You hear about those terrible explosions at Reliant Stadium an hour ago?" her supervisor, Willy Susch asked. Ladonna went rigid and looked intently at the two cops.

"No, I didn't," she replied, barely able to breathe. Her fear skyrocketed. "I've been too busy stocking shelves. What happened?"

"A whole bunch of explosions at half time," one cop said. His nametag read, Patterson. "Looks like deliberate sabotage; maybe terrorists. Ambulances and fire trucks from all over the city, and outside, have been called in. Our radio said hundreds of people, maybe even thousands, are likely dead and thousands more hurt. We're on our way to help with traffic control."

As he spoke, Ladonna's heart suddenly felt heavy in her chest. Her breathing became labored. She reached for a shelf to steady her. Willy grabbed her arm. The cops helped him guide her into the office. Willy insisted she sit down and try to calm herself. He urged Ladonna to go home in case her children arrived there. He offered to drive her. She still had three hours left in her shift. Ladonna refused, hoping desperately to hear from Jammal or Roshona. She knew they'd try calling her first at work, if they needed to . . . if they were able to. She wanted to be there, just in case.

Finally, her shift over, Ladonna reluctantly went home. She hadn't heard from Jammal and Roshona. Her sense of foreboding became overwhelming. Two friends called after she got home and she hurried them both off the phone to keep it free, telling them why. She asked them to call around to friends and neighbors, and ask if anyone had seen her two children. She knew the answer, but denial was in control, for now. No one called back. She couldn't get through on the overloaded police phone lines to report them missing or ask about them.

Ladonna kept a vigil beside the phone through the night. The only other time her phone was in use was when she called in to work the next morning and was told to take the day off. Later that day, at 2 p.m., a knock on her apartment door startled her from a daze. She didn't want to answer it.

"Ladonna Garvey?" a woman in uniform asked softly. A shoulder patch on her uniform said 'University of Houston Police'. A male colleague stood behind her. Ladonna nodded, holding onto the door with one hand and the doorframe with the other, barely able to stand.

"I'm Constable Alicia Jefferson, University of Houston Police. This is my partner Constable Jorge Carranza. We need to speak with you. May we come in?"

"Yes . . . of course," Ladonna replied, her fear shifting to panic as she stepped back. "What's this all about . . . please?"

There was no answer as the three walked into the tidy, sparsely furnished living room. She tried to tell herself it might be about her jailed husband Tyrone, due for release on parole anytime now. She knew better. Ladonna could see they were university police. She tried to tell herself, *I hope Jammal didn't do something. Naw, surely not! He's doing so well.* The delusion wasn't working. After fighting the thought, she could no longer suppress it: *Oh, God! Surely nothing's happened to my babies.*

Constable Jefferson broke into her near hysteria and denial, motioning both of them to sit on the sofa.

Const. Carranza remained standing, looking around uneasily.

"I'm sure you've heard about those terrible explosions yesterday afternoon at Reliant Stadium?" Jefferson said after they were seated. She was half-turned toward Ladonna, their knees almost touching.

Ladonna nodded, fighting tears.

"We understand your son Jammal and daughter Roshona were attending the game," Jefferson said.

Ladonna nodded again. Now, tears began flowing freely down both of her ebony cheeks.

"We're very, very sorry to have to tell you this, Mrs. Garvey. It appears your children were among those who died in those explosions. Your son's wallet and your daughter's purse with their identification were found on bodies recovered from the wreckage of the stadium. I'm very sorry, Mrs. Garvey.

"The Houston police and the FBI have asked us to help with identification and notification of next of kin."

It took the strength of both fit young police officers to keep a wildly hysterical Ladonna under control until an emergency call brought paramedics to administer a sedative.

Ten days after the deaths of her only children, Ladonna was released from Kindred Hospital-Bay Area 16. She was never the same although she received sustained care, support and attention from a large circle of family and friends. Her appetite disappeared. Once considered borderline obese, her weight had dropped sharply. She would be considered thin now. Ladonna felt herself being drained emotionally by the many kindly visitors. She appreciated their desire to ease her grief but it didn't help. Ladonna never went out except to her job. She walked slowly there and back in a daze, always on time, her clothing hanging loosely on a body that had become little more than a skeleton.

When not working, Ladonna spent most of her waking hours rocking forward and backwards on her living room sofa until late into the evening, every evening. The sofa developed a permanent vertical groove where her now skeletal back slammed repeatedly into the sofa. Family, friends and neighbors concluded her isolation was Ladonna's way of trying to nurture back to health her severely damaged emotional state.

One hot afternoon in late August, Ladonna failed to show up for work. It was one year to the day after the deaths of her precious children, Jammal and Roshona. She had only ever missed one day of work. Her supervisor, Willy Susch, phoned the emergency number in her personnel file. Her building supervisor found Ladonna's emaciated body in a sitting position held upright by a deep vertical grove in her living room sofa. Cause of death was ruled as organ failure brought on by starvation. Ladonna was 37 years old.

Chapter 24

East Harlem, NYC

Rhamir was in his latest Harlem apartment with Larigani watching a special report following up on the terrorist attacks. Both of their faces bore huge smiles. They exchanged high fives. Everything had gone according to his plan.

These attacks would provide the momentum he wanted to help with recruiting as he began planning for the much-expanded next phase of his War on America.

*

Danbury

Mark received a call from Khaled. The undercover agent told Mark he was using a payphone in Fort Worth, TX, a third of the 866-mile trip back to a new terrorist camp in Albuquerque, NM.

Khaled struggled to contain his anger and grief while describing the horror he'd witnessed in Houston. He told Mark that he was quitting and to get him out immediately. Mark reassured Khaled that plans were in the works for a raid soon on Rhamir's new camp.

"If you leave the camp," Mark told him sternly, "all you'll be doing is sending those bastards a signal that something is amiss. You could jeopardize our raid. There has to be absolute surprise, otherwise we'll lose some very good men."

Khaled reluctantly agreed to stay after Mark reminded him that he was in the best possible position to help put an early stop to the terrorists' savagery.

*

Albuquerque

Three weeks after the attacks, Rhamir arrived at the new camp in New Mexico. He ordered his Islamic Army of America to hold a special ceremony honoring their fighters who'd returned from the four cities: Tempe, Houston, Durham and Washington. They were also to honor the martyrs who'd gone to Paradise for their holy cause. He called them, 'Heroes of the Jihad'.

Singled out for special praise was the crew of the radio-controlled model airplane used in Houston. Rhamir told the two men:

"Your skill has brought us sweet revenge! Now the infidels have seen that we can attack them with our own drones, as they have been attacking our sons and daughters, and mothers and fathers!"

Rhamir was referring to the drones America had been using successfully to attack ISIS, al-Qaeda and Taliban sites in Syria, Iraq, Afghanistan and northern Pakistan.

"We will use our own drones again and again in our holy jihad against these imperialists. I hereby appoint the two of you to lead our Islamic State Air Force in America!"

Everyone laughed, enjoying the rare humor but appreciating the serious intent behind it. They applauded loudly. All of the assembled fighters were excited and emboldened by the success of the first attacks. They were eagerly looking forward to their next assignments. Those who had not participated in the first attacks were hoping to be chosen for roles in the ones to follow. A few volunteered to become martyrs, to ensure they would be included.

Rhamir, Larigani and Shahid decided momentum was on their side. But they also knew the attacks made it essential to become more cautious. America's national security levels had been increased sharply. Now, anyone of middle-eastern origin who appeared the least bit suspicious could be hauled in for questioning any time on almost any pretext. It had started already. They'd heard about dozens of people with no connection to their jihad being taken in for questioning. Muslim groups were objecting about racial profiling.

Rhamir ordered the assembled fighters to be on guard, to "dress American" so they blended as much as possible with the population. He'd shaved his beard and ordered his jihadists to do the same. Rhamir also urged them to maintain a constant vigilance, and to report anything suspicious like possible surveillance, to him, Larigani or Shahid.

After the meeting, Rhamir called Larigani and Shahid aside.

"Our glorious leaders in ISIS are anxious for us to proceed to the next phase," he said.

Rhamir told Larigani and Shahid he wanted to use the next phase of attacks to 'further energize' the network of cells and to give more fighters 'combat experience'. This phase would bring them closer to their nation-wide revolutionary war. Then, Americans could no longer have any doubt their country was on its way to becoming a fundamentalist Islamic state.

Rhamir busied himself for weeks carefully researching the 12 American cities he'd decided on for the expanded attacks prior to the nuclear explosion in Times Square. In each, he identified specific targets and how the attacks should be carried out. His motives were varied but deadly: he wanted to kill and injure as many Americans as possible to create widespread panic, to disrupt services and to cause maximum damage.

He would demonstrate all of this with a special attack he was planning – on Lincoln Centre. It would be the prelude to Phase Two.

Rhamir finally realized that planning had become so complicated now he could no longer keep all of the details in his head. Despite his obsession with secrecy, he decided it was necessary to write his plans down. Besides, he wanted a record that he could show his ISIS superiors someday soon. He was confident also that his notes would become part of the recorded history of America once it became governed by his version of Sharia Law. His notes included specific targets within each of the 12 cities and the methods of attack he was considering:

• Seattle, Space Needle, multiple car bombs;

• Tulsa, Bank of Oklahoma Tower, truck bomb in parking garage;
• Phoenix, Sky Harbor Airport control tower, truck bomb in parking garage next to the control tower;
• Las Vegas, Caesar's Palace Coliseum, briefcase and suitcase bombs in main theater and under gaming tables;
• Dallas, World Aquarium, timed backpack bombs in tunnel through the 22,000-gallon water tank;
• Atlanta, Centennial Olympic Park, car bombs in parking lots and backpack bombs in the crowds;
• Minneapolis, Mall of Americas underwater aquarium, suitcase and briefcase bombs;
• Indianapolis, Indy 500 Speedway, car alarm bombs and timed backpack bombs at the stadium during a major race;
• Nashville, Grand Ole Opry, truck bomb during a high profile multi-star fund-raising concert;
• Detroit, Ford Motor Company assembly plants, multiple car alarm bombs next to plant entrances at shift change;
• Billings, Montana, three oil refineries (Chevron, Exxon/Mobile, Cenex), multiple radio controlled model aircraft targeting oil storage tanks (multiple teams needed for each refinery attack);
• Philadelphia, the Liberty Bell, multiple suitcase bombs to ensure destruction.

Chapter 25

Danbury

The distinctive ringtone on his iPhone drew their attention. Mark and Paige were enjoying a rare quiet evening after putting the kids to bed. Paige took the phone from Mark's hands, smiled coyly at him and said into the phone:
"This is Mark Tremblay's line. How may I help you?"

As she listened, wrinkles began to appear on her smooth forehead, and then became deeper and deeper. Paige held the phone to her chest and said, "I think it's your Grandpa. Something's terribly wrong, Mark." She pushed Mark's iPhone toward him, shaking her head. A look of fear crossed her face. He took the phone.

"This is Mark. Who's calling please?"

"Mark," said a familiar voice. It was unsteady. The strain in his grandfather's voice was unmistakable.

"I've some terrible news, son," his grandfather said. There was a long pause. He heard his grandfather clear his throat.

"It's about Warren," Paul Winston said, his voice shaking. "There's been an accident . . . a plane crash. Warren was on board, Mark. I'm terribly sorry, son, but I'm afraid we lost him in the crash."

There was a long pause.

Mark sat back heavily on the loveseat, stunned.

"Warren was on his way to Washington," his grandfather continued in a voice choked with emotion. "He stopped over here in Kansas City. We had a meeting about your alliance. The FBI jet . . . it exploded on take-off! It happened just a few minutes ago. I was seeing him off. I wasn't sure when you'd hear about it. Thought it best that I call you. This is terrible!"

There was another long pause. Mark fought to maintain his composure. Paul sensed his grandson's grief. Warren had been as much a friend and mentor to Mark as he'd been his boss.

Paige watched Mark's expressions with growing alarm. She walked over beside the chair and put her arms around his shoulders. She wondered if something had happened to his grandmother, Anne.

"What is it?" Paige asked, clearly alarmed. "What's happened?

Paige felt terror welling up in her chest. She was still dealing with the horror of the kidnapping ordeal that Edward and Caylyn had been through. It began flashing through her mind again.

"Grandpa's calling about Warren," he said looking up at her, his eyes red and glistening. "There's been a plane crash at the Kansas City Airport. Warren was on board. He was killed."

"Oh my God!" she said, breaking down sobbing. "I knew something had to be wrong. Your grandfather sounded awful."

"I appreciate the call, Grandpa," Mark finally managed to say quietly. His voice was low and clouded with grief as he struggled to maintain control. "Thanks for thinking of us."

He paused to regain his composure.

"Will you let me know when you get more details?" Mark said. "I'm going to call headquarters."

"Okay, son," Paul said gently to his grandson. "It's good Paige is there with you."

"Shit!" Mark said forcefully after he hung up, his eyes filling with tears. "Shit! Those bastards! Those goddamned bastards! I'm going to get them if it's the last thing I do! Damn them all to hell!"

Mark stood and wrapped Paige in his arms. They held each other for a long time, trying to bring a measure of mutual comfort . . . trying to make sense of yet another senseless act. It had been just a few weeks since the four barbaric terrorist attacks across America.

I'll bet those savages expected I'd be on board, too, he was thinking. He did not share that with Paige.

The couple would spend the next 10 hours almost glued to the phone. It would be the following morning before an exhausted Paige was able to collapse into bed.

Mark headed for the shower. He knew that immediately after, he would be subjecting his exhausted body to a round of scrub football in their back yard with an excited and impatient Edward. The youngster had risen early – unaware of his parents' all-nighter – hoping for some time to play with the man who he proudly called 'Dad'.

Chapter 26

Chapman, NY

Rhamir's home-trained ISIS team was almost ready for the attack on Lincoln Centre in New York City. The excitement was mounting.

Months before the attacks across America, Rhamir's fighters had converted a farmhouse near Chapman into a military operations center, a recruit training facility and a bomb factory. The living room, dining room and one of the three bedrooms of the old clapboard farmhouse had been converted to classrooms. The large kitchen was the heart of the bomb factory. Specially trained jihadists mixed the chemicals there to make PETN and then mixed the result with a plasticizer. This produced a waterproof plastic explosive they could mold into shaped charges.

Four men comprised Larigani's bomb-manufacturing team: two 'jihad heroes' from the attacks and two fighters just back from training in Syria. They also helped build fitness training structures and courses for new recruits on the heavily treed acreage.

Larigani was especially proud that Rhamir had chosen him to lead the upcoming attack on Lincoln Center. Logically, a senior fighter not a Rhamir lieutenant could have handled the assignment. But Larigani craved the action and had convinced Rhamir to give him a break from planning the 12 attacks in the next phase. Rhamir had reluctantly agreed.

A white panel truck purchased online had been turned into a huge bomb. Larigani could barely contain his excitement as his team finished placing shaped charges of PETN in the truck. It would be detonated remotely in the parking garage beneath Lincoln Center on the last night of the New York International Film Festival.

The attack would draw immense attention and in the aftermath there would be another flood of recriminations, further dividing Americans.

The other attack in New York was still months away – Times Square on New Year's Eve where a million people would gather. That would be the 'big one', the nuclear attack. It would be their 'pièce de résistance' and would follow the dozen attacks Rhamir was now obsessed with planning. Larigani also hoped he'd be given the overall responsibility for the Times Square assignment. He could hardly wait.

Chapter 27

Manhattan, NYC

Douglas called a meeting at Prescott Center in mid-town Manhattan to review developments of the four attacks and the sabotage of the FBI plane. Attending were Mark, Paige, Mark's grandparents Paul and Anne, Emile Bilodeaux and representatives of companies participating in Mark's alliance. Douglas had agreed to lead the civilian team and chair their planning sessions.

Mark struggled to maintain his composure while updating the others on the investigation into the plane crash that killed Warren. Two pilots, three other special agents and a flight attendant on board the chartered jet were also killed when it exploded on take-off from Kansas City International. He told them FBI investigators found remnants of a remotely operated explosive device in the wreckage.

"We arrested a baggage handler at KCI shortly after the crash," Mark said. "He was a recent hire by one of the baggage handling contractors. Our interrogators tell us he's been singing up a storm . . . hoping to minimize his sentence. Good luck with that!"

The plane crash amounted to the seventh attack, including the two on Mark and Paige's home. Mark's anger grew as he described the numerous warnings from intelligence sources his task force had passed along to national, state and local law enforcement agencies. The warnings had been ignored. There could be no excuses.

Mark was impatient to fight back. Months earlier, executives at all of the federal security agencies, including Warren's supervisors at the FBI, had listened skeptically, refusing to take seriously reports of impending attacks. And the intelligence Khalid Mahmoud had provided about a possible nuclear attack had been met with open derision bordering on hostility.

"The good news is these attacks have most top decision makers in the Bureau and the intelligence community now willing to accept they are the work of ISIS," Mark said. "But not everyone. I'm astounded that some still attribute these attacks to local drug gangs or organized crime trying to intimidate local authorities.

"We do have a number of allies high up, now. One is Bjorn Sorensen," Mark added. "Bjorn's in charge of all FBI undercover and counterterrorism work along the east coast. Our taskforce reports to him. He has stuck his neck out a mile by supporting what we're doing. I hope you don't mind, but when I spoke with him earlier today I told him about this meeting. I took the liberty of invited him to join us. I know you'll agree it's important that he meet all of you. He'll be here shortly"

Mark paused, and then added in a low unsteady voice, "I report directly to Bjorn now. He's asked me to take over from Warren."

Sorensen had agreed to attend, but only after Mark had briefed him thoroughly on the alliance plan he was proposing. Bjorn had done an about face after the attacks, Warren's murder and the attempts on Mark and Paige's lives.

"I owe you an apology, Mark," Sorensen had said then. "Warren and you have been right all along about these terrorists. Your warnings were right on; we should have been listening.

"In fact, I'm going to ask my superiors to actively encourage our counterparts in NSA, the CIA and others in the intelligence community to support your initiative. We should have been throwing resources into what you've been doing long ago, not trying to thwart the efforts of your task force."

*

Following the attacks, Douglas had formed a civilian operating committee coordinated by Paige. It would liaise with their FBI contact: Mark. The committee's primary job was to make use of thousands of available eyes and ears in the companies owned by or connected with Prescott Enterprises and Continental Oil and Gas, in the U.S., Canada and Mexico, and all the other companies they were bringing on board the alliance. They knew many of these companies also had community involvement programs like Prescott's and Continental's.

The original concept was that employees from the companies would be passive observers, reporting sightings as they occurred. But Paige had developed a plan to make their work more proactive. They would spearhead local surveillance projects . . . acting like an assertive CrimeStoppers program. The result was a nation-wide surveillance network of people trained and committed to actively looking for suspicious behavior in hundreds of cities and towns across America, Canada and Mexico.

Paige realized the plan had one huge geographic weakness – the ghettos and other low-income areas where the religious fanatics were known to be recruiting disillusioned youths most successfully. She knew and applauded what Mark had up his sleeve to address that critical deficiency.

In the meeting, no one mentioned but everyone understood that if law enforcement authorities found themselves hamstrung by proselytizing politicians and ass-covering bureaucrats, it would increase considerably the risk of a 'Vigilante War on Terrorism' erupting. They understood the possibility was real and would draw untrained civilians onto the battlefield, putting them and innocent people at risk. The alliance provided opportunities for civilians to join the battle against ISIS directly, helping to diffuse vigilantism.

The steering committee was waiting for Sorensen's arrival when Douglas told the group:

"The other day, I had a long conversation with someone who could be a valuable resource for our alliance. His name is Mohammed Al-Hashimi, a professor of religious studies at Columbia University.

"Mohammed and I met at Duke," Douglas said. "He's a good guy. We both lived on campus. We became friends. Now, he's an Islamic scholar and religious leader.

"He's deeply worried that Muslims are being tarnished by the outrageous ways those barbarians are misrepresenting their faith. They're all doing it: ISIS, al-Qaeda, Boko Haram and the other extremist groups. And it serves their cause to incite prejudice among Americans against Muslims living peacefully here. If that prejudice becomes widespread, then ISIS and their like will have won. Sadly, it's looking more and more like honest Muslims are becoming the other innocent victims of these depraved sub-humans.

"I thought it useful for us to understand better how cleverly these extremists are using falsehood and rhetoric in their war against us. I asked Mohammed to share with us his thoughts about the religious underpinnings claimed by ISIS, and the others. Here's a copy of what he sent over."

Douglas distributed a document. It read:

Whither The Real Infidels
By Professor Mohammed Al-Hashimi
Department of Religion, Columbia University
Conventional wisdom tells us ISIS and a host of other terrorist groups (al-Qaeda, Taliban, Hezbollah, Haqqani, Islamic Jihad, Boko Haram and al-Shabaab, among others) are Muslim extremists. That's not true. They are not Muslims. To be sure, they are extremists and claim to be Muslim, but that is a lie. What they espouse as religion has nothing to do with the Quran, Islam's most holy book. Legitimate Muslims are deeply offended by such claims, and rightly so. They disavow any connection whatsoever with these false pretenders to Islam.

Ironically, ISIS accuses others of what they really are – infidels. It is they who are the godless ones, the apostates and blasphemers, seeking to legitimize their mindless savagery by wrapping themselves in a cloak of phony secular pretense. They have no more to do with legitimate

Islam than the murderous rampages of the Crusaders, or the religious inquisitions, or the witch-hunts of Salem, NC and elsewhere, had to do with true Christianity. Tragically, there is a larger irony here, and that irony is that so many of us believe the myths that the terrorists have perpetrated.

While it may come as a surprise to some, religious scholars of both the Quran and the Holy Bible agree that the two sacred books have an overwhelming number of similarities and surprisingly few differences. Most notable among these similarities are teachings that advocate peaceful and harmonious coexistence by those of their faith and with those of other faiths. The basic premise of each holy book is to foster civility and the wellbeing of the societies they serve.

Religious scholars agree that a few passages in both the Bible and the Quran are written in such a way that people with malicious intent can take these passages out of context, that is deliberately misrepresent them, in order to make them appear to support violence and other uncivilized behavior. Such misrepresentations are inconsistent with the entreaties of peace that are the prime messages in both holy books. Extremists from both ancient and modern times have done this. These deliberately misleading versions have been used also down the ages in attempts to legitimize oppressive laws and to support patriarchal tyrannies.

These insights by religious scholars help us to understand that radical extremists are not the agents of Mohammed they claim to be. Quite the opposite; they are the worst kind of criminals and they are putting peace-loving peoples everywhere in grave danger. As we know, driven by their own deeply rooted self-loathing, these criminals have committed countless horrendous attacks upon innocent people, as evidenced by those barbaric beheadings, mass killings and burnings of people alive in the Middle East, and now the recent heinous attacks here in America, as well as by 9/11 and a mounting toll of other atrocities around the world.

Finally, we must remember to not underestimate these barbarians. They are as fiendishly clever as they are vicious. There is abundant evidence these extremists are fomenting the prejudice against Muslims we are experiencing more and more in western countries. It serves their purpose. Their leaders know that every flare-up of prejudice turns people who are otherwise committed to peace and goodwill into losers and them into winners. We would do well to remember that how we treat people usually determines how they treat us: so, when we behave toward innocent people as if they are the enemy, chances are they will respond accordingly.

While everyone at the meeting was absorbing what they had just read, Bjorn Sorensen arrived with an inquiring look in his eyes. It piqued everyone's curiosity.

"I had a call from the top," he said, his voice and the look on his face unable to hide the awe he was experiencing. "From the Hoover Building . . .

"Joe Foster wanted to be sure you were in on this meeting, Mr. Winston," Sorensen said looking with deference at the fit and distinguished 75-year-old Paul.

Surprise and pleasure registered on Paul's face.

"He said the two of you know each other from 'way back'," Sorenson continued. "He has quite a high regard for you, sir. Mr. Foster asked us to call on his direct line as soon as I got here. He's standing by."

Foster was the FBI's long-time executive assistant director for counterterrorism, based in Washington, one of the most senior FBI executives. Years ago, he'd declined to be considered for the position of Director of the FBI. More recently, he'd been allowed to postpone retirement to continue devoting his considerable talents and experience to counterterrorism.

Paul and Foster had met decades earlier while investigating an elaborate plot to murder Paul and Anne. The goal of that conspiracy had been to take control illegally of key portions of Prescott Enterprises, their rapidly expanding international business empire.

"The regard is mutual, indeed," Paul smiled at Sorensen. "It's been years. Douglas?"

Sorensen handed Douglas a slip of paper with Foster's direct number.

"Foster here," said a voice over the speakerphone. "Is that you Paul?

"Yes, Joe," Paul said. "It's good to hear your voice again. It's been much too long."

"Yes it has." Foster said, getting right to business. "I was pleased to learn, Paul, that you're involved in this unconventional initiative. I will assume that with you on board, there's no need to worry that some lawless bunch of vigilantes will go off half-cocked, now will I?"

"Count on it, Joe," Paul replied. "I'm a little old now for that sort of thing.

"But first, Joe, let me say how very sorry we are about the loss of Warren and his colleagues. He'd stopped in to see me that morning, as you know. An awful shock and a terrible loss to all of us."

"Thank you, Paul," a subdued Foster said quietly. "A huge loss to the Bureau and to this country. Warren was an invaluable asset to us and to the American people. We'll miss him and his knowledge. He was a strong supporter of this alliance thing your grandson's trying to set up. I'd like to hear more about it."

"I'm going to ask my son Douglas to outline our plan for you," Paul replied.

"Sir, thank you for joining us," Douglas began. "Briefly, our group can provide Mark's task force with on-the-street support from employees of Prescott Enterprises and Continental Oil and Gas, as well as our suppliers and dozens of other large companies across the country. Let me assure you, Mr. Foster, our sole purpose is to bring whatever resources we can make available to support law enforcement agencies . . . emphasis on the word 'support'. We are now poised to begin providing that support."

"I'm pleased to hear that," Foster said. "And as unusual as it may be, I must say I like the sound of it."

"Mr. Foster," Douglas said. "I believe we are agreed those horrible attacks and Warren's murder have removed any doubt that ISIS is out to cause America even more serious harm. And from the intelligence we've been getting, it's highly likely there will be more attacks, unless we can stop them and soon."

"I believe you're right, Douglas," Foster replied. "I want you to know, we'll be listening very carefully from now on to the intelligence provided by that undercover agent of ours. You have my word on that. It's the best intelligence we've had yet on this latest threat. I'm personally looking into why our people failed to respond properly, failed to take it seriously, and failed to bring this to my attention.

Good God, solid intelligence about a terrorist group planning attacks on American soil, much less a nuclear attack, is ignored? That's inconceivable . . . it's totally unacceptable!"

"Mark," Foster said, "I know how frustrated you must have been, young man. Bjorn told me that both you and Warren had tried repeatedly to warn our folks and other law enforcement agencies that attacks were imminent.

"Well, Mark, you can count on this." Foster's voice became a growl. "There's going to be an accounting, and a change of attitude all the way up and down the chain of command! I'm going to see to it personally!"

"Thank you, sir," Mark said, glancing around the room, his face alight with relief and anticipation.

"Mr. Foster," Douglas said. "I'm sure you will agree further escalations of domestic violence like these attacks have the potential to damage America's economic wellbeing. And a nuclear attack would be devastating. Our group of companies is stepping forward, Mr. Foster, because we believe more and more Americans are looking for ways to take part actively in this fight. Let's just hope we're not too late."

"I couldn't agree more," Foster replied. "Good Heavens, we work for the American people, after all. You pay our salaries. And I'm embarrassed to admit that over the years we've isolated ourselves, and our work, from the very people we're sworn to protect. Of course, we want your help. Of course, we need your help. What I'm hearing you offer is the help of responsible civilians across the country. I like that idea. How could we possibly refuse?"

"We appreciate that very much, sir," Douglas replied. "So, allow me to give you a more detailed overview of the resources we have available, and how we plan to deploy them. We'd also like to offer a number of specific suggestions on how we might be of assistance to the FBI and to other authorities."

"Go ahead," Foster replied.

Chapter 28

"Mark, get over here right now. My father wants to see you."

The caller was Vinny Caprionni. Mark saw Vinny's name on the iPhone caller ID and thought, *Christ! That useless son of a bitch . . . what's up now!*

"Did your father say what it's about?" Mark asked, struggling to exercise restraint.

"You don't ask such things of the Godfather!" Vinny snapped back arrogantly. "He said you're to be in his office at 2 o'clock. Be there!"

The phone went dead.

"Dumb shit!" Mark sighed. He remembered vividly the last phone call received from Vinny. It nearly got him killed. Fortunately, that experience had ended with a bizarre twist of irony: Joe Caprionni had guardedly agreed to help the FBI track down ISIS.

He was looking forward to seeing Caprionni. Mark had learned enough about the mafia to be convinced they were well situated strategically to provide valuable intelligence. But he knew that many of his colleagues and other agencies would balk at inviting organized crime to assist law enforcement. They'd consider it an unholy alliance, at the very least, hopping into bed with the enemy. And maybe it was, but it could work.

Mark grinned to himself, confident about his plan. And while perhaps outrageous to many, some elements of the mafia's twisted set of principles were in fact laudable. Their deep respect for family values, sense of honor and their admittedly perverse form of patriotism, came to mind. Besides, Mark's esteem for Caprionni had risen considerably after seeing a softer side of the crusty old mafia boss after being told about the brutal murder of Anashi and the kidnapping of Edward and Caylyn. And then, Caprionni had become both furious and concerned over the beheading in Washington, the attacks in Tempe, Research Triangle Park and Houston, and then Warren's murder. Self-interest and bizarre, perhaps, but Caprionni was genuinely and deeply concerned about his country.

*

Caprionni Mansion, Staten Island

Mark arrived just before 2 p.m. Arnie Ravelo was waiting for him under the portico at the front entry. The mafia soldier reached out for the offered car keys and then gave Mark a big friendly bear hug, as he usually did. Arnie's job was to frisk Mark for weapons. He didn't bother. After Vinny's attempt to have Mark murdered, and Mark's restraint when he could have shot Arnie, the two men had formed an even stronger bond of mutual respect. A connection like that was a big deal in La Cosa Nostra culture. The two men valued the special relationship they now shared.

"Nice to see you again, Mr. Mark," the tall burly mafia lieutenant said with a friendly smile, holding Mark by his shoulders.

"It's nice to see you too, Arnie," Mark replied warmly.

He strode up to the heavy oak door. Vinny opened it as he approached, looking disapprovingly as he always did at where Mark had parked on the wide driveway.

"Follow me," Vinny said, turning abruptly. He walked briskly across the elegant marble floor of the two-story foyer and down the wide carpeted hallway to his father's den.

Vinny opened the door without knocking and walked in.

"He's here," Vinny said to his father.

"Come in! Come in!" Caprionni said. The mafia godfather hurried from behind his huge desk and stepped across the richly carpeted floor, hand outstretched. Mark felt his hand grasped firmly by the wiry mobster, who put great meaning in such gestures.

Mark thought: *What a turnaround from a few weeks ago!*

Caprionni placed his arm around Mark's shoulder and directed him to a meeting table beside his desk; more gestures full of meaning. Previously, Mark had sat across the desk from Caprionni, along with Vinny and other mafia soldiers. Meeting at the round oak table signaled a privilege. Vinny walked over to the table and paused, apparently deciding where he would sit.

"Not this time," the elder Caprionni said looking at his son, waving him away. "This is a personal meeting; just me and Mark."

Vinny was taken aback. He shot an angry look at Mark, then whirled around and marched from the room, slamming the door. The mafia don was embarrassed by his son's immature behavior.

When seated, Caprionni looked into Mark's eyes for a long moment, and then said:

"You know that I sit with The Commission."

"Yes, sir," Mark nodded. The comment was an understatement. Mark knew Caprionni had been chosen recently to chair The Commission. The mafia's fabled group set policy and tried to avoid mafia wars by adjudicating differences among the five New York mafia families. The families controlled most organized crime in New York City, along the eastern seaboard and in numerous other areas across the country.

With his appointment as chairman, Joe Caprionni became the most powerful crime boss in America. Everyone listened carefully to whatever the chairman of The Commission had to say, be it La Cosa Nostra, the Black Mafia Families (BMF) on the west coast, motorcycle gangs, or ordinary street gangs. The decisions of the chairman usually affected everyone in some way.

"I brought to The Commission the matter of those terrorists you told me about," Caprionni said. "The Maniero family admitted they were misled. They maintain they did not know the people they employed for other purposes were connected to ISIS. They have been dismissed. The Maniero's claim they knew nothing about the hit on your home. But they still say you were trying to set up a drug network that would distribute product directly from

216

Columbia, bypassing our families. Everyone knows better, and I think so do the Maniero's.

"But Mark, we both know they are partly right. You did sneak into my family to spy on us. I know now, however, that the things the Maniero's are saying about you are not to be believed. I am deeply embarrassed to admit also, that what my son said about you is not to be believed either. I have spoken to Vincenza about that. He is alive today only because he is my son. The Commission has chosen to do nothing about the Maniero's, for now. They are going to see about this thing later. And I will deal with Vincenza.

"What I do believe, Mark, is what you have told me: that you are with the FBI. I had you checked out by your real name. We have sources.

"Mark, I also had my people investigate what you said was going on with the terrorists. You were right. And those terrible attacks removed any doubt. I informed The Commission that these people seem to think they can simply move in and take over all of our drug operations, and then use that to finance a war on America, a war on our way of life! And you are telling me they might even try to use a nuclear bomb on Americans?"

Mark nodded. "Yes, sir."

"Are they crazy?" the Godfather said. "The Commission is very upset by all of this. I must tell you, when I said to them that more of these attacks are expected and that these could do much harm to our businesses . . . to their livelihoods . . . it got their attention. I pointed out that the extremists want to breed fear, to create so much fear it will damage the economy of our great country. We are business people, too, you know. They understood.

"The Commission recognizes that fearful people do not spend money on big items like homes and cars and vacations. Nor do such people spend money on drugs or gambling or prostitutes, or with the many other legitimate services we are providing. And in such a climate of fear, companies do not invest in growth. They understood all of this."

Caprionni paused for a moment, again looking Mark directly in his eyes.

Then he said:

"The Commission has done something I never thought I would live to see, Mark. They want you, of all people, you an FBI agent who betrayed us, to come and meet with them. It must be just you alone . . . no one else. I told them that I had trusted you with my son's life, that you are a man of his word, a man of honor. They want to talk."

Mark was taken aback and delighted. He looked at Caprionni, careful to hide his surprise and excitement. He'd told himself the best he could expect was a measure of cooperation from the Caprionni family. But now The Commission was interested, and to be invited to meet with his sworn enemies, perhaps to discuss a deal? It was ironic and it was exactly what he had hoped might happen.

Understandably, The Commission's motivation was self-interest. Their immediate concern was protecting their highly profitable illegal operations. After all, organized crime in America was taking in more than $50 billion a year. But the mafia leaders saw the bigger picture, too. All were business-savvy with massive multi-faceted operations: drugs, prostitution, money laundering, gambling, loan sharking, protection rackets, influence peddling, control of unions, construction price fixing, among others, plus quickly growing portfolios of legitimate businesses.

"Yes, Mr. Caprionni," Mark said solemnly, trying to contain his excitement. "I am willing to meet with The Commission at a time and at a place of their choosing."

He understood offering The Commission the choice of place and timing was an important gesture of respect. It would not be lost on the members, and they would of course decide on the location anyway.

"I will come alone, as they ask," Mark added. "But I will come only as your guest, Mr. Caprionni."

Mark knew he was invoking the mafia code of honor by asking Caprionni to take him to the Commission meeting as his guest. It was a safety precaution in case anything went wrong, in particular any nasty shenanigans the Maniero's might have up their sleeves.

"That is good, Mark," the powerful mafia boss said with just a hint of a grin, understanding Mark's strategy.

"Of course you will be my guest. I will tell you when the meeting is arranged. When a date and time is agreed, I will ask you to go to a location where you and I will meet. Okay? It is a precaution, you understand. Someone will pick us up and take us to the meeting. Are you okay with that?"

Mark nodded. He understood mafia soldiers would be concealed around where they would join up, protecting Caprionni and ensuring Mark had come alone. More than likely they would change vehicles at least once. Mafia soldiers would provide security during the travel there and back, and many more would be in hiding around The Commission's meeting location.

"Yes, Mr. Caprionni. That will be fine." Mark answered. "Sir, might I ask you a question?"

"Of course, young man," Caprionni replied, curious.

"I don't mean to pry and I do not wish to appear disrespectful, sir," Mark said, "but will I hear from you about this meeting, or from Vincenza?"

"From me," Caprionni replied abruptly, a cold look in his eyes. "Vincenza will not be part of this."

Mark understood. Vinny would not be privy to any of the arrangements being negotiated between The Commission and the FBI. He was relieved.

*

Mark returned to his office. His private number rang.

"Hi Love," he said, recognizing his home private line on the caller ID. "How're ya doing? Everything all right, you gorgeous woman, you?"

"Have you got your TV on?" Paige said. She was barely able to contain her excitement.

"No," he replied. "I've been out."

"Well you missed it, then!" she said. "The Secretary of Homeland Security was on TV. He was announcing the counterterrorism task force, and your appointment, as he said he would. For some reason, he felt it necessary to tell the world that you're not only a former Navy SEAL but also a former undercover agent. And he called you a rising star in the FBI. Quite the buildup, Hon."

"Oh shit!" Mark said. "I was told it would be low profile. That SOB promised to leave my background out of it. Damn it all! Politicians! Did he mention anything else or anyone else specifically?"

"Oh yes!" Paige said. "Listen to this. He said the President has signed an executive order authorizing you and your taskforce to requisition any assistance you require from federal law enforcement agencies, as well as local and state national guard, police forces, and even the armed forces anywhere in the country.

"It looks, Love, like the political pendulum has swung the other way. Did you know about this other stuff?"

"Well, I'll be damned!" he replied. "Yes, sort of. We asked for the moon but we've learned to expect much less or nothing. It seems we've hit the jackpot. Now, we have all the emergency authority we need. Wow! This is just terrific! That's huge. Huge!

"You were at the regular alliance board meeting this morning, right?" Mark said.

"Yes," Paige said excitedly. Mark could tell something more was coming. In his mind's eye, he saw her wriggling excitedly as he'd seen her do, and every time she did that she commanded his full male attention. His breath caught in his throat.

But back to business.

Page said: "Your uncle asked me to take on a wider responsibility, to lead the team in charge of the entire operating plan that Prescott, Continental and the others are setting up across the country. It's going to be a handful, but I'm delighted . . . I'll be helping you directly!"

"Wow!" Mark replied, feeling a burst of pride for his bright young wife. It was a much bigger role than his uncle had first planned for Paige. It was obvious she'd earned it.

"Good for you! You're going to do a sensational job, my love. Thank you, thank you, for agreeing to come on board to help. You and I working together . . . that's really cool!"

Chapter 29

Chapman, NY

Just after dark, 25 heavily armed members of a special joint assault team quietly surrounded a remote farmhouse near Chapman, NY. The team under Mark's command included members of the FBI special task force, as well as SWAT team members from local law enforcement and the New York State Police.

The previous day, Mark had received a call from Khaled Mahmoud, the FBI's undercover agent in Abdul Rhamir's other terrorist camp near Albuquerque, NM.

"Mark, from what I'm overhearing, activity at the Chapman camp is ramping up," Khaled said. "They're up to something. I've no details yet, but it sure looks like they're preparing for an attack at any moment, probably in New York."

"Many thanks, Khalid," Mark had said. "This confirms what we've been picking up via satellite and on-site surveillance at Chapman. Looks like it's time to move."

All the reports led to one conclusion: the farmhouse was the center of preparations for more terrorist attacks. The toll of dead and injured from the three earlier bombings was staggering. More than 3,200 had now been confirmed dead, almost reaching the death toll from 9/11. Another 6,300 had been injured. Estimated total losses were approaching $10.5 billion.

At the farm, Mark and his deputy Sam Bedford crawled close to the house behind the cover of a dense 20-foot cedar hedge. A voice in his earpiece said:

"Mark, we've just observed a white panel truck pull out of the barn at the back of the property. It's heading down the road now. Should we intercept?"

Sam was on the same channel. Both understood an armed confrontation might alert suspects in the farmhouse. It could spook them into detonating the PETN they suspected was stored there. An explosion of that amount, if even near accurate, would be enormous. It would kill most of the assembled law enforcement officers and threaten people in nearby homes. Civilians adjacent to the property were being evacuated quietly but that job was far from complete.

"Let the truck go," Mark said into his headset, cupping his hand around the microphone to contain his voice.

He called the joint task force operations center and provided an update.

"Ask the highway patrol dispatcher to pass along the truck's description to their cruisers. We need them to maintain surveillance, with as many unmarked vehicles as are available, but tell them to keep well back, at least a half-mile clearance. Repeat, at least a half-mile clearance. That panel truck could be a huge bomb. We'll let them know if and when it's safe to approach.

"Oh, and patch me through to Lt. Rick Atwood in the chopper, please."

Atwood came on the line.

"Rick," Mark said, "See if you can find an open stretch of highway a few miles ahead of the truck, one without as few buildings as possible. As you probably heard, that vehicle might be filled with PETN. Maintain visual contact but keep as far back as you can. We've asked the highway patrol to keep its distance, too, and to wait for our signal before attempting any roadblocks or intercept."

"Roger," Atwood replied. "I've got the target on my night scope. When we see the target coming up to a sparsely populated stretch of road, we'll let you know. Out."

Mark and Sam crawled closer to the farmhouse. No lights were visible. Four camouflaged members of NYSP's SWAT team had joined them. All were trained in bomb disposal. Everyone knew the risks. Two were assigned to the back door, and two to the front door. The place looked deserted. All six checked for booby traps. They found none. Mark quietly began a count down over the intercom.

"On the count of three," Mark said, pausing. "One . . . two . . . three!"

They stormed the doors, weapons ready to take out anyone armed or who appeared ready to detonate explosives inside. The four SWAT officers charged through the ground floor rooms checking for occupants, then the basement and second floor, and then the attic. The place was empty. It was cluttered with the remnants of what had been going on just a few minutes earlier. They found PETN in various sized chunks littering the kitchen. Chemicals to make more were found in large quantities in the basement along with plasticizing chemicals. They also found briefcases and dozens of pressure switches. The kitchen table and counter were covered with shaped charges, wire, and parts of cell phones. Under some maps they found one complete cell phone. It was turned on.

"I wonder," Mark said as the live cell phone was handed to him. "I wonder if they used this cell phone to test the trigger mechanisms on the phones they were making. Don't anyone touch this. The phone might be programmed to a detonator somewhere here. Let's not set it off accidentally."

The live cell phone gave Mark an idea, but also a concern.

"Check all the PETN you can find for attached wires and detonators, and disconnect them," he told Sam and the SWAT officers. "Then grab everything that looks suspicious and take it all outside. Spread it out, at least 50 yards away from the house. As you know, a piece of PETN the size of a chocolate bar could flatten this house."

"Look at this!" Sam said, motioning Mark over to the kitchen counter. "Oh shit! See this? It looks like diagrams and notes for an attack they're planning in New York. I'll bet that's where they're going . . . and I'll bet that van is filled with PETN.

"Good God, Mark, they're going to attack something tonight!"

"It sure looks like it," Mark agreed. "See, here's an inventory of the stuff, and here's a diagram of the shapes for the charges and placement in the van.

Holy shit, that is one enormous bomb . . . maybe 600 or 700 pounds. That's big enough to topple an office building.

"Oh my God! The address!" Mark said pointing to a map of downtown New York stapled to a wall. "It's circled – the Lincoln Center. Jesus Christ, that must be their target. They're going to blow up the Lincoln Center! See these arrows? I'll bet they're going to park the van underground, using the 62nd Street entrance, and then detonate it by cell phone."

"Mark," Sam said. His face turned grey. "Tonight is the grand finale for the New York City International Film Festival! It's at Lincoln Center. Good God, Mark! Vice President Stuart Gonzales is going to be there, along with some heads of state.

"We'd better call them right away!" Sam added. "They need to vacate that place immediately. It's going to take time."

"How long's the van been gone?" Mark replied calmly. Sam was digging out his mobile phone. They both checked their watches. It had taken close to 15 minutes to search and clear the house, and another 10 minutes to go through the notes they'd found. Twenty-five minutes.

"That van could be half way to the suburbs of New York by now. Hopefully that gravel road they're on is slowing them down some," Sam said. "We've got to call the Secret Service to start the evacuation right away. And we've got to stop that damned van before it gets into a heavily populated area. If it reaches the city and detonates prematurely, it could be a disaster."

"Here's a thought, Sam," Mark said, still calm. His face bore a Machiavellian smile. He alerted the operations center to his next move; he radioed Atwood:

"Can you confirm your visual on the white panel truck?" Mark asked.

"Roger that," Atwood replied. "A large white panel is kicking up dust on a gravel road about 25 or 30 miles from your location. I'm seeing brake lights often so the road must be rough. If you're planning an intercept, they'll be in a valley in a minute or two. That's about the only location I've seen so far without a lot of homes and other buildings. And there's been little vehicular traffic."

"Roger that. Thanks," Mark answered. "I have a better idea than an intercept. But first, pull your bird well back from the van ASAP. Pull back at least a mile and drop down low. We could have fireworks in just a few seconds. Pull back now. Acknowledge."

"Roger that," Atwood replied. "I'm backing off."

Mark turned to Sam.

"I'll just bet this cell phone was used to test phone detonation mechanisms," he said holding it up, "to make sure they worked. Agreed?"

"I see what you mean," Sam replied with a grin. He realized he might not need to make that call to Lincoln Center after all. "Guess we should make sure it's a working cell phone. It could become important evidence."

"Yup," Mark said. "But first, let's make sure we've got all the wired PETN disconnected and well clear of the farmhouse."

He called the SWAT team over and explained what he planned to do. All scoured the house quickly a second time, gathering up any PETN that looked even remotely like it was being prepared for detonation. All members of the assault took the PETN 40 yards in different directions, double-checking that the evacuated PETN had been separated from any wires and placed in depressions in the ground. Everyone was ordered away from the house. It had taken another 12 minutes.

"Let's hope the truck is all by itself on the road," Mark said as he walked outside away from the farmhouse.

"That's what Atwood told us," Sam answered, following Mark into the dark backyard, stumbling over stakes in what appeared to have been a vegetable garden.

Mark pushed the 'redial' button on the cell phone. In seconds, shock waves rattled the windows and doors of the farmhouse, followed immediately by an even larger explosion. They felt the ground under their feet shudder slightly like a minor earthquake tremor. In the distance, a massive orange cloud of flames rose, cutting the darkness. They heard a muffled 'boom', 'boom', echoing off the hills around the countryside.

"Holy shit!" Atwood shouted over the radio. "That was one hell of a fireworks display, Mark. That little valley helped direct the blast upward. We saw flaming pieces going in all directions. I'm setting down at your location. You'll need us again at first light to track down the pieces. I can tell you they're scattered over a wide area."

Ten minutes later, Atwood walked into the farmhouse where Mark, Sam and their team awaited the NYSP crime scene investigators. They made 'high-fives' all around. Everyone knew this was a small victory in a long and arduous battle ahead.

"Tell me something, Mark?" Atwood asked. "What would you have done had that truck not exploded?"

"Don't ask," Mark replied. He didn't tell them he had a Cobra attack helicopter on alert.

In the days following, investigators found pieces of the truck and remnants of clothing and body parts scattered around the blast scene. Scraps of singed passports, drivers' licenses and visas, and other personal effects were recovered by investigators and turned in by neighbors. NYSP concluded that five people were on board the truck when it exploded.

It took highway crews three full days to repair the crater 32 miles southeast of the farmhouse.

Chapter 30

Albuquerque

"That fucking infidel bastard!" Abdul Rhamir screamed, slamming his fist on his desk. "That son of a bitch!" he added.

He was at his new training camp near Albuquerque watching TV reports about an explosion in southern New York State. Authorities told reporters they believed it was caused by a truck-bomb. Rhamir knew his top lieutenant, Frank Larigani, was dead along with two of his trainers and two other experienced jihadi. He was relieved the new recruits he planned to train in bomb making had not yet gone to Chapman.

"That sheep fucking illegitimate son of a camel!" he said, ranting obscenities about Mark, who he correctly assumed was responsible. "How did he find out about our camp? There must be a traitor! There must be!

"Ali-Mumar," Rhamir shouted angrily, calling over his remaining lieutenant. "Find me the traitor. Find him now! He will pay for this treachery!"

Ali-Mumar Shahid was the second of Rhamir's lieutenants. Larigani had been his senior lieutenant and the one he relied on most. Larigani and Shahid had been with Rhamir for years, as members of the New York sleeper cell. He'd made them his lieutenants when his war on America grew too large for one man to manage directly.

Shahid was delighted with his assignment.

At last! he thought, *when I find that traitor it will prove I'm just as worthy a lieutenant as Larigani.*

Shahid secretly welcomed Larigani's death. With him out of the way, Shahid expected to become Rhamir's main deputy and someday perhaps even succeed Rhamir. Shahid wanted that more than anything else he could imagine. The key was finding a traitor somewhere within The Islamic Army of America, and fast.

He faced a dilemma.

Should he go through a tedious investigation and assemble a short list of possible traitors? The truth was, he didn't know how to go about it. He'd never done anything like this before. Perhaps he should simply finger someone, a likely suspect, who could be the one of course, but without being positive? He was sure Rhamir would never know the difference. No one would believe anyone he decided to accuse. Shahid didn't care. He could deal with the real traitor later. The accused could deny it all he wanted. He'd be dead, after being subjected to horrible torture intended especially for traitors.

Having been designated as a Rhamir deputy, he'd be acknowledged as the leader in waiting if he could successfully expose the traitor, and soon! The thought exhilarated Shahid. And once the Islamic Army of America became victorious, he'd have power and wealth beyond belief. He'd have access to women in abundance.

I must find a traitor soon, before Rhamir has a chance to doubt me, he told himself.

Chapter 31

Manhattan, NY

Mark opened his black leather briefcase and removed notes for the meeting. Paige sat beside him at the boardroom table. His uncle, Douglas, chaired these meetings. Also present were Paul and Anne Winston, and Emile Bilodeaux. The five were the alliance steering committee, the de facto brain trust. Mark was an ex-officio member.

"I've some good news," Mark said, beginning his report to the meeting. "The task force has received approval to expand our civilian initiative. And I'm pleased to tell you that it includes adding the allies I'm about to suggest. We've just completed an understanding with them."

"Are you absolutely sure you want to bring organized crime into this alliance?" Douglas interrupted. Mark had discussed his plans on and off for weeks with his uncle, hoping to gain his unconditional support. Douglas had remained skeptical.

"Yes I am," Mark replied firmly.

"If I might wax philosophically for a moment," he said with a grin, "There are times when situations may appear to be a problem, yet upon a closer look may have within them the means to solve that problem. Well, this is one of those times."

Mark described the deal he'd struck with Joe Caprionni and The Commission, with the consent of the New York state attorney general. The New Jersey, Connecticut and Pennsylvania attorneys general had also come on board, and attorney generals in other states were considering it.

"Suspected terrorist activity reported by organized crime and their associates, sent to us anonymously, has the potential to yield an enormous intelligence bonanza," Mark said.

"Are we cleared to do this?" Douglas said. "We're working with an alphabet soup of federal agencies – the NSA, DNI, DEA, FBI, Homeland Security, Justice, the State Department's Coordinator for Counterterrorism and a host of others. Are we putting ourselves offside with these folks? It seems to me that bringing the mafia into our alliance could be like pouring gasoline on a fire."

"The only clearances we need are from Bjorn Sorensen and Joe Foster," Mark said with a hint of impatience. "And they're on side. Agreed, I've been getting static from a few official quarters, but they can damned well answer to Sorensen and if necessary, to Foster!

"What's more, the mafia's Commission realizes it's in their best interests to cooperate," Mark said. "It also involves their perverse sense of honor and their patriotism for America, however twisted. Agreed, when this is all over, they must still answer for much of what they have done. They know that there will be a reckoning. But they know their cooperation with our alliance is certain to mitigate things for them. And in the process, they will also have been exposed to alternatives. Some will respond, some will not.

"The bottom line, Uncle Doug, is this: Joe Caprionni has given us access to many more eyes and ears, tens of thousands of them, in places exactly where ISIS has been most successful with its recruiting, online and in person. That's an enormous resource. And The Commission is willing to approach organized crime around the country, including the Hell's Angels.

"By the way," Mark continued. "Paige came up with an excellent idea. I'll let her explain it to you."

"As we all know," Paige said, "people involved with organized crime want nothing to do with law enforcement, regardless of the reason.

"At the same time, we have a network of corporate employees trained to watch for potentially threatening situations and unusual behavior in their neighborhoods. So we thought, why not invite volunteers from our network to act as anonymous contact points for the mafia. The fact is people in organized crime need a way to report tips anonymously, separate from law enforcement. They need people to receive their tips and follow up on them. This covers a huge weak spot in our alliance.

"We're in the process now of setting up phone numbers, email addresses and texting numbers, as well as other contact coordinates on social media networking sites using codes. I'm quite familiar with social media, as you know. What do you think?"

"That's excellent! You've been busy." Paul said. "Douglas, we can alert our teams from this end and get to work on Paige's terrific idea. I'm sure you'll have all the volunteers you need."

"And Paige," Paul said, "the proactive way you've suggested Prescott and Continental expand their involvement will encourage organized crime families to come forward."

"All right, all right!" Douglas said. "I suppose I have to admit it does make sense, in a crazy sort of way."

During the next few weeks, Mark increased his meetings with the civilian task force to exchange briefings and to work on enhancing liaison between the civilians and his task force. Paige's role had expanded to include setting up call-in and follow-up sites for the mafia across the country. Mark also began meeting once a week with Joe Caprionni and was in even more frequent contact with him by phone.

During one meeting, Douglas's executive assistant came in, saying Mark had a call.

"It's a Mr. Bjorn Sorensen," she said. "He asked me to tell you he wants to see you right away."

Twelve minutes later Mark was sitting in a meeting room at the FBI's New York field headquarters, on the 23rd floor of 26 Federal Plaza. Bjorn was in New York for other meetings.

"A call came in here from our undercover agent in the Maniero family," Sorensen said, dispensing with the usual pleasantries. "He left a message for you. He said that someone from the Caprionni's called the Maniero's about making a deal . . . some kind of merger between the two families. You're close to Caprionni; do you know what this might be about?"

Mark shook his head.

"Want to take a guess who made the call?" Bjorn said.

Without waiting for Mark to respond, he continued, "It was none other than Vincenza Caprionni."

"Vinny?" Mark replied, shocked. "What the hell is he up to . . . trying to make a deal with the Maniero's? His father hates the Maniero's. Are you sure it was about a deal? Could it have been Commission business?"

"Definitely about a deal," Bjorn said. "Our agent overheard the Maniero's discussing it. Vinny was talking with Salvatore Maniero Jr., eldest son of the Maniero godfather."

"That stupid little son of a bitch!" Mark said. "Those two simpletons don't realize something like this could start a mafia war. Mr. Caprionni would see to that! And that would lead to the five families being raided immediately. Everyone would be arrested. Everything shut down. When Mr. Caprionni finds out about this you can be damn sure he will be even more displeased with that loose cannon of a son of his."

"Life just keeps getting more interesting for you, doesn't it?" Sorensen said with gentle sarcasm.

"You could say that," Mark replied with a grin. "But the first priorities of my task force right now, of course, are to figure out what that thug Abdul Rhamir is planning next, and to track down that nuclear device.

"If I could find him, I'd be tempted to have him picked up and sweated. But we're being told we don't have enough evidence to hold him, much less convince a grand jury or get a conviction, certainly not the way judges pander to the accused these days."

"I know, I know," Sorensen said. "Sometimes, it does seem like we protect the guilty and victimize the victims."

"You got that!" Mark said. "Unfortunately, our folks have lost track of him. That son of a bitch left his latest apartment a few days ago and took his mother with him. He's the key to finding that nuclear bomb, but we've no way to keep tabs on him until we find him. I have an APB out, for what that's worth. Our agent is in New Mexico."

Chapter 32

ISIS Camp

"Come with me!" Shahid ordered.

The command sent fear rocketing through young Khaled Mahmoud's athletic body.

They were in a trailer serving as a bunkhouse Khaled shared with five other fighters.

After prayers, he was lying on his bed reading a copy of Time magazine when Shahid had come to the bedroom door and ordered him to follow. Trembling inwardly, Khaled was certain Shahid had discovered he was an FBI undercover agent. He knew traitors were punished with horrific torture and a gruesome death. He began thinking about possible ways to escape.

Albuquerque had been intended as their second camp. After the raid on his Chapman camp, Rhamir was certain there was a traitor among them. He'd also become paranoid about being tracked and captured. After the first four attacks he'd moved repeatedly in New York and again after Chapman. He finally decided to abandon New York City and relocate his headquarters to the camp in the mountains of New Mexico. Besides, he had plans for New York. He did not want to be living there when that happened. After arriving, Rhamir reminded Shahid constantly about the urgency of finding the traitor.

"Next to getting this camp fully operational, that's my top priority," Rhamir said. "It's the most important thing you can do for our glorious Jihad. We must find this traitor or all of our work will come to nothing! It will be destroyed!

"Track him down, Ali-Mumar!" Rhamir had said, glaring fiercely into Shahid's eyes. "Track him down and you will become my confidante. You do this for me and I will officially appoint you as my deputy commander!"

At last! Shahid told himself. *At last, Rhamir will make it official!*

He was so excited by the prospect he could not focus on anything else except finding the traitor within their midst, or a reasonable facsimile.

Khaled followed Shahid into the kitchen of the bunkhouse. The young undercover agent shivered with fear. Shahid told the five others who lived there to go outside and shut the door. The order made Khaled's scalp prickly.

"Look," Shahid said, gesturing for Khaled to sit at the only table. It was littered with dirty dishes, cups and glasses, smelly half-empty frozen food containers and discarded magazines. "You grew up in America. I need you to help me see things I cannot see."

"Of course," Khaled said nervously. "What do you need me to do?"

Shahid explained that he and Rhamir were convinced there was a spy within the Islamic Army of America, most likely American-born. He said that he needed someone he could trust with instincts about American-born or American-raised jihadists.

A fighter raised in America like him would be more likely to have these instincts.

Shahid would come to realize too late that he'd recruited the very 'traitor' he was trying to find.

"Look, Khaled," Shahid said. "This is vitally important. We must move quickly. I suspect three people. One is a Hispanic and one a black. Both of them are assigned to the trailer next to the dining hall. The other is in this trailer. I want you to get close to each of them . . . see what you can find out. Let me know what you think. Okay?"

Khaled nodded, concealing his discomfort with the assignment. Shahid gave him the names and left. One was born in America to Middle Eastern parents. In New York, that young man had also been among Khaled's eight roommates. The other two were among the last 15 to arrive at the New Mexico camp. Three others left behind in New York all had been born in Iraq. No one including Shahid seemed to know why.

Chapter 33

Danbury, CT

Joe Caprionni and The Commission were becoming more receptive to working with the alliance. Accordingly, Mark had arranged for regular contact with the mafia boss of bosses. The two met weekly now, and were on the phone almost every second day. As a courtesy to the older man, Mark suggested that between meetings Caprionni could phone him when it was convenient for him, rather than the other way around.

Mark was amused to realize that he'd begun to look forward to their frequent phone conversations and especially their regular meetings. He was also surprised by the powerful mafia don's new willingness to talk at length on the phone. He'd always been paranoid about wiretapping.

Even more bizarre, the same man who only a few months ago had ordered him murdered, now apparently wanted to be his friend, despite their age difference. Mark wasn't sure what to make of it. Nor did he know what to make of his growing fondness for 'the old bandit' as he now referred affectionately to Caprionni. He realized that he'd tapped into a long-hidden softer side of the mafia don.

But today, Mark was worried. Arnie had called three days ago to cancel the regular weekly meeting with Caprionni. He wouldn't say why. That was unusual. There'd been no further word, and no phone calls from the mafia don. Mark began to worry that the aging mafia boss might be ill or something else had happened. He reached for his iPhone.

"Mr. Caprionni," Mark said when he heard Caprionni's voice on his direct number.

"Yeah, Trimonti," Caprionni said faintly, forgetting for the moment that name had been Mark's undercover name. "I mean Tremblay. Yeah, Mark. Yeah. Yeah. Whad'ya want?"

His normally brusk voice was weak, although he sounded as impatient as always. The mafia godfather was upset about something. He sounded confused, even disoriented. It was not like him.

"You cancelled our meeting and we haven't talked for a while, sir. I would like to come over to see you, Mr. Caprionni," Mark said. "Would this afternoon be all right with you?"

"Uh, okay, yeah I guess," Caprionni said, evidently distracted by something. "Yeah, I guess so."

There was a long pause, and then he added, his voice weak and flat.

"Yeah . . . I must see you. We must talk."

The old man's behavior worried Mark. He seemed befuddled. Caprionni didn't sound anything like the strong and confident Giovanni Caprionni who'd become the most powerful organized crime boss in America. Most important, the mafia would soon be playing a major role in Mark's alliance. Without them, the effectiveness of the alliance would diminish substantially.

"Would two o'clock be convenient, sir?" Mark said.

"Yeah, okay," Caprionni replied. "Come then." His voice sounded hollow, almost a lifeless monotone. He promptly hung up.

Well, that much is normal, Mark thought, bemused.

*

Caprionni Mansion, Staten Island

Mark drove up the wide curved driveway to Caprionni's mansion at 1:45 p.m. He parked as he usually did under the portico leading to the imposing front entrance. Two Caprionni soldiers with assault rifles were standing on alert at both ends of the portico. That was different. Others armed in a similar manner were trying to be invisible behind huge oak trees and bushes that dotted the expansive lawns surrounding the mansion. Mark had not seen such a show of force before.

Arnie stood at the open front door, holding an Uzi tucked behind his right thigh. That was odd. Even more unusual was Vinny's absence. The useless pipsqueak always complained about where Mark parked, and insisted on escorting Mark to meetings with his father. The guards, and the look in Arnie's eyes, told him something was seriously amiss in the Caprionni family. Arnie beckoned him to come in.

"Hi Arnie." Mark greeted his gangster friend warmly as usual.

"Good afternoon, Mr. Mark," Arnie replied formally, almost stiffly. Mark was taken aback. They usually embraced. Arnie always took the initiative.

Not this time. Mark was even more surprised when Arnie offered no further conversation. He just stood there, looking away, waiting for Mark to make the next move.

Mark could hardly keep himself from asking, 'What the hell's going on, Arnie?' but decided to simply say:

"Mr. Caprionni's expecting me, Arnie. Is it okay if I go ahead in?"

"Yes, Mr. Mark," Arnie answered, nodding his head toward the hallway. There was a hollow sound in his voice. "The godfather told me you were coming."

The high ceiling of the two-story entry carried the echo of his shoes on the spotless marble floor, until they were muted by the plush carpet of the picture-lined 'rogue's gallery' ending at the door to Caprionni's den, on the left. He knocked on the door.

"Come." The mafia don's voice sounded faint through the heavy oak door. It was ajar. Mark pushed it open.

Caprionni's chair was turned away from him. This had never happened before. Mark closed the door behind him. It made a soft 'thud' as the latch engaged.

"It's Mark, Mr. Caprionni, " he said, announcing himself to the back of the mobster's black high-back chair behind the oak desk. "Mark Tremblay", he repeated. "May I come in?"

Caprionni slowly turned the chair, gesturing with a limp right hand for Mark to come forward.

As he got closer, Mark's breath caught in his throat.

Caprionni's normal build was tall and slender. But today he looked as if he'd lost a lot of weight since Mark last saw him. That was just 10 days earlier. The mafia don's face was gray, unshaven for days and heavily creased. His eyes were deep set, red rimmed and bloodshot. Mark could hardly believe what he was seeing before him . . . and he was certain that the old man had been crying!

"Are you okay?" Mark heard himself say, stepping forward quickly. He would have been more subtle and diplomatic, had he caught himself quicker. Shock and concern about Caprionni's appearance had overtaken him.

"It's okay, Mark. Come here," Caprionni said kindly, pushing himself up slowly and gesturing to the round table where they always met now. "Sit down. I must tell you some things."

When both were seated, Caprionni looked Mark in the eyes and said:

"Vincenza is dead."

Mark was stunned.

"What?" he said, uncertain he had heard correctly. "But how? What happened? Who did this?"

"The Maniero family," Caprionni said. He paused, struggling to regain control.

"The Maniero's killed Vinny?" Mark asked, incredulous. He began to envision a fierce mafia war. There could be a bloodbath before anyone was able to stop it.

"No! No!" Caprionni said quickly. "The Maniero's and Vincenza. They're all dead . . . all dead . . .

slaughtered! Someone shot all of them . . . every one of them!"

A tear made its way down the old man's right cheek. Caprionni turned away quickly and wiped his face with a white crumpled handkerchief. Mark didn't know whether to look away in deference to his dignity or to try comforting the grieving old man. Instinctively, he reached over, putting his hand on Caprionni's saying:

"Are you sure you're feeling up to telling me how this awful thing happened, Mr. Caprionni?" Mark said. "I will come back later, if that would be a better time for you . . . as you wish."

"No, no!" Caprionni said, pulling his hand away from under Mark's and reaching for his handkerchief, still struggling with his composure. "You must stay. I . . . I need you here."

The proud mafia don paused. He looked away for a moment, then turned to Mark:

"Today, I am ashamed, Mark. And I am grieving, for my son, for his death. I grieve also for what he has done to this family, and for the distress he has caused his mother. I have to tell you, she is in a terrible way. It is much for a mother to deal with, and for me. You are a good man, Mark. I know that now. I trust you. I am going to tell you about some important matters. You need to know these things."

Caprionni paused again, obviously steeling himself.

"I trusted my son completely," Caprionni said. "But I have learned he was trying to make deals behind my back, deals with the Maniero's. Deals to take over the family's drug business. Can you

247

believe this? My own son, a traitor to his family! And this . . . this . . . he accused *you* of doing! He lied to his own father!

"When he was young, I had such high hopes for Vincenza. I wanted to teach him, so he could succeed me one day. So why this? How could he do such a thing to his family? How could this happen?"

Mark remembered the brief media reports a few days earlier about a multiple murder on Staten Island. In New York, murders were a daily occurrence, even multiple murders. They were routine to the news media. The reports gave no hint of a connection between the murders and organized crime. Someone had got to the NYPD to limit the amount of information released. News reports made it sound like a domestic mass murder, which was bad enough. But reports of a mass murder involving the mafia would have raised speculation about a mafia war, attracting huge media attention.

Mark knew from the FBI's undercover agent that Vinny had been trying to make a deal with the Maniero family but there was no way he could tell the old man. Caprionni would have taken offence and not believed him. It could have ended The Commission's participation in their alliance.

"This is what I know," Caprionni said.

He paused again to regain his composure, and then continued:

"Four nights ago, three men shot their way into Salvatore Maniero's home. It was suppertime. The family was gathered to celebrate the first birthday of Salvatore's grandson, Salvatore Junior's baby boy, Salvatore III. Vinny was there, too. It's a terrible

irony, you know. He was killed because he was there
. . . there to conspire against his own family.

"Everyone is dead, even the baby. Can you believe
it? Everyone that is, except Salvatore's teenage
daughter. She is why I know what happened. Grace
was upstairs in the bathroom when the hit came. She
climbed into the attic and hid. She thinks there were
three men, maybe four. She is under my protection
now. My people think the attackers used AK-47s.
We don't know for sure. There are no shell casings.
Nothing! The killers spread gasoline everywhere and
burned the house to the ground. Grace broke her leg
jumping to escape the fire after the killers left. My
doctor fixed her leg and is treating her burns.

"What is so strange, Mark, there are no bodies!
Can you believe that? Nothing! Nothing at all! The
killers must have taken them before the fire. By the
time the fire was reported, it was too late. The house
is gone. I shouldn't wonder no one heard the shots.
The house is on 50 acres down at the end of Staten
Island, maybe five miles from here. Maybe the guns
had silencers. You know the place. Anyway, Grace
walked all that way here through bush and back
alleys, with a broken leg and burns to her hands and
legs. Can you believe that? She made a splint and a
crutch from old fence boards she found. Grace is a
very brave young woman. Too bad for Vincenza that
she didn't like him."

Caprionni paused, giving Mark time to digest this
latest bombshell. Mark now had more of his own
grief to deal with – the death of his undercover agent
in the Maniero crime family, a fellow law
enforcement officer. He was certain to have been

among those murdered. Mark realized someone at the NYPD was doing one hell of a job covering this up.

The distinguished old mafia don walked slowly over to a sideboard beside his desk and returned with two cups of coffee. Black for him, Mark noticed. It surprised and pleased him that Caprionni had remembered, despite his grief. Caprionni always took cream, no sugar for himself.

"I think you know, Mark," Caprionni said, making an effort to sound more businesslike. "We have sources of information inside NYPD. We hear they're stymied. They don't want the details of these murders to get out until they know something more about what happened. There had to be 10 or 12 people there on Saturday night, counting the bodyguards. But there were no bodies! No bodies? How do you figure that? No one is going to tell the police about Grace. Maybe later. It's too risky for the girl if word gets out. She's an important witness, I know. That makes her a target.

"Grace told me she heard the screaming but saw very little, only what she could see from an attic window. Three or four men dressed in black were running away in the dark. I am calling on your sense of honor, Mark, to keep this to yourself, at least for now. NYPD has too many leaks. She is in great danger. We must arrange for her protection before we tell the cops. Then I will see that investigators get to question her. Will you accept that?"

Mark nodded, reluctantly: "For now, Mr. Caprionni, but just for a while."

Concealing evidence of a crime was a crime, he was thinking. That applied to everyone, including him. Mark was determined to find a way to get this compromising secret about Grace Maniero to investigators without putting her in danger. As the only witness, she would have invaluable information they needed quickly, but she would also be in great danger. Mark knew the head of the FBI's witness protection program. He made a mental note to call her as soon as he left the meeting. He wasn't sure how he was going to square this with the deal he'd made with the New York attorney general.

Caprionni's voice had trailed away. He was staring off into the distance. Mark thought perhaps the old man was reflecting on how the Caprionni family disposed of people they'd murdered. Something similar was possible, Mark thought. Then Caprionni spoke again:

"I'm positive it was those goddamned terrorists, Mark!" he said. "It had to be those fucking ISIS bastards who made the hit! They were making a deal with the Maniero's to get my drug operations. You know that. You told me. They're vicious savages. We're in a war, Mark, a war against a bunch of fucking wild animals!"

Caprionni's profanity astounded Mark. He'd never heard the mafia don use such coarse language, ever, even when furious about something. The godfather continued:

"Here is why I think those terrorists are responsible. My people are telling me that since my son and the Maniero's were murdered, someone else is running the Maniero drug operations. They have never seen this person before. He is Middle Eastern . . . tall . . . dark hair . . . heavy eyebrows. I am told the man speaks very good English. Everywhere he goes three men are with him. I think probably these are lieutenants or bodyguards. I am thinking they are those terrorists . . . and the murderers . . . maybe the same ones that hit your house. What do you think?"

"First, Mr. Caprionni, let me say how very sorry I am for your loss," Mark said, showing genuine respect and concern. "Please accept my deepest sympathies, to you and to your wife. I know Vincenza was your only child. It must be very hard for you and Mrs. Caprionni."

Caprionni simply nodded back. Mark saw he was struggling again with his composure.

"We both know these terrorists have been trying to take over a drug operation to get cash," Mark said. "You and I have discussed this. They need money to finance their operations and can't get ISIS money into America. May I ask, have you told The Commission about what's happened to Vinny and the Maniero's?"

"Yes, yes, of course," Caprionni replied. "I called the heads of the other three families right away. We have all increased our security. And you should know I have named Arnie to replace Vincenza as my lieutenant."

"May I say that I'm pleased to hear about that, Mr. Caprionni," Mark said. "Arnie's a good man . . . an honorable man and completely loyal to you. If you will forgive me for saying so, sir . . . you couldn't have made a better choice."

"I knew that you would think so," he replied. A slight hint of a smile eased for an instant the deep furrows crisscrossing his grief-stricken face.

Chapter 34

Danbury, CT

"Hi my love," Mark said answering his iPhone. He admired the photo of Paige on his phone. She was calling from her New York office. His heart jumped every time her picture appeared.

"You're one gorgeous creature!" he said crooning into the phone. "Want to go somewhere private? Right now? Just you and me! We could get naked together, you know! We've got a license for that!"

"Mark!" Paige said fondly, trying to stifle a giggle. Then her tone changed:

"P-l-e-a-s-e, Mark! This is a business call! And you're going to like this one, oh gorgeous man whom I love. Listen, I'm calling to tell you that much-criticized inclusion of the mob in the alliance is starting to pay off."

"What've you got, Love?" Mark said. Now he was all business, too.

"Just had a call from a volunteer contact in Albuquerque," Paige said. "Someone from the Banditos biker gang called her. They found the number on our Facebook page. A few bikers there came across a group of young men yesterday. Some looked middle-eastern. They were acting unusual . . . kinda awkward . . . like they were not wanting to let on about being new to the city. It got the bikers attention.

"Anyway, Mark, she told me the bikers followed the men and watched them pile a huge bunch of groceries and other stuff into a one-ton pickup," Paige added.

"Here's where it gets interesting. Three of the bikers decided to shadow them. Gotta give those guys credit. That's not easy to do that quietly on a Harley. They followed the strangers out of town. The truck had to be souped up. The bikers were forced to hustle just to stay in visual contact. The truck headed east on I-40 and then south on Highway 337. When the truck pulled into a farm, the bikers tucked their rides into the trees and snuck up close. They told our caller they saw at least 40 to 45 people, probably more.

"The bikers at first thought it was a cult or weird retreat facility. Some people were dressed like middle-easterners, you know, robes and turbans. They saw a whole bunch of AK-47s and a firing range. That reminded them about all those terrorist attacks. They decided to tell someone. That someone was their regular drug contact. She's involved with our alliance. It's working, Mark! It's working!"

"I'll be damned!" Mark exclaimed. "We may have found a big jihadist camp, maybe a new training camp to replace Chapman. Please thank your contact in Albuquerque, and hers in the Banditos. Never thought I'd ever say that!"

After they hung up, Mark made some quick calls and then phoned Bjorn Sorensen with the update.

"That sounds like a large camp," Sorensen said. "What resources do we have in the area?"

"We've our undercover guy there and a one-person field office in Santa Fe," Mark said. "That's it, and the guy in Santa Fe is quite new. I'd bring in some of my task force but everyone's committed to our first priority, finding that damned nuclear bomb."

"Shit! I didn't know we were that thin down there," Sorensen said. "Damned budget cuts. You'll just have to do the best you can for now, Mark. I'll see what I can do at this end. Have you heard from your guy yet? He must be due to report by now, isn't he?"

"Yes, Khaled's overdue", Mark said. "I'm getting worried. I've not heard from him in over a week. Maybe he's on his way to that camp, or maybe he's already there and having trouble finding a way to check in. All we can do for now is wait."

Chapter 35

Albuquerque

"I'm in Albuquerque for supplies," Khaled told Mark. His voice on the phone was rushed. "I haven't had a chance to call you. And I don't have much time. Here's a quick update. We arrived a few days ago at a farm about 50 miles southeast of here."

"Good to hear from you," Mark interrupted, speaking more calmly than he felt. "It's been a while. We had a tip about the camp. Glad to hear you're there and okay."

"Yeah," Khaled said. "No opportunity to get away to call you. I'm on a payphone in a Walgreen's store. Not many of those phones around anymore.

"The camp looks like an old farm, maybe 100 acres. About 45 to 50 people are in the camp, now. They're expecting more. Apparently Rhamir chose New Mexico because a deputy of bin Laden was born not far from here, in Las Cruces. Anwar al-Awlaki. Goofy! You know, he's that guy the CIA killed with a drone attack in Pakistan."

Mark understood that travel between New York and Albuquerque explained the lack of calls. They'd probably taken a circuitous route. A group of young men traveling together, some black, some Hispanic and some with middle-eastern appearances would draw attention, especially after the terrorist attacks.

"Look," Mark said. "We need to track down Rhamir urgently. He knows where that damned nuclear bomb is. We need to get him and sweat him. I wonder if he's planning to bring it to your camp. Have you heard about it from anyone else?"

"No one's said a thing about it here," Khaled said. "Rhamir seems to be the only who knows anything about it. He was at the camp for a few days . . . gave us one of his pep talks then left. Don't know where he's gone. Shahid told me that Rhamir has some kind of special services team that he's gone to see. Maybe it's his nuclear team.

"It could also be connected to other news I have for you. They're planning another round of attacks, many more than before, possibly up to a dozen. I haven't heard how soon or where. Shahid was bragging to me about them. He said that I'll be helping him. He wouldn't tell me anything else. No one seems to know much except he and Rhamir. I'll keep you posted.

"Quickly, here are a few other things," Khaled added, his voice tense. "First, they've closed down the New York apartments, except one. They left three jihadists there. I don't know what that's all about."

"I do," Mark replied. "The Maniero crime family was massacred last week. I'm damned sure that group did it. Rhamir and three others have taken over the Maniero drug operations."

"Holy shit!" Khaled said. "That son of a bitch is on the move! I'm not surprised. He's desperate for money. Guess he's gonna get it any way he can.

"Oh, I got a chance to mail you that report on the programs at the training camp in Syria I attended. Rhamir wanted some notes about how the training was organized. He's using it for the camp here. I made copies. He asked me to mail a copy to a guy named Fahim Tahir in DC. While I was in the post office mailing him a copy I addressed one to you. I included a sketch of the layout of the camp.

"Holy shit!" Khaled said. "Here they come. Gotta go!"

"Hang on!" Mark shot back quickly. "The attacks. When are they?"

It was too late. The phone was dead.

Shahid with three other jihadists rounded the corner of the Walgreen's store. They walked in through the automatic sliding glass doors barely a second after Khaled had hung up. He'd caught a glimpse of them through the store's tinted windows crossing the parking lot. They'd gone to fill the pickup with gas and buy weapons and ammunition while Khaled shopped for cleaning supplies and paper products.

Khaled had bought a USA Today newspaper before making the call to Mark, just in case. It proved a lucky choice. He was leaning against the shopping cart pretending to read the newspaper when Shahid and the others walked up. Shahid was the only one with enough money to pay for the supplies.

"Making sure we're not in the paper?" Shahid asked, joking.

"Not today," Khaled replied with a wide grin, relieved Shahid obviously hadn't suspected a thing.

Shahid gestured for Khaled to follow him outside after giving one of the others money to check out the supplies in Khaled's cart. The two men walked across the parking lot.

"Well, what do you think?" Shahid asked in Urdu.

"About what?" Khaled responded, also in Urdu, genuinely puzzled.

"Farouk Mohammed and the two guys from New York," Shahid answered impatiently. "Which one do you think is the traitor? I deliberately brought them with us today so we could observe them. We're running out of time."

"Awe, shit! I wish you'd said something earlier, Ali-Mumar," Khaled said. "I'd have been more observant. I'm afraid my attention has been on that write-up for Rhamir on the training camp in Syria. I'll be more vigilant from now on."

"Damn it man, Rhamir is expecting an answer, and soon," Shahid said, visibly exasperated. "He wants the traitor badly and he's counting on us. And I'm counting on you!"

They turned and walked silently back across the parking lot to the four-door pickup where the others were loading the supplies. The pickup looked like it was aging, but Rhamir had arranged for the engine to be souped up and the drive train restored next to new. Khalid had assumed Rhamir was some kind of automotive enthusiast. The real reason was much less innocent.

Chapter 36

Danbury, CT

Edward had wakened early that Sunday morning expecting to play football in the back yard with his dad. His mother was in New York with Aunt Jennifer on a combined shopping-Broadway play weekend. Caylyn was still asleep. He was happy to hear his Dad's shower running. Soon they'd be outside playing a pickup game of football. Lately, Edward had been experiencing long waits for one-on-one time with his Dad.

He sat on an upholstered bench outside his parents' walk-in closet. Beside him was one of the iPhones his Dad used for business. He knew by the color of the cover this was the one with an unlisted number. It had no voice mail, deliberately. When someone called it would just keep ringing. Edward and Caylyn had been given strict instructions to never answer it, not under any circumstances.

The phone began ringing while Edward sat looking at it, annoyed. It wouldn't stop. The ringing became irritating. Finally, it got the better of him. He knew that he shouldn't but he answered it, just to stop the persistent ringing. Edward tried to mimic his father's grown up manner:

"This is Mark Tremblay's line," he said in a voice as firm and deep as an elementary school boy could manage, which wasn't much. "Who's calling please?"

The phone went dead. Edward shrugged his shoulders. He put the phone back where he'd found it, annoyed at the experience but relieved for the quiet.

Neither Edward nor his father would know that Abdul Rhamir had made the call from his new camp in New Mexico.

*

ISIS Camp

Rhamir was startled by the familiar young voice. He'd been dialing numbers from phone bills brought from the now-abandoned apartments in New York City. He was trying to determine who owned the numbers shown on the bills. Rhamir had become obsessed with tracking the traitor who'd caused their losses at Chapman.

He was angry that the suspect call had been made to Mark Tremblay's phone from one of his apartments! But who of the fighters there could be the traitor? The terrorist leader decided to keep this to himself for now, and take time to consider what he'd learned. He would discuss his finding later with Shahid.

The day after arriving at the camp he delivered to recruits and jihadi what was, by his own assessment, one of his better morale boosting speeches. After the speech Rhamir called Shahid to a meeting.

"Ali-Mumar," he said. "I have been doing some investigating on my own to uncover the traitor. I have no time for this! It is work you should be doing!"

"What have you discovered, Rhamir?" Shahid said, embarrassed and confused. He hoped to bring the traitor to Rhamir.

"The traitor was living with other faithful fighters in one of the New York apartments," Rhamir said, describing what he'd found. "All you have to do now is narrow down the suspects and unmask the traitor."

"I've done most of your work for you already," Rhamir said derisively. "Now you need to finish it quickly! Do you hear me?"

"Your information confirms something that I've been working on," Shahid lied. "I need to talk to some of our fighters first. I think we can solve this quickly."

Now that Shahid had lied trying to limit Rhamir's scorn, he'd forced himself into having to come up with a plan, and quickly.

Within minutes following his meeting with Rhamir, Shahid called Khaled over to his trailer and said excitedly: "Khaled, we've found the traitor!"

"Who is it?" Khaled asked, struggling to hide his apprehension. "How did you find him?" He'd still not given Shahid feedback on the three suspects Shahid kept asking about. Khaled couldn't bring himself to condemn anyone to hideous torture and a gruesome death.

"Phone records," Shahid said, trying to hide his shame for not having thought of them. "Phone records in New York. Rhamir keeps everything. Your old apartment . . . he figured it out!"

Khaled felt a cold sweat on his body. He'd made several calls to Mark while alone in the apartment. He didn't realize the bills showed numbers for local calls as well as long distance calls. No one had mentioned it.

"The traitor is Farouk Mohammed! I'm absolutely sure of it," Shahid said, making an entirely random choice. "It all fits with all the other things that I have found! It's him!"

Shahid had found nothing. The only wrong Farouk had committed was letting Mark's children escape from Rhamir's apartment.

"You look surprised!" Shahid said.

Khaled's mind froze.

"You had no idea Farouk was the one . . . the traitor?" Shahid asked misreading the startled look on Khaled's face. His 'understudy' knew full well he was accusing Farouk with no evidence whatever.

"No, I didn't," Khaled said truthfully.

"I've learned that sometimes it's very easy to be mistaken about others," he added, in a faint hope to raise doubts about the accusation against Farouk.

"Exactly!" Shahid said, again misreading Khaled. "We trusted that traitor. The dirty scum made phone calls to a number we've tracked to that FBI infidel. You know, the one Rhamir's been trying to kill. I'm sure you've heard Rhamir talk about him. His name is Mark Tremblay."

"Yeah," Khaled said, feeling another prickly sweat. "That name sounds familiar. I think Rhamir mentioned him once or twice."

"Yeah, he did. Look, Khaled, before I forget," Shahid said handing his understudy a cell phone.

"As my deputy you'll need this. You and I may have to be in different places while planning our next attacks. This'll make it easier for us stay in touch."

Shahid handed Khaled a cell phone. It was both a huge gesture and a great opportunity for Khaled. Shahid was showing confidence in him, but most important, Khaled could use the phone to reach Mark's unlisted mobile.

Shahid left Khaled and headed back to Rhamir's trailer.

"I had to check with some of our fighters before telling you this," Shahid said to Rhamir. "I can confirm now who the traitor is. It's Farouk!"

"You mean the one who let those Tremblay brats escape?" Rhamir said. "Are you absolutely certain?"

"Yes!" Shahid said simply. Then he made up a story on the spot for Rhamir, claiming falsely that others confirmed Farouk had made the calls to Mark. It convinced an already agitated Rhamir of Farouk's guilt. Besides, Rhamir was still angry with Farouk for the escape of Mark's children.

Shahid hurried back to find Khalid. He'd joined a crew building an obstacle course to train new recruits.

"Is that traitor Farouk back yet?" Shahid demanded. "Have you seen him?"

Shahid had given money to one of the other jihadi to go into Albuquerque for groceries, and for more ammunition for target practice. Farouk had gone with him.

"I'm not sure when they'll be back," Khaled said.

"Go back to your trailer!" Shahid said, meaning the old bunkhouse Farouk shared with Khaled and four other fighters. "Come get me as soon as he's back. Say nothing to anyone. Go now!"

Housing at the camp consisted of eight second-hand bunkhouse trailers and four newer two-bedroom park model trailers arranged in a rough circle around an assembly area. The old bunkhouses were on site when they arrived, left from some earlier occupant. One of the big new park model trailers Rhamir had bought was his personal residence, shared with his aged mother. Another served as both camp headquarters and Shahid's residence. A third was the cookhouse. The fourth was the dining hall where fighters ate in shifts.

The bunkhouses were for fighters, trainers and jihadi recruits. At the head of 'the square', as Rhamir called it, was a large hip roof barn with wing additions on both sides that once contained cattle stalls. The barn housed the bomb factory and three classrooms. The hayloft had a large open area used for large gatherings, as well as for fitness and hand-to-hand combat training, and now for extra sleeping quarters filled with new recruits. Also stored in the barn were three ATV's and Rhamir's pride and joy, a powerful dune buggy.

As Khalid turned to leave, Shahid said:

"By the way, Rhamir asked me how it was that the car bomb you were responsible for in Houston didn't explode. I didn't have an answer. What went wrong? I was embarrassed, not having an answer. For a moment, I was worried that he might think you were the traitor."

Shahid laughed loudly. Khaled felt another bolt of tension shudder up and down his spine.

"I'm embarrassed, too, Shahid," Khaled said, lying and trying to stay calm. He prayed his voice was convincing. "Yes, I heard the car did not explode. Two other fighters made the final preparations for me. I should have checked it out myself, personally. It's my mistake . . . my fault. I'm really very sorry. But as you know, you asked me to make copies for everyone of the layouts for the parking lots and the stadium. I was away making the copies when I should have been checking the car. I ran outta time. I take responsibility."

"Okay, okay, Khaled," Shahid said, holding up his right hand in a gesture of resignation. "Never mind. I just need an answer for Rhamir. He was very pleased with our attack; thought it was incredibly successful. He just wondered about your car. You are one of our best fighters and he knows it."

"Thank you very much," Khaled replied. "I appreciate your faith in me. It is very reassuring."

It was late in the day when Farouk returned from Albuquerque with his companion and began unloading supplies from the back of the pickup into the barn.

Reluctantly, Khaled walked over to Shahid's trailer. He was hunched over some papers. Khaled told him Farouk was back. He knew that he had no other choice.

"Okay," Shahid said. "Go find Naeim Azhadi and Mohsen Rouhani. Tell them to bring their Kalashnikovs and come find me. Then go and ask Rhamir to join us at your trailer. He knows why. He's in his trailer with his mother. You should come too."

Joining them was the last thing Khaled wanted. He knew Farouk was far from pure but didn't deserve to be treated as a traitor. He'd taken part in the murders of hundreds of innocent people, including the massive Houston attack; Farouk had personally built and placed one of the briefcase bombs. And he'd let Mark's kids escape. But he wasn't the traitor. Khaled wanted no part of what he knew happened to traitors. He'd seen it in Syria.

A crowd was gathering as he arrived with Rhamir outside the bunkhouse. While waiting for Rhamir, Khaled watched him strap a long curved sword to his waist. Earlier, Khaled had seen the sword hanging on the wall in the trailer. He thought it was a souvenir, a decoration. He'd never seen Rhamir wear it. The sword evidently served some kind of ceremonial purpose.

Shahid walked into the square. Behind him, hands tied, was Farouk. He eyes showed total panic. Azhadi gripped Farouk's right upper arm tightly. His left arm was held firmly by Rouhani. Each was holding an AK-47 in their other hand.

"Why are you doing this?" Farouk said to Shahid. "What do you think I've done? Tell me, please! I've done nothing wrong! You have to believe me! Please! Please!"

Both guards pushed Farouk toward Rhamir. Azhadi hit Farouk on the back of his neck with the butt of his AK-47. Farouk fell to his knees in front of Rhamir.

Meanwhile, Khaled began working his way to one side and around to the back of the crowd of some 55 jihadist fighters and recruits gathered at the scene.

"Stand him up and tie him over there!" Rhamir said, pointing to the remains of an old horse-drawn wagon. Azhadi and Rouhani lashed Farouk's hands to the side of the wagon, and then stripped off his clothing.

"What have I done?" Farouk said again, terrified and still dazed by the blow from Azhadi's weapon.

"You're a traitor!" Rhamir said, hoping to arouse the crowd of fighters gathered. He succeeded. A few of them shouted insults at Farouk.

"You are a traitor for the FBI," Rhamir said. "I have proof! Because of your treachery, the infidels murdered five of our best fighters and destroyed Chapman. You will pay for betraying our glorious Islamic Army of America!"

A few in the crowd began shouting, "Death to the traitor!" "Death to the spy!"

"I don't know what you're talking about!" Farouk cried. "I didn't do that. I've done nothing!" He shouted as loud as he could, trying to be heard over the noisy crowd. "Nothing! Why are you doing this to me? You have the wrong man!"

"You are a traitor!" Rhamir shouted again, further arousing the crowd.

Farouk's panicky cries were drowned out by the rowdy crowd shouting: "Traitor! Traitor! Kill the Traitor!"

As the dusk grew deeper, Rhamir ordered that a pile of old wood be gathered and set on fire. Shahid found a three-foot length of iron rebar in the barn and placed it in the fire.

The growing darkness and milling crowd gave Khaled the chance he needed to get away.

He slipped around behind a bunkhouse and ran down a wash into the bushes. After dialing Mark's iPhone, he waited as it rang and rang. Then he remembered that number had no voice mail. Before leaving New York, Mark had given him another number, a dedicated secret number to memorize. It had an anonymous sounding voice mailbox. Khaled dialed it and left a quick message about what was happening.

As he hung up, Khaled heard Farouk scream. He shuddered as Farouk's long piercing screams of agony were repeated, time after time after time. On hands and knees in his hiding place, in bushes beside a wash 30 yards behind the trailers, Khaled fought back the urge to vomit. He'd never heard such excruciating and pitiful screams from a human being. He tried without success to block out images in his mind of what he knew was happening to Farouk. He'd witnessed terrible things at the camp in Syria. Then he lost the battle, vomiting until there were only dry heaves.

Finally, sitting in the sand, exhausted and with sweat pouring off his body, he heard a loud 'whack' and a cheer go up from the crowd. Khaled realized he'd better clean up as best he could and slip back or he'd be missed, even though it was totally dark now.

The crowd was starting to disperse by the time he got back. In the light from the fire and lanterns, he saw Rhamir wiping blood from his sword. Lying in the sand at his feet was Farouk's naked decapitated body. His head was on the ground three feet away. Khaled's stomach heaved again. He almost lost it. Shahid was holding a large clear plastic bag in one hand and a cardboard shipping box in the other. Khaled turned and walked unsteadily into his bunkhouse. He knew he had to stop this unspeakable savagery, somehow and soon.

Chapter 37

Miami, FL

Late one morning, the phone rang in Jack Brewster's office in Miami.

"S-E-A Containers," he said. "Jack Brewster here. How may I help you?"

Many people knew his direct line. He always tried to answer it himself. Jack had learned the value of that personal touch from Paul Winston, who'd help rescue the company during a rough patch years earlier.

"We need help with container," a heavily accented voice replied. "You have mobile crane? On boat? Yes?"

"As a matter of fact yes we do, sir," Jack said. "We have a crane mounted on a 65-foot barge. I assume you want us to lift your container? Is it loaded on something now? Is it full or empty?"

"Full," came the reply. "Very full. And it is in water."

"Okay, sir," Jack said. "Look, give me your phone number and I'll have the head of that crew give you a call to make arrangements."

"No!" came the sharp reply. "I meet only with you. Here is location."

Jack copied down the directions. He asked the caller's name but heard only:

"We will meet there in two hours." The phone went dead.

He looked at the address. North Key Largo was at least 90 minutes away on Highway 821 from his plant and offices near the Port of Miami. Jack didn't like the sound of the voice, but his curiosity got the better of him. He decided to meet the guy.

Jack was president of South East Asia (SEA) Containers Ltd. He gave much credit for the survival of his company to Prescott Enterprises and the example Paul Winston had set for him. Jack had founded the company years earlier after returning from Vietnam, an idea flourishing in his fertile mind.

He was a Master Sergeant, a logistics expert for the U.S. Army's combat support group, in South Vietnam. During his years there, Jack's unit was responsible for moving enormous amounts of war materiel from coastal areas to American and South Vietnamese military units. In the process, he'd acquired valuable knowledge, important contacts and an impressive track record.

Jack's closest brush with death during the war came when he helped uncover a drug trafficking operation using the combat support group to transport drugs. An ambush planned by ringleaders failed when authorities had received an anonymous tip.

SEA Containers had grown quickly. Jack's reputation for getting things done became known widely back home, as was his integrity. The company built and repaired custom shipping containers for 103 large export-import companies around the world. Its manufacturing division alone was selling more than 7,000 containers a year when it faltered a decade ago. Emilio Hernandez, a trusted army buddy and fellow logistics sergeant, was head of manufacturing until the late 1990s. Hernandez turned out to have a secret gambling addiction. To pay gambling debts, he was making illegal deals behind Jack's back that had driven the company to the brink of bankruptcy.

Prescott Enterprises had rescued SEA Containers, preserving more than 230 jobs. Paul described it as 'angel investing'. During almost half a century, Prescott had built a highly profitable merchant banking and investment enterprise. A big part of Prescott success was based on rescuing companies like SEA that had good leadership and a sound business, but were experiencing financial difficulties. Paul sensed SEA Containers was a perfect candidate for a Prescott investment. It turned out that way for both parties.

*

Key Largo, FL

When Jack arrived to meet the anonymous caller, a small tramp freighter was just visible heading east toward the horizon. A decrepit 35-foot aluminum fishing boat was tied to a crumbling cement pier. Backed up to the pier was a flatbed trailer hooked to an transport truck. Wording on the door had been spray painted over.

"I take you," said a man who walked up as Jack got out of his pickup. The voice sounded like the caller. Jack followed him. Silently, they climbed into the aluminum boat with a half-cab and went out to a round bright orange buoy bobbing on the ocean swells.

"It is down four meters . . . maybe more," the man said in his halting accent. "Your crane can pick up and put on trailer . . . yes?" he added, pointing to the parked truck and trailer.

Jack quickly sized up the job. It was pretty simple.

"Yeah, sure," he said. "No problem. What happened? What's in the container?"

"Parts for machines," the man answered a bit too quickly. "Only machine parts.

"That old boat," the man added, gesturing with his thumb toward the tramper disappearing over the horizon. "They getting container ready when big wave come up. Tip boat. Container slide overboard. Stupid sailors! Good riddance!

"How much for this? To lift from water and put on truck?" he added.

"Let's see, we've got to bring the barge and crew up from Miami. And we'll need a scuba crew to hook up the cables to the container. Say about $4,500 plus expenses to bring the crane, do the job and return the crane," Jack said. "Maybe another $2,000 to $2,500 for expenses. We'll need to do a detailed estimate for you."

"This is much," the man said. "But okay. How soon?"

"The crane and lift crew can be here tomorrow morning. I'll send our dive crew over at the same time."

The man offered him a manila envelope filled with $100 bills as a retainer. It turned out to be $4,200.

Jack made a mental note to remind his crew chief to collect the balance.

*

Miami

The following afternoon, Jack's direct line rang again.

"Geraldo here," a voice said.

Geraldo was the shop steward for the union representing workers at Jack's company.

"Hey, Geraldo! Good to hear from you," Jack said with a mixture of enthusiasm and curiosity.

The two men had a distant but cordial relationship. It was an open secret between the men that the union was controlled by organized crime. Jack suspected they were a descendent of the Santo Trafficante Jr. crime family that once ruled the Miami underworld.

"Jack, you know that job lifting the container out of the water near North Key Largo?" Geraldo said.

"Yeah, Geraldo," Jack replied. "How'd it go?"

"The job went fine. And we got paid in full. But it's an odd one, Jack," Geraldo said. "I don't like the feel of it. Too much like an illegal import to me. The client didn't show us any paperwork, like they usually do, and the container didn't have any seals. This one stinks, Jack. Thought you should know."

Jack was aware organized crime gave a wide berth to unusual situations that looked blatantly illegal . . . unless, of course, they had full control over everything, including any cops that might become involved.

"Look, Jack," Geraldo said, "I remember you mentioned a few weeks ago some kind of civilian counterterrorism program run by Prescott Enterprises. Wasn't it Prescott that helped you out, uh helped us all out, when things got tough around here a few years back?"

"The same," Jack said. "Are you saying we should have someone look into this? It could bring in the authorities."

He was coming close to subject matter both had silently agreed to avoid.

"That's what I'm saying, Jack," Geraldo said firmly. "I spoke about it with friends. They thought I should call you. especially after those terrorist attacks. I remember you telling the workers the other day that you're going to set up contacts for us to report anything suspicious around here. Right?"

"That's true," Jack said.

He knew the people Geraldo referred to as 'friends' were in fact contacts in the crime family that controlled the union. Jack recalled hearing years ago that Prescott had some kind of a connection with the Chicago mafia, something to do with the Bay of Pigs fiasco. Other organized crime families respected the connection. He didn't know the details but wondered if that might be why SEA had never experienced serious union problems.

"What makes you think that container you pulled up has anything to do with those sick bastards?" Jack said.

"A couple of Middle Eastern guys were on board the barge when we lifted the container," Geraldo replied. "I was alone in the pilothouse when one of them came in with a funny look on his face. He seemed frightened.

"He pointed down into the water where our divers were hooking up the container and said something like, 'That's for bad things.' Then he handed me a folded up note. It was taped tightly closed. He put his index finger over his lips and said, 'You read it later, okay?' The guy slipped out of the pilothouse before I could ask any questions. I didn't understand at first what he meant.

"Well, Jack, after the container was loaded onto the flatbed, one of their own people tried to open a door a little way, I guess to drain the water," Geraldo said. "Pressure of the water inside pushed the door open wide and knocked their guy aside. A soggy cardboard box fell out onto the ground. It broke open. Our worker pretended not to notice but he saw packages in waxed paper he swears looked just like the plastic explosive PETN he saw in Afghanistan."

"Holy shit!" Jack said. "Is he absolutely certain? I've seen what that stuff can do. If that container is full of PETN, those jokers are up to some serious trouble. Tell your guy thanks. We need to check it out. I'll make some calls right now. But what about that note?"

"Oh, yeah," Geraldo said. "There's some guy's name and phone number on it, and the name of an organization I've never heard of. The name is Mohamed Jamshid Fahim and the phone number 1-202-457-5892. The name of the organization is the Council on American-Islamic Relations. When the guy handed me the note his voice became very respectful, and then he mumbled something. It sounded like 'Imam'. Do you know what that is?"

"Yeah, I do," Jack said. "An Imam is a Muslim religious leader. You know, much like our church ministers and priests. They're respected in the Muslim culture, but there are fanatical Imams, too. Like those guys in Iran. I'll pass that information along, too; might be a good contact for the Prescott program. Did the guy say anything else?"

"Naw, that was about it," Geraldo said. "He was scared and I was busy. He left before I could ask him any questions."

Neither Jack or Geraldo knew the man in charge of the container was Anwar Chegini, part of Rhamir's three-man nuclear team. The guy who spoke to Geraldo was a kid Rhamir had tried to recruit.

After recovering the container, Chegini decided not to tell anyone that the nuclear device had taken a dip in the Atlantic Ocean on arrival off Miami. He felt that since it had been packed for shipping in shrink-wrap it should be fine. Just to be sure, he swore his two partners and the new recruit to silence, under threat of death.

Jack and Geraldo were about to hang up when Jack added:

"Geraldo, there's something your friends might want to do."

"What's that Jack?" he said.

"When you mentioned that Prescott program, I remembered a note I got the other day," Jack said. "It was sent to companies in the Prescott network. I forgot to call you about it. It'll interest your friends. Here's what it says:

Prescott Enterprises and Continental Del Rio Oil and Gas have been advised of an unusual arrangement in the fight to protect America from terrorist attacks. The agreement is between the FBI and a group in New York called The Commission. This group represents five organized crime families in that city, as well as other cities on the east coast, in Los Angeles and elsewhere. We understand The Commission has instructed its affiliates to be on the lookout for suspicious activities in the wake of those horrendous attacks across America. Authorities believe that a terrorist group operating in America and linked to ISIS and al-Qaeda is responsible.

Not surprising, members of organized crime are reluctant to approach law enforcement agencies directly. Through an intermediary, The Commission has asked Prescott and Continental offices across America to provide points of contact for them to pass along tips on suspicious activities. While this is most irregular, so are the terrorists' attacks on innocent people in our country, and elsewhere. We have agreed to assist. Paige Tremblay is coordinating the Prescott/Continental program and will be responsible for this special project. Her contact information is below. The tips and leads we hope to gather will be turned over anonymously as they are received to a special FBI task force. All companies in the Prescott network are asked to arrange for confidential email addresses and phone numbers that members of organized crime families can access for this purpose.

"What a great idea!" Geraldo said. "Can you scan that letter and email it? I'll see that my friends get copies."

"I'll send it right away," Jack replied.

Neither man was aware that the most valuable cargo the battered container had been carrying was a shrink-wrapped nuclear device.

Chapter 38

Danbury, CT

Mark pulled his car in beside Paige's on the driveway of their new home in Danbury. She slipped out quickly and ran over to Mark. He jumped out, threw his arms around her and gave her a long affectionate kiss. Paige struggled to get free, breathless from his kisses. Mark was puzzled.

"Mark!" she cried, struggling to catch her breath after his passionate greeting. "I have wonderful news!"

"You're pregnant?" he asked. They'd been trying.

"No, silly!" she laughed. "Remember that guy I told you about at the Council on American-Islamic Relations? I called him; we talked about what's going on. He just phoned back on my mobile in the car. The Council is 100 percent behind your alliance, Mark! Isn't that wonderful?"

"Our alliance," Mark corrected her. "Hey, you pulled it all together; you're making it work. And yes, that's wonderful news. Tell me, who is he and what did he say, Love?"

"His name is Dr. Mohamed Jamshid Fahim. He's an Imam at a mosque in DC. Dr. Fahim was trained as an orthopedic surgeon before becoming a fulltime Islamic Imam. He's also a member of the CAIR board of directors.

"Dr. Fahim took our proposal to their board. They unanimously agreed to actively support the alliance. The board appointed a five-member task force to contact all mosques throughout America, Canada and Mexico. He's confident most of the 2,000 mosques represented will encourage followers to add their eyes and ears to our alliance.

"Wow!" Mark said excitedly, as they walked up the driveway to their front door. "Congratulations, My Love. This is awesome."

"It's timely," Paige replied. "Dr. Fahim told me that strong feelings are spreading rapidly among genuine Muslims since those attacks. They're fed up with being blamed for actions by a few terrorists who call themselves Muslims but are not. He said legitimate Muslims hate it when the news media call these psychopaths 'Muslim extremists' or 'Islamic extremists'.

"CAIR would be an enormous help tracking down those SOB's by having legitimate Muslims on the alert," Mark said. "Maybe, just maybe, we're beginning to tighten the noose. Let's hope so."

Chapter 39

ISIS Camp

"Just a few more weeks," Rhamir shouted to the crowd. "In just a few more weeks, we will force those infidels to see . . . and to fear!"

Rhamir was standing before his enthusiastic followers at their camp 40 miles southeast of Albuquerque.

"We'll send the infidels a message . . . a bigger message than before. A message that we, the Islamic Army of America, can and will strike freely, whenever and wherever we choose!

"We are winning!" he said to loud cheers from his jihadist fighters.

"Allahu Akbar!" he said.

"Allahu Akbar!" his assembled followers shouted back.

"Islam is pushing forward. We are winning! Very soon, we will conquer these weak-kneed imperialists!"

Rhamir had gathered his fighters in the loft of the cavernous barn. His goal was to bolster morale, sensing that some fighters had become doubtful about Farouk's gruesome murder, wondering if he really was a traitor. Shahid had told him about grumblings. The pretext for the gathering was to announce officially the appointment of Shahid as his second in command. Shahid would be responsible for helping draw up tactical plans for the next phase of the Islamic Army's expanding war.

He'd also decided to make a surprise announcement. It would be a break from his rigid secrecy. The surprise would energize his fighters. He would reveal when the Islamic Army would launch its next attacks. He would also name the target cities. Rhamir wanted his jihadists to follow up on ISIS social media recruiting by contacting potential fighters in the cities where they were about to be sent, recruits he could use in future for lone wolf attacks or to set up more self-perpetuating cells. Guerilla warfare like this was the most difficult to gather intelligence on and to stop.

"In this next phase of our holy war," Rhamir told his assembled fighters, "we will attack not three but a dozen targets in cities all across America!"

His assembled fighters erupted into roars of excitement and more cries of "Allahu Akbar!"

"And among them," he continued, "will be the prize – Times Square in New York. All of our next attacks will be on New Year's Eve. The one in Times Square will be the biggest one. Over a million people will be there! It will be glorious!"

"Allahu Akbar!" his fighters shouted at the top of their lungs, their fists pounding the air. The few still seated jumped to their feet. "Allahu Akbar!"

"Tonight, I will give you the gift of my trust. I know it is the will of Allah for me to do so. Tonight for the first time you will learn about all of our next targets."

The assembly grew silent. They understood the importance of the secrets with which they were about to be entrusted. The eerie quiet was interrupted only by the sounds of birds chasing each other in and around the rafters above them.

Rhamir paused for effect. He looked out over the crowd in the dim light of evening. A single floodlight illuminated Rhamir. He began:

"This time, our glorious Islamic Army will attack targets that have been chosen especially for their unique significance in each of the dozen cities," Rhamir said loudly. "Among these chosen cities is Washington, DC."

Rhamir was interrupted again by even louder roars of approval and cheering, and by more shouts of "Allahu Akbar". When the crowd calmed Rhamir continued to share his list of targets.

"You will be assigned to teams for each city. The teams will recruit and train more fighters locally for their attacks in each city. Those of you who know potential recruits in these cities are to let us know right away. Okay, here is the list:

"In addition to New York and Washington, the target cities are: Seattle, San Francisco, Philadelphia, St. Louis, Dallas, Phoenix, Detroit, Las Vegas, Miami and Billings, Montana."

"We will strike these targets all at once, all across America, all on New Year's Eve!"

Rhamir was interrupted by the wildly enthusiastic fighters, who began chanting, "Allahu Akbar! Allahu Akbar!" When they drew quiet again, he said:

"And we will have an extra special surprise for the infidels," he continued. "I will tell you about that as time draws closer. These attacks will mark a huge

advance for our Islamic Army of the Americas! The
infidels will not see these coming. It will be a
glorious, a magnificent triumph!

"And Ali-Mumar Shahid will be our master
planner for these glorious tributes to our martyrs. He
will divide you into attack teams for specific training
requirements and work with the team leaders to
develop tactics for each attack."

Rhamir's fighters, now totaling more than 60,
again roared their approval.

Shahid was startled. The announcement that he'd
been chosen to plan the attacks came as news to
Shahid, standing beside Rhamir. He was already
elated over his newly announced official position.
As the crowd roared its approval, he turned to
Rhamir and stammered:

"I . . . I am honored Rhamir, that you would place
such faith in me. I will not let you down in our holy
war to rid the Earth of these infidels."

"You have combat experience now, Shahid,"
Rhamir told him quietly. Secretly, he desperately
wished Frank Larijani was still alive.

Rhamir dismissed the gathering and sent the
jihadists back to their assigned training tasks. He
told Shahid to join him at his trailer. There, he and
Shahid began developing a master plan for 11 of the
12 attacks. Rhamir told Shahid the New York attack
would be planned separately.

"In this new assignment, it will also be your job to
oversee logistics for our fighters assigned to each
city," Rhamir said. "I will handle New York
personally. It is complicated. I'll tell you about that
later.

"Pick a deputy. You seem to like Khaled. Put him in charge of training. He did very well in Pakistan, and he wrote an excellent and useful report for me."

Shahid was almost giddy with excitement.

"I have figured out how we will overcome the heavy security at the Capitol Building, in Washington," Shahid boasted. "Four of our glorious drones will be launched from many blocks away. The pilots will guide the model airplanes to their targets using reports from fighters with mobile phones stationed along the streets leading to the Capitol building.

"It will be a triumph . . . another great achievement for our glorious Islamic Army of the America's! Just think, we will take our war right to the heart of the infidels' government!"

Rhamir smiled. Shahid's strategy had impressed him. It improved his confidence in Shahid. He moved on:

"One of our most important economic targets is just outside of Billings, Montana. You will assemble an assault team that is larger than the others. This is really three targets in one. Just outside of Billings are three separate oil refineries. Three capitalist corporations own these refineries, Chevron, Exxon/Mobile and Cenex. Crude oil is piped there from Canada to be refined and shipped in pipelines everywhere, including back to Canada.

"For those heroic attacks, you will use our wonderfully successful drones and blow up as many storage tanks as you can. You must begin now to find more recruits and plan the training for our glorious fighters.

"Think what a great, massive disaster those burning refineries will create!" Rhamir said. "It will be huge. It will take days, maybe weeks to extinguish! And it will cripple the supply of gasoline and oils all over America and Canada. It will be glorious! Glorious! Praise be to Allah!"

The Ultimate Threat

Chapter 40

New York City

"Caprionni here!"

The mafia godfather's unmistakable brusk voice boomed out from Mark's iPhone.

Mark was meeting with his task force in an FBI conference room one floor above their offices in New York. At first, he was going to ignore his iPhone. It was on 'silent' mode sitting on the table. It began flashing. He saw Caprionni's name on the caller ID. When he phoned it was always around suppertime. This had to be important.

"Yes, Mr. Caprionni," Mark said, turning away from the table, "Good to hear from you, sir. What can I do for you?"

"It's not what you can do for me, son. It is what we are *trying* to do for you, but *cannot!*" Caprionni said. His voice had a strength Mark hadn't heard since before Vinny was murdered. "That plan of yours . . . it is supposed to be working, but it is not. There are problems."

"What do you mean, sir?" Mark said.

"The Commission tells me that since we sent out the word the families are getting calls from all over," Caprionni said. "From New York, Miami, Los Angeles, Detroit, Chicago, Jersey . . . many other places. Everywhere! Everywhere! You name it! Everywhere! But this information . . . it is not going anywhere. Do you understand? Nowhere!

"My people do not call the cops. You know that. But they want to help your alliance. What do I tell them?"

"Mr. Caprionni," Mark said patiently, getting up and walking from the room. "What seems to be the problem, sir? The last time you and I met with The Commission I left each of you a package with the names of contacts and how to reach them. It was all there: names, email addresses, regular phone and texting numbers, social media sites and confidential codes, and websites. Paige had it all organized by city especially for you and your colleagues. Is that not working?"

The boss of bosses of organized crime in America paused, and then said quietly, with hesitation in his voice:

"Mark, I will tell you what is wrong. My colleagues on The Commission . . . they are like me . . . my age. You understand? We know phone numbers, of course! But these email and text and social media things. Well, I . . . they . . . don't know about such things.

"That package you gave us. We . . . none of us understand what it is. Only phone numbers. And Mark, they don't want to admit there is something they do not know. You understand? They cannot order their people to do something they do not understand. They could lose face, son. They could lose respect. This cannot happen. What can we do about this?"

"Okay, Mr. Caprionni," Mark said, trying to keep the grin on his face out of the sound of his voice. "We can solve this for them very easily. I will arrange to set up web links, and email and texting numbers for each member of The Commission."

"What is this mail thing all about . . . and what is this . . . this . . . texting business . . . and this web link thing?" Caprionni interrupted impatiently. "Is that what you call it?"

"Look, sir, I will personally call the consigliore in each family. They will know people who are knowledgeable about what I'm saying, if they don't. I'll write messages for your colleagues that each consigliore can arrange to have sent out. Everyone will get the contact details that they need in order to pass on important information. They will know how to make use of it or how to find someone who does. What do you think of that?"

"You will do all that for us?" Caprionni replied. "That is a very big job."

Poor man, Mark thought. *He has absolutely no idea what I'm saying.*

"Of course I will, sir," Mark said. "It's important for the alliance . . . for the arrangement that you and I and The Commission have agreed to.

"Mr. Caprionni, you and the other godfathers will look computer savvy, Internet wise and very smart, and no one but us needs to know about it. Okay?"

"This is very good, Mark," Caprionni said, sounding relieved. "I will tell The Commission about your kindness and respectfulness. We do not forget such things."

Caprionni abruptly hung up. Mark sighed, smiling to himself and thinking. *That old   bandit is never going to learn good manners. But at least he and*

The Commission are on our side . . . and working for us. That's all that matters.

"That was Joe Caprionni," Mark said when he returned to the meeting. "As you know, he chairs the New York mafia commission. We needed to solve a little glitch about getting The Commission on board the alliance."

A knock on the open door of the meeting room drew everyone's attention. Mark, his boss Bjorn Sorensen and nine other FBI special agents on his task force were gathered for the meeting. Bjorn had come from Washington for two reasons: to show his support and to organize an FBI-led raid on the terrorists' training camp near Albuquerque.

"Mr. Sorensen, Mark . . . can I interrupt for a minute?"

Enrique Cardinal, an FBI special agent stood in the doorway.

"There's something you'll want to know about," Enrique said. He stepped into the room and closed the door behind him. "NYPD just called. It was about that suspicious package they recovered on the street this morning from a doorway next to our building.

"For those who haven't heard," Enrique said, "a package addressed to the FBI was dropped off sometime early this morning in the Starbucks doorway next to our main entrance. A Starbucks employee arriving early for work called NYPD when she spotted blood leaking from a corner. Naturally, the cops treated it as suspicious, a potential booby-trap. It turned out to be gruesome but not dangerous.

"The bomb squad removed the package to their secure site," he said. "A robot was used to open the box, rather than explode it. Good thing. Inside was a human head."

"What?" Mark blurted out, fearing the head might be that of Khaled Mahmoud, his undercover agent in the camp. The attention of everyone at the meeting was riveted on Cardinal.

"Yeah," he said. "A human head."

Cardinal added: "There was no identification . . . just a note addressed to you, Mark."

"To me?" Mark said, surprised. Now he was more fearful than ever about Khaled. "Let me guess . . . the note's from those goddamned terrorists."

"Yup," Enrique replied. "The ones calling themselves The Islamic Army of America. A copy's being emailed over as we speak. The note said something to the effect, 'This is what we do to traitors who spy for the FBI'. It was signed, 'The Islamic Army of America'."

"Is there any identification?" Mark asked, his worry in high gear. "Do we know who the head belongs to?"

"We know it's not our undercover agent," Cardinal reassured him, much to Mark's relief. "I had our undercover supervisor check out a photo of the head that NYPD sent over; almost made him toss his breakfast. As you all know, photos of our active undercover agents are closely guarded. Anyway, he's confirmed it's not our guy. We don't have an ID yet on the victim"

Mark sat back grateful it wasn't Khaled, but concerned whom the victim might turn out to be. Mark and Bjorn exchanged relieved glances.

"Do we have any idea how the package was delivered?" Mark said. "Is there any security video of the entrances?"

"The package was left sometime after midnight," Enrique replied. "It was dark. There's some surveillance video but it's indistinct. Wish these guys didn't use cheap surveillance cameras. All we have are blurred figures walking past the Starbucks door at different times. Nothing useful. Even digital enhancements don't help.

"I'm afraid that's not all," Enrique continued. "NYPD sent the head to the coroner's office. A forensic pathologist said the victim was male, of Middle Eastern origin and in his early 20s. He said the victim was cruelly tortured before being beheaded. The victim's tongue was missing. The pathologist believes it was severed while the victim was still alive, the same regarding the victim's ears. And the poor devil's eyes had been burned out, likely with a red-hot metal bar or something like that. Again, the pathologist believes the victim was alive when all this happened. Traces of wood chips in the hair suggest the victim may have been positioned over a wooden chopping block and then beheaded using a machete or a sword."

A long silence settled over the room after Enrique finished his gruesome description. There were muffled epithets and groans as images of what they'd just heard flooded their minds. One female agent clasped a hand over her mouth and hurried from the room.

"Jesus Christ!" Mark blurted out, remembering the terrible acts of unspeakable brutality inflicted on Anashi and on informants he'd seen in Afghanistan. "You can bet Abdul Rhamir is responsible. I've no doubt about it. That depraved bastard! I wonder if this murder is what my phone message was about?"

"What do you mean, Mark?" Bjorn asked.

"I got a message yesterday from our guy on my secure voice mail line," Mark replied. "Thank God the head's not his. He was very upset. He said something terrible was happening, but he was okay for now . . . promised to call me again when he can get away from the camp."

"Camp?" Enrique said.

"Yeah," Mark replied. "We've confirmed that a bunch of terrorists working here for ISIS have set up a training camp and bomb factory in New Mexico. We've asked the Pentagon for satellite surveillance. Some brass hat over there is taking his own sweet time getting back to us."

Chapter 41

ISIS Camp

"I've a great opportunity for you, Khaled!"

Shahid had walked unannounced into the living room of the bunkhouse Khaled shared with four other jihad fighters. There'd been one other, Farouk, who'd been savagely murdered three days earlier.

"What would that be?" Khaled asked, with false cheerfulness, concealing the grief and anger he was still feeling over Farouk's gruesome slaughter.

"As you know, as deputy commander of our glorious Islamic Army of America," Shahid said proudly, "I've been ordered to develop the tactics for our next attacks on the American infidels! I want you to assist me as my deputy commander."

Shahid looked around. "Are we alone?" he added lowering his voice, nodding his head in the direction of the sleeping area.

"Yeah," Khaled replied. "Everyone's over at the barn. Rhamir's showing some recruits how to install pressure detonators on briefcase bombs. The others are building the obstacle course for the new recruits. I was just going over to help."

"They'll get along without you," Shahid said abruptly. "This is more important."

Shahid told Khaled where in each of the targeted cities the attacks were to be carried out. Khaled realized that all Shahid wanted from him right now were ideas he could pass along to impress Rhamir.

Khaled decided to go along with Shahid, not that he had much choice.

My God, I hope we can shut these cruel bastards down before they kill and hurt any more people, he thought.

For days, Khaled and Shahid drafted plans and then re-drafted them, and pondered the selection of teams and training requirements for each attack. Khaled kept listening for word about the nuclear weapon during overheard conversations between Shahid and Rhamir. Nothing. Meanwhile, he struggled to keep his revulsion in check and to control his frustration over not being able to get information about the planned attacks out to Mark.

Finally, one evening, Khaled found an opportunity to slip away after dark. He went to a place he'd used before. It was a clump of bushes beside a wash. He phoned Mark to tell him about Rhamir's plans and the targets.

Khaled was unaware that Mark had flown to Albuquerque a few hours earlier. Mark was there to set up a command center for the raid he would lead next week. He'd just checked in at La Quinta Inn, off I-40 on San Mateo Blvd. Mark's first priority was to get Khaled away from the camp before the raid.

Bjorn's operations team was using Mark's office to direct the raid and to provide liaison with FBI senior executives and other law enforcement agencies.

"I was beginning to worry," Mark said when Khaled called.

"It's been difficult to get away," Khaled replied. "Everything at the camp is in an uproar. Rhamir has announced to everyone where and when the new attacks will take place. There will be 12 of them.

"I've detailed notes on how 11 of the attacks will be carried out," Khaled said. "I'll find some way of getting them to you. They'll be sending teams of fighters to those cities very soon. And there's one more thing."

"What's that?" Mark asked.

"I overheard comments about where Rhamir and his people might be getting some of their explosives. They're making some PETN here but it's not enough for what they're planning next. They lost a lot at Chapman. I heard a rumor that some ready-made explosive is being smuggled in by sea, on tramp steamers.

"Look," Mark added, "I'm in Albuquerque. Got in this afternoon. I need you to leave the camp tomorrow night . . . the next day at the very latest. We're planning to raid the camp this weekend. I'll be leading it.

"I want you out of there before the raid starts. Let's plan on you sneaking out tomorrow night. I checked a roadmap. There's a place called La Jara Springs Estates. I'll drive out tomorrow and pick you up there. If you can't get out tomorrow, and we're unable to communicate, I'll drive out again the next night."

"I'm staying here, Mark," Khaled said firmly. "I want to make sure those two bastards, Rhamir and Shahid, don't try to become martyrs when you hit the camp. Those sons of bitches need to be kept alive to face trial for what they've done."

Argue as he might, Mark couldn't persuade Khaled to leave. He thought it would be easy to get Khaled out, after the murder of Farouk. Mark couldn't help admire Khaled's change of mind. He had to let it go; besides, the call was getting too long. They hung up. Their conversation got Khaled thinking about possible raid scenarios, and how he might capture Shahid and possibly even Rhamir to keep them from committing suicide to escape accountability when 'the cavalry' arrived.

Unknown to Khaled, his late night exit from the camp had been observed. He was followed.

Alfred Naughton, a close friend of Farouk's, blamed Shahid and Khaled for his friend's horrific death. He'd seen Khaled speaking with Shahid just before Farouk was grabbed and then publicly condemned by Shahid.

Naughton noticed when Khaled had slipped away. He followed him down a wash to the bend where Khaled phoned Mark. Naughton overheard enough to know Khaled was the spy, not Farouk. Furious, Naughton quietly made his way back to camp, and then ran straight for Rhamir's trailer. He burst into the middle of an online video meeting.

Chapter 42

"Is it ready?" Rhamir was asking his nuclear attack team on Skype when Alfred Naughton burst in. He'd been meeting online weekly with the three-man team, occasionally more often. This was one of those extra calls. He had an announcement and orders for them.

Rhamir turned angrily to Naughton and ordered him to wait outside. He noticed Naughton was agitated, not his normal laid-back self.

The Skype meeting resumed:

"It is ready!" said Mohamed Shokar, who despite his poor English skills was by mutual consent the team leader. "We just need transport and set up."

"Allahu Akbar!" Rhamir said, pleasantly surprised. "That's excellent news!" Early preparation fit perfectly with what he had in mind.

"Allahu Akbar!" The three replied.

"I have decided to move up the date for our Times Square attack," Rhamir said to the surprised team. "No one but the four of us knows or needs to know right now.

"I want you to head for New York right away. I've decided on a pre-emptive standalone nuclear attack. It will cause massive panic. And it will be a distraction. The infidels will be so confused and demoralized they'll not be expecting the other attacks. It will be easier for us to proceed with them on New Year's Eve."

Rhamir laughed. The other three joined in, but not with quite the same enthusiasm.

"Don't you want to catch those million shameful partiers on New Year's Eve in Times Square?" Shokar asked.

"That was my plan," Rhamir replied. "But as it is, our nuclear bomb will easily kill a million in the city, probably many more. That's enough. It will provide the diversion we need to set up the other attacks. But it will also mean that the Americans will increase their security hugely, so I will need everyone in place in each city beforehand.

"Just think of it!" Rhamir said to appease the three. "You will conduct the very first nuclear attack on America!

"Allahu Akbar!" he said.

"Allahu Akbar," they replied, showing more enthusiasm.

Chapter 43

New York City

"Bjorn Sorensen here," he said, answering the phone in Mark's office. "How may I help you?"

"This is Captain Robert Beckett, sir," a crisp military voice replied. "I'm with the United States Marine Corps. I'm assigned to satellite surveillance operations at the Pentagon.

"Sir, I just came across the FBI's request for satellite surveillance in my boss's inbox. Major Alfredo Ramirez was called away on a family emergency yesterday and asked me to take over while he's gone. Your email was marked 'urgent' but it's dated yesterday. I must apologize, sir. I'm terribly sorry about that."

"Urgent it is, Captain," Sorensen said. After confirming Capt. Beckett's security clearance using known code words, he continued: "It concerns those recent terrorist attacks. We've received intelligence reports they've set up a training camp and bomb factory southeast of Albuquerque.

"There's an undercover agent in that camp. We need to get him out immediately. Can your satellites help us locate the place and keep an eye on what they're up to?"

"Yes we can, sir," the Marine captain replied without hesitation.

"I should tell you, captain, the FBI is planning to raid the camp this weekend. With your help, we hope to get a better understanding of the camp layout and the terrain out there. Then we'll be ready to raid the camp and round up those terrorists. Everything has to be precise, of course, and timed to the second. We'll be depending on the best imaging you can give us. We know the location is heavily treed and rugged. How much of a close-up can you get us, how detailed?"

"We can give you all the ground detail you're going to need, day and night," Beckett replied. "We are at your service, sir. I've a copy of Homeland Security's authorization for us to assist the FBI. We'll locate that camp and be prepared to provide you real time operational coverage when you're ready.

"I'll see this gets priority, sir," Capt. Beckett added. "Can you give me a better idea of the approximate location?"

Sorensen replied: "The camp is about 40 miles southeast of Albuquerque, and five to 10 miles southwest of a little community called Chilili, at the junction of Highway 337 and La Jara Road. The camp is in the mountains somewhere east of there along La Jara Road."

"That's close enough, sir," Capt. Beckett said. "Leave it with me. I'll get back to you as soon as I can. Here's my direct line and my home number."

Bjorn copied down the numbers. It was just after 4 p.m. Washington time. He didn't expect to hear back from Beckett until sometime the next day, considering all of the bureaucracy Beckett would face.

*

At 1:05 a.m. Bjorn was in his hotel room fast asleep when his phone rang. He saw from the caller ID it was Mark.

"What's up, Mark?" Bjorn said, instantly alert. He knew it wouldn't be good news. Mark wouldn't call in the middle of the night.

"We've got trouble," Mark said. "I just had a call from our guy. His cover's been blown. He's on the run out in the bush. It happened sometime after we spoke a few hours ago.

"He told me someone must have overheard his call to me and blew the whistle. He's out there unarmed with only the clothes on his back. I'm heading for the area to try and find him. Would you alert those state and local police contacts we've been planning the raid with? I need their help out here, right now! And could you ask Kirtland Air Force Base for a chopper to pick us up near a place called La Jara Estates, just in case we need a backup plan?"

"Mark, hold on!" Bjorn shouted. Too late. The phone was dead. He would have ordered Mark to wait until local law enforcement officers could provide him with support. He tried calling Mark back. The phone just kept ringing.

Damn it, he thought. The mobile's voice mail was not responding. *Damn it, he's turned it off so I can't order him back! That hot head could get himself killed!*

He almost did.

*

Forty minutes after Mark's call, Sorensen was at 26 Federal Plaza in Mark's office. It was 1:45 a.m., New York time. That made it 11:45 p.m. in New Mexico. Before leaving, he'd called Capt. Beckett at his home in North Rosslyn, VA and alerted him to the emergency. A sleepy Beckett snapped wide awake and said he would go immediately to the Pentagon, and get satellite surveillance set up as soon as possible. The emergency nature would help him clear red tape.

En route to Mark's office, Bjorn had called Douglas Winston. He'd made a commitment to alert him any time his nephew was placing himself in harm's way. This was one of those times. Mark didn't know it, but his uncle and Mark's grandfather had made this a condition of Prescott and Continental Del Rio's participation in the alliance. Bjorn also learned Mark's grandfather was visiting Douglas. In minutes, both uncle and grandfather were headed for Mark's office in downtown New York. Bjorn alerted security on his arrival to admit both Winston's.

Ninety minutes later, Capt. Beckett called Bjorn that the satellite surveillance was operational. He'd managed to finesse his way through the security and bureaucratic roadblocks in the middle of the night. It helped that decision makers in the Pentagon knew he'd been awarded the Medal of Honor while a young sergeant during the first Gulf War.

"Sorensen here, Capt. Beckett," Bjorn said. "Before we go on, the reason we're on speakerphone is I have two people with me. Douglas Winston and Paul Winston are heading up a civilian counterterrorism project for us.

"When we spoke yesterday, Captain, we talked about an undercover agent. Unfortunately, his cover was blown last night. Right now, he's being pursued by a bunch of those terrorists determined to butcher him. He's alone, on foot and unarmed. About 50-60 bad guys are after him. All of them are armed. Most are on foot. But we understand they also have three ATV's and a dune buggy. I'm hoping your satellite will be able to spot them and the vehicles."

"Yes we can, sir," Capt. Beckett replied. "We can spot all of them, and probably your guy too. We'll get a fix on everyone for you right away."

"Thank you Captain," Bjorn said. "There's someone else I need you to look for. The head of our counterterrorism task force has gone out there to try recovering our guy. He's alone in a white Ford Explorer.

"Needless to say, we'll need to get both out of there as quickly as possible," Bjorn said. "Those terrorists are packing AK-47s and Uzi's. We also think they have some RPG's.

"As you know, we were originally planning to raid the camp next week. But that raid's in motion as of right now, with whatever resources we can muster on short notice. Of course, top priority is the recovery of those agents."

"Roger that, sir," Beckett replied.

"The guy who's on his way out there is Mark Tremblay," Bjorn said. "I expect he's somewhere on Highway 337 by now. He'll be trying to link up with our undercover agent along La Jara Road. Between the two of them, their total armament is one .357 Magnum, maybe a handful of ammo, and a rented SUV. It could get pretty damned one sided."

"I hear you," Beckett agreed. "If you don't mind my asking, sir, what other resources can you get into that location quickly?"

"Not much," Sorensen replied. "The one person in our Albuquerque office is on his way. It's going to take a while to get local law enforcement mobilized. Can you get clearance at this hour to feed your data through Kirtland Air Force Base?

"I'm sure I can, sir," Beckett replied.

"That's terrific Captain," Bjorn replied. "Earlier I was able to get word to the commanding officer at Kirtland. Col. Gene Saxton has authorized the use of a Huey to extract our guys. It's unarmed; being used for training but available immediately. The chopper's been doing security patrol overnight. It'll be taking off any minute.

"When your satellite folks contact the base, is there a way you can patch them directly to the chopper?" Bjorn said, noticing the worried looks etched across Paul and Douglas's faces.

"Good as done, sir," the Marine captain replied.

"The airspace could get busy," Bjorn said. "Col. Saxton has offered to send in three Sea Stallion choppers with 50 combat-equipped Marines once they can get mobilized. That'll take a couple of hours, best-case scenario. Luckily, the Marines happen to be training with the 58th Special Ops Unit. Saxton's also scrambling a pair of Huey

307

assault choppers but that's going to take an hour or so as well.

"Captain, the Marines have been ordered to treat this as live combat. It will still be dark when they take off. So, like the Huey's they'll be relying on your satellite relays to guide them in. The good news is it'll probably be daylight by the time the Marines arrive on site. That should help with rounding up those bandits."

Bjorn turned to Paul and Douglas:

"Before you got here, I called Chief Eduardo Watson of the New Mexico State Police about this. He's on the planning team for the raid. Chief Watson is sending in his six-man Tactical Unit from Albuquerque. They don't have a large helicopter available, so they're sending them in an SUV. I'm afraid it's the best they can do."

Turning back to the speakerphone, Bjorn said: "Captain, your satellite intelligence will be needed also to deploy those NMSP assets. Bottom line, a lot is riding on that Huey and on your intelligence information."

"Roger that, sir," Beckett replied.

Chapter 44

ISIS Camp

"Everyone spread out and circle around! Find the traitor! Find that fucking traitor!"

Rhamir was furious as he hastily assembled his jihadist fighters in the camp's central 'Square'.

"Use your flashlights, look for tracks, for any fresh signs of him. Fire your weapons in the air if you see any trace of that camel turd of a spy.

"Get going, now! Hurry up! Remember the reward!"

Three pairs of senior fighters scrambled onto the only ATV's. The rest ran off in all directions, stumbling in the dark over rocks and brush, falling into washes, and crashing through groves of pines and juniper trees.

Rhamir had assembled the jihadists to get them worked up, and to convince them "the traitor Khaled" had been working with Farouk. He knew now that Farouk was innocent, that he'd murdered an innocent man just because he'd listened to Shahid. Rhamir was concerned that some fighters, in addition to Naughton, might also know the truth. Naughton was a dilemma – he was valuable but was he too valuable to be killed? Rhamir made a mental note to talk with him.

Rhamir and Shahid jumped into Rhamir's dune buggy.

"He can't get far!" Shahid shouted, as Rhamir drove northwest across the high foothills landscape toward La Jara Road. "The traitor's on foot. We'll get him! And the reward will help."

Rhamir had offered $5,000 cash to anyone who captured Khaled. He wanted Khaled alive. He was furious over being misled into accusing the wrong man of being a traitor, and then torturing and killing him. Khaled would face an even more brutal fate. But his biggest worry was how much the real spy could tell the outside world if he managed to escape.

"We damned well better get him!" Rhamir shouted back angrily. "He can expose our plans, and us too. He'll destroy everything, all of our progress if he gets away, because you fucked things up again, Shahid! You told him everything!"

"I know my apologies will change nothing," Shahid replied contritely. They were paused on a rise watching flashlights flickering in the darkness through the trees and brush all around them.

Shahid was consumed with fear over what Rhamir might do to him. He'd seen what Rhamir had done to Farouk without the slightest hesitation or emotion.

"There he is!" they heard an excited fighter shout off to their right. Then they heard rapid gunfire, punctuated by a loud scream of agony.

"There! There!" Shahid shouted to Rhamir, standing up and pointing to their right. "They got him. They got him! Over there!"

Rhamir wheeled the dune buggy down the hill toward the shouts. Trees swept past them, threatening to wipe Shahid off the side as he stood, clinging to the roll bars, trying to see better. They almost hit a stand of pines. Then the buggy swept over a rise. It headed for the bottom of a large brush-filled hollow. Rhamir slammed on the brakes. The dune buggy came to a skidding halt in a cloud of desert sand, almost on top of three fighters.

The trio was bent over a prone figure. In the light of the dune buggy's headlights and hand-held flashlights, the fighters could see blood covering the shirt of a fellow jihadist. He was sprawled awkwardly on his back. The three fighters stood up slowly as Rhamir and Shahid jumped out of the dune buggy and walked over rapidly.

"Did the traitor shoot him and get away?" Rhamir said.

"No, I'm very sorry, Rhamir," one of them said. "It was an accident!"

Rhamir bent over to look. The young man's arms were spread out. An AK-47 lay in the dirt inches from his right hand. His body was bent at a crooked angle, one leg folded beneath his body. The young man's eyes were open and glassy. He was dead.

"It was a mistake!" the young man stammered, clearly frightened. The words came spilling out of him. "He looked like the traitor. I thought he was pointing something at me. Now, I think he was just waving his rifle. Oh, I'm so sorry."

"Shut up!" Rhamir said angrily to the distressed shooter. "Go back to the camp. Right now. If you see one of the ATV's, send it over to get this body.

"The rest of you, get on with finding that fucking traitor! We must get him! That's what we're here to do. On your way!" Rhamir said, firing his AK-47 in the air.

The startled men turned and ran in all directions. No one dared to speak to anyone else until they were far away.

Chapter 45

On board 'Green Dog One'

"Kirtland Tower. This is Green Dog One. Over"
"This is Kirtland Tower. Go ahead Green Dog
One. Over."
"Kirtland Tower, we have a visual on the beacon at
Manzano Lookout. We are proceeding east-southeast
toward the search area. ETA is approximately 12
minutes. Acknowledge."
"Roger that, Green Dog One," said the air traffic
controller at Kirtland Air Force Base. The readout on
the control console was 3:15 a.m.

The training helicopter called Green Dog One was
an unarmed US Air Force Huey (UH-1D) hurriedly
scrambled minutes earlier. The pilot, Lt. Hugo
Alvarez, and co-pilot Sgt. Will Sifton trained
helicopter pilots on Huey's. But they were also
required to stand overnight security patrol shifts just
like everyone else. It was part of the base's standard
operating procedures (SOP's).

At a hasty briefing, Alvarez and Sifton were told
they were to take off immediately on an urgent
mission to rescue two FBI special agents. One was
an undercover agent. His cover had been blown. He
was in grave danger. His name was Khaled
Mahmoud. He was their first priority. Mahmoud
was unarmed and being hunted by 50 to 60 terrorists
from a nearby camp. Alvarez and Sifton were given
rendezvous coordinates that were five to six miles

east of La Jara Springs Estates. The other man was FBI Special Agent Mark Tremblay, trying to reach Mahmoud from the east end of La Jara Road. Tremblay was driving a rented white Ford Explorer.

"We understand the terrorists are well armed," Major Casey Amundsen, the squadron commander, had warned them at the briefing. "We believe they have AK-47s and Uzi's, and maybe even some RPG's. So watch yourselves fellas."

He said there wasn't time to scramble an armed Huey immediately. Two would follow once they were fueled and armed, and the crews briefed. Alvarez and Sifton had looked at each other with raised eyebrows. This would be their first time in the line of fire. They were looking forward to some real action after being bored by weeks of training duty. Their only armaments were two standard M-4 Carbines and sidearms issued for security patrol duty.

The helicopter's route was across the corner of Isleta Pueblo Indian Reservation. They gained altitude to clear the mountains on the reservation. Minutes later, they dropped down from 8,700 to 3,000 feet. Sgt. Sifton caught sight of the bend on La Jara Road where it turned from east west to north south.

Below them somewhere, this FBI special agent named Khaled Mahmoud was running for his life.

"Green Dog One, this is Kirtland Tower," the air traffic controller said. "Acknowledge."

"Roger, Kirtland Tower," Lt. Alvarez replied. "This is Green Dog One."

"Green Dog One, we have the satellite relay people on the line," Kirtland ATC said. "I'm patching them through to you, Green Dog One. Acknowledge."

"Roger that, Kirtland Tower," Alvarez said.

Alvarez and Sifton listened as MSgt. Lawrence Ducie gave them a running commentary on the visual activities at their rendezvous point a few minutes ahead.

"Wish we had an armed drone to turn loose on those ISIS bastards," Ducie said.

"Roger, that," Alvarez said. "Sounds like we could use some armed back up, and right now." Sifton worked with Ducie to coordinate the satellite visuals with the helicopter.

*

Far below, Khaled was out of breath and scrambling through the bush. He'd been running hard for an hour.

Darkness had helped him evade the roving groups of terrorists searching for him. But it would be dawn in a couple of hours. Often he'd hear shouts, and twice heard gunfire in the distance. Thoughts of what had happened to Farouk sent chills up and down his spine, spurring him on. Farouk's fate would also be his, or worse, if he were caught.

Khaled guessed he was half a mile south of La Jara Road, and about three miles east of La Jara Springs Estates where Mark was to meet him. It was tough slogging through the uneven ground and thick underbrush in the dark. He still had some distance to go before reaching the rendezvous. He was relieved it was a cloudless night. His only navigational aid was the stars and he wasn't all that confident about how he was reading them.

Coming upon a grove of Ponderosa pine, Khaled stopped for a brief rest. His strength was almost gone.

"I should kill you where you sit, you treacherous bastard," a familiar voice said. A powerful LED flashlight went on, almost blinding him. "I'd shoot you if Rhamir hadn't ordered us to take you alive . . . well mostly alive."

Khaled froze.

Ah, shit! he thought.

He felt simultaneous waves of panic, over what he knew was coming and disappointment that now he would not be in on the FBI-led raid.

Khaled tried to focus on the voice, and away from the torture and horrible death that awaited him. The voice was Alfred Naughton's, Farouk's buddy. Naughton would take much pleasure from what was about to happen to him. In the glaring light from Naughton's flashlight the muzzle of an AK-47 was just barely visible. A second LED flashlight went on, to Naughton's right.

"Here," Naughton's voice said, apparently speaking to his companion. "Don't fire yet. I have a score to settle with this infidel spy before we turn him over to Rhamir. I'm going to enjoy this."

Then, turning to Khaled, Naughton said: "Stand up traitor!"

Khaled was getting to his feet when he felt a heavy boot slam into his ribs, knocking him prone. Then he felt another blow, and another. He could just make out Naughton's companion begin to step forward, holding Naughton's weapon, as he struggled painfully to get to his feet. Just then, Naughton's companion tripped on a root and began to fall. In each hand was an AK-47, making it difficult for him to get his balance without one of the weapons hitting the dirt and sand.

As he fell, the man thrust out the rifle in his right hand trying to use it to steady himself. It slipped from his grasp, throwing him off balance as he fell. Still in a crouch, Khaled lunged forward and caught the weapon. He whirled his body as his finger reached for the trigger. Landing on his back, Khaled took aim at Naughton, whose boot was about to hit him again. He squeezed the trigger hoping the safety was off. A burst of gunfire caught Naughton in the midsection and chest. Khaled quickly rolled and fired another burst into the face of the second man raising his weapon. It was over in seconds.

Khaled sat, trying to regain his composure. He listened intently for fear Rhamir's men would converge on the sound of the gunfire. At first, all he heard were shouted questions asking what was going on. Then someone shouted orders that everyone hold their fire. Khaled understood with relief his pursuers had assumed the gunfire was a false alarm, just trigger-happy jihadists.

He got up and ran again. Minutes later, Khaled thought he was imagining sounds. Exhaustion was overtaking him. His heavy breathing was making it difficult to hear. He forced himself to hold his breath and listen carefully. Then he was sure . . . the sound of a helicopter in the distance. His heart jumped. He began running toward where he hoped La Jara Road would be. The road was his only hope. Maybe he could flag down the helicopter, if he got there in time, if they went that way . . . if they saw him.

Khaled knew Rhamir and his murderous fanatics didn't have access to a helicopter, so it must be friendly. He knew it was risky but he stripped off the dark brown coat over his white hoodie. He took off the hoodie to use as a flag. He heard more shots and then heard the helicopter pass.

They must be shooting at it, Khaled thought. He still couldn't see the chopper; too many pine trees around him. It sounded high and moving fast.

If I can just get closer to the road, maybe I can get their attention, he thought. *Maybe they can get me out of here, if they come back . . . if they can see me.*

*

Sgt. Sifton's voice came over the intercom:

"That looks like the road, La Jara Road, Lieutenant."

"Roger that, Sergeant," Alvarez replied.

Sifton and Alvarez kept their talk over the intercom professional, this time. It was unusual for them. They'd become friends and kibitzed a lot when off duty, and sometimes even during missions when no one else could listen in. This time their radio was patched into the satellite surveillance units and into control tower communications, monitored by their commander, Major Amundsen. On their intercom, Sifton normally used Alvarez's nickname 'Chief', knowing Alvarez' grandfather was Navajo.

Not surprisingly, Alvarez had nicknamed his tall weightlifter co-pilot, 'Tiny'.

Alvarez was guiding the Huey according to voice directions from the satellite unit. They coordinated the helicopter's location with a digital image of a lone man on foot. The top-secret high-resolution satellite technology showed dozens of others nearby in stunning detail, all with flashlights and assault rifles. Some appeared to be within a few hundred yards of the man on foot.

"Hey, look at the lights over there!" Sifton said, now able to see the ground. "Is that a bunch of flashlights? Yeah, most are bouncing around. Must be flashlights. The others look like the headlights of ATV's or dune buggies. Betcha those are the bad guys!"

"Hold on," Lt. Alvarez said calmly over the intercom. "I'm giving those guys a wide berth. Don't want to get shot down. That'd mess up our mission."

"Yeah," Sifton said. "Gettin' killed out here could spoil our whole day."

"I'll go around and come in from the east," Alvarez said. "That way we can make a sweep along the road toward the bandits, and try to get a visual on that guy Khaled Mahmoud before we come too close to them. Time for the night vision gear."

As they circled the area, the two airmen saw muzzle flashes and tracers aimed in their direction. Both realized it was the first time they'd been shot at with live ammunition. They understood the shooters were out to kill them too, if they could. It was sobering.

"Dropping altitude," Alvarez said, listening to the satellite feed guide him closer to the lone man. He maneuvered the Huey to about 400 feet over the road, slowing down as they swept along still trying to get a visual on the fleeing FBI undercover agent. The satellite voice feed and digital image told the pilot that Khalid was nearby.

"See anything?" Alvarez asked Sifton. Both searched forward and along their respective sides of the road as the trees whizzed by under the Huey. Alvarez had never done anything like this before. He realized he was too high and moving too fast to see much in the dark, even with their night vision equipment.

"Negative, Lieutenant," Sifton replied.

Alvarez pulled the helicopter up and brought it around in a tight turn. He eased the chopper down to 250 feet and headed back along La Jara Road. No sign of Khaled. They were told they were almost on target. Again, he lifted up and turned the Huey, heading back for a second pass. This time he brought the chopper down to just above the treetops along the road. He slowed the chopper as much as he possibly could without enveloping the helicopter in clouds of dust and sand from the road. Through their night vision gear, they could make out the landmarks for La Jara Springs Estates. Still no sign of Khalid. Alvarez pulled the helicopter up again, and started to turn it west once more.

Just as the Huey came around and headed back, Alvarez and Sifton heard a loud explosion in the tail assembly. The Huey began to rotate out of control and loose altitude.

"Mayday! Mayday! Mayday!" Alvarez shouted into the mike. "We've taken a hit! Green Dog One going down! Going down! Satellite: mark location!"

Khaled was heading north toward the road when he heard the explosion and saw the brilliant flash and then flames, 50 yards ahead and to his left.

"Oh shit!" he said out loud, crestfallen as he watched the tail disappear in a red-orange fireball. The rotor assembly was blown into thousands of pieces.

Khaled scrambled toward the helicopter as fast as his tired body would take him. Forgetting his own safety, he raced to get there in time to pull out anyone who'd survived the crash, fearing the helicopter might explode. He estimated the chopper went down just a few yards off the road. As Khaled charged forward he tried to think about how he was going to hide any survivors and himself from Rhamir's men.

*

"You okay, Tiny?" Alvarez said, looking down through thick smoke at his big co-pilot.

Below him, Sifton's helmet and facemask were gone. His face was streaked with blood from a cut above one eyebrow.

"Yeah, Chief," Sifton said, his voice strained. "But for Christ's sake, in future please make your fuckin' landings a bit softer, okay?"

"Yeah, sure, I'll make a note of that," Alvarez smiled relieved his co-pilot seemed to be okay.

Alvarez was dangling in his harness. Below him, Sgt. Sifton was covered in pieces of wreckage.

The Huey had crash-landed and rolled onto its left side, up against a grove of juniper trees, 10 yards north of the road. They were lucky. The chopper had been cruising slowly and was below 200 feet when hit. The main rotor had provided just enough lift to avoid a potentially lethal crash.

Alvarez braced himself and released his harness. He held onto the frame of the broken windshield to keep from falling on Sifton. His partner was struggling urgently and unsuccessfully to release his own harness. They knew the chopper could erupt in a fireball any second. Alvarez noticed that Sifton was using his left hand. Sifton was right handed.

Aw shit! Alvarez thought. *His arm's broken.*

Alvarez hurried to clear away debris that had fallen on Sifton and then hit the button on the co-pilot's harness. It wouldn't release. Alvarez tried a second time. It was jammed. He could smell fuel leaking from a ruptured tank. Alvarez pulled a knife from the leg sheath in his flying suit. He sliced the webbing, gently easing Sifton to a sitting position. Sifton didn't say a word. Alvarez could see his partner's teeth were clenched tightly against the pain.

"Okay, let's get the hell out here in case it blows," Alvarez said.

He slipped his hands under Sifton's armpits to begin dragging him to safety. Sifton let out a labored scream. Alvarez stopped and looked down. Sifton's arm wasn't broken. His right shoulder was dislocated. Relief washed over him. He'd dealt with dislocated shoulders before. He told Sifton to roll onto his left side. Alvarez stepped over Sifton and yanked on his right arm as he'd been taught. Sifton let out a horrific yell, and then looked surprised. The piercing pain of the dislocated shoulder was gone. The shoulder still hurt like hell, but he was able to scramble out of the crash on his own.

"Damned good thing we have these M4 Carbines," Alvarez said. "With those bloody fanatics in the neighborhood, having a bit of firepower is going to come in mighty handy. Do you think your arm's up to it?"

"Mine are," came an answer from behind the bottom of the Huey, now vertical. Khaled poked his head around the smashed nose of the chopper. Alvarez pointed an M4 Carbine at the sound. "I sure am glad you fellas got here. Sorry about your chopper. You both okay?"

"Oh sure. Just thought we'd drop in," Sifton said, his left hand holding his right arm, his sense of humor still intact.

"You must be Khaled Mahmoud," Alvarez said, lowering his weapon and extending his hand.

"That's me," the blown undercover agent replied. "Sorry to have gotten you into this. We'd better find cover." He glanced at the thin skin of the downed helicopter. "Your chopper offers about as much protection from bullets as a pup tent. There are 55 to 60 bad guys out looking for me . . . us . . . and most are armed with AK-47s or Uzi's. Oh yeah, as you fellas discovered, at least one of them was packin' an RPG."

"We have a couple of M4 carbines and buckets of ammo in the chopper," Alvarez said. "Both of us have side arms. That's it. How are you with a rifle?"

"I'm okay," Khaled replied. He showed them the AK-47, wishing he'd checked the pockets of the two guys he'd shot for more clips of ammo.

Khaled and Alvarez agreed their odds were not good. Two M4 carbines, an AK-47 and a couple of side arms were not much against dozens of AK-47s, Uzis, and RPG's.

"Chief?" Sifton said, glancing over at his boss. "I didn't tell you this, but I tossed on board a bit of insurance, just in case. You could say this is one of those 'just in case' situations."

"Okay, spit it out, Tiny," Alvarez said. After two years as a team, he'd learned not to underestimate Sifton and to expect surprises, some brilliant, some not.

"Yes, sir," Sifton said, his eyes sparkling. "Before we left, I stuck a box of hand grenades in the back."

"You what?" a startled Alvarez said in disbelief, a wide grin lighting up his face. "I'll be damned. By God, your call was a bloody good one this time, Tiny!"

Khaled looked at the two with amusement, and concern. He could hear approaching shouts. The jihadists had seen the chopper go down, and he'd heard cheers and gunshots. Now, the terrorists were closing in on the crash site, and on them.

"I'll get those little pineapples," Alvarez said. "Tell me where you stowed 'em." Sifton described the location and Alvarez headed off into the rear of the wrecked helicopter. He emerged with a funny look on his face, calling Khaled over to help him carry the large box back to their position.

"Holy shit," Alvarez said. "There are two dozen of these things. No wonder the damned box was so freakin' heavy. Where'd you get them? Uh, cancel that. I don't want to know."

"Trade secret," Sifton replied. "These outta do; not quite one for each of them. But they should help even the odds, don't you think?"

"You bet," the FBI agent said smiling. "Let's go find some trees to hide behind."

As they turned, they heard the roar of an ATV rushing down the road toward them. Alvarez used his knife to pry the lid off the box of grenades, stuffing one in each breast pocket of his flying suit. Alvarez told them to go on ahead; he'd catch up in a minute. Then he grabbed his M4 and ran the few yards to some brush in front of the chopper. It was the side farthest from the road.

Khaled picked up the other M4, a backpack with the ammo, and grabbed one side of the box of hand grenades.

"You okay using your left hand?" he asked Sifton.

"Yup," the sergeant said. "Let's get the hell outta here!"

They ran into the trees, angling away from the road and the chopper. The pair tried to stay close enough to spot any approaching vehicles carrying help but far enough off the road to find cover.

Mark should be here soon, Khaled thought.

Sifton, like Alvarez, had combat training but no experience. Khaled had none of either. Sifton spotted a tight grove of stout Ponderosa pines behind a low hill. A few deadfall trees provided makeshift protection. They were 20 yards from the road.

The two men had just put down the box of grenades when they heard a loud explosion and saw the helicopter turn into a fireball. Seconds later, they saw Alvarez running toward them silhouetted in the fire of the burning helicopter.

"Over here!" Sifton said, waving his left arm. Alvarez looked around, saw them and headed in their direction, crouching low as he ran. Shots rang out from near the burning helicopter.

"Wasn't that just beautiful!" Alvarez exclaimed. "A couple of those bastards drove their ATV right up to the chopper. One of them got off and went inside. They didn't see me 'til I tossed in the grenades. They all went up together. Grenades got the fuel tanks. Whew! Beautiful!"

"Good for you!" Khaled said. He and Sifton both gave Alvarez high fives. Sifton used his left hand again. "Two down and maybe 55 or so to go."

"These babies are coming in damned handy," Alvarez said, reaching into the box for two more grenades.

"Good for you for thinking of them!" he added, holding a grenade in his right hand and looking at Sifton. "But we're gonna have some explaining to do."

"You know something?' Sifton replied. "Explaining how we got back alive would be a nice way to open that conversation," Sifton said as a rocket propelled grenade explosed in the trees to their right.

"Anyone see where that came from?" Alvarez said. Another burst of gunfire brought pine needles raining down on them. The terrorists' fire was getting closer. "Guess they're trying to provoke us into firing back, to show 'em where we're hiding. Not bloody likely!"

Alvarez, who'd pitched semi-pro baseball before joining the USAF, used his training to throw two more grenades toward where the gunfire seemed to be coming from. They saw two explosions in quick succession and were rewarded with loud screams when the second grenade exploded.

Chapter 46

Southwest of Chilili, AZ

Khaled's cell phone vibrated. It was the first time he'd received an incoming call. He'd given Mark the number after Shahid had given him the phone.

"I'm about a mile from where the map says La Jara Springs Estates is supposed to be," Mark said. "I don't see any buildings yet. Where are you?"

"There aren't any buildings. Just keep going," Khaled said. "We're straight ahead of you, about 30 yards off the road, in a stand of Ponderosa pine. It's on your right. Any minute you'll see a fire ahead of you."

"Yeah," Mark said. "I can see a glow over a low ridge. What's that?"

"A downed air force helicopter. The two pilots are okay. They're with me. Rhamir's guys shot 'em down with an RPG. Watch yourself, Mark! We're under fire here. What have you got for weapons?"

"Not much," Mark said. "Just my .357 Magnum. I'm expecting backup but haven't heard from them. Oops, hold on Khaled. Got a call. Could be them. Hang on a sec."

Khaled held, impatiently sitting on the damp soil, his back to a stout pine tree. A few bullets hit the trees randomly above them from time to time. He, Alvarez and Sifton looked at each other and shrugged their shoulders. They watched the muzzle flashes, getting fixes on the jihadists' positions.

Alvarez was itching to throw a few more grenades. But waiting was in their favor, for now.

Mark came back on the line.

"Our only agent in the Albuquerque office is about 15-20 minutes behind me. Six guys from New Mexico's tactical squad are somewhere along I-40. But it sounds like you could use some help right now. What's your situation?"

"Between the three of us, we have two M4 carbines, plenty of ammo, an AK-47 with maybe 60 rounds, a couple of nearly-useless side arms and 20 hand grenades. You heard me right, hand grenades. Somewhere out there, around 50 or 55 of Rhamir's killers are trying to find us. They're armed with AK-47's, some Uzi's and a bunch of RPG's. For what it's worth, we managed to get two of them a few minutes ago and maybe a couple more just before you called."

"I'm coming in," Mark said.

"That's not a good idea, Mark," Khaled said. "You'd best wait for backup and then bring them here, assuming they have some heavy assault weapons. Your .357 will be useless against Rhamir's AK-47s."

"I'm coming in," Mark repeated. "We need to buy some time until more firepower arrives. I can help. Kirtland has a couple of assault Huey's in the air and heading this way. Each has a pair of heavy machine guns. They should even things up a bit.

"Listen," Mark continued, "When you see my headlights, I want you to use a few of those grenades of yours to create diversions. Your guys okay with that?"

"Hold on Mark." Khaled explained to the pilots what Mark had told him about the two choppers en route and what he'd asked them to do. They nodded enthusiastically. Both were itching for more action, especially with backup on its way. And the muzzle flashes were giving them targets for the grenades they were itching to throw.

"Okay, you got it, Mark," Khaled said. "My companions say they could use another grenade chucker. We'll create a diversion as soon as we see your headlights. Watch for the burning chopper. Just before you reach it, drive off the road and into the trees. There doesn't seem to be any fences around here to get in the way."

A few minutes later, the headlights of Mark's car appeared in the distance. As the SUV drew closer the jihadi fighters opened fire from numerous locations. The Explorer was still out of accuracy range. But the gunshots gave the three defenders a better fix on the terrorists' positions.

Khaled, Alvarez and Sifton grabbed four hand grenades each and crept away from their hiding place, fanning out. They'd agreed on separate targets. Alvarez would throw the first grenade. He did. On that signal, Sifton and Khaled threw their grenades at the targets they'd agreed on. Sifton used his left arm with surprising accuracy. Alvarez threw his second grenade. With the gunfire, tracer bullets and grenade explosions, the area became a mini-war zone.

They'd identified nine targets based on muzzle flashes and thrown nine grenades. The resulting explosions caused numerous loud screams. Under cover of the confusion, they regrouped quickly back in the pine grove. As soon as Mark's vehicle came to a stop on a slight rise, a hundred yards back from their position, Alvarez and Sifton opened fire with the M4's on the few jihadist positions still firing at the Explorer. Khaled joined them with the AK-47.

"I'm going to bring him in," Khaled told the others as the headlights went off. They agreed he should circle to the left. Most of the active enemy positions were on their right, on the far side of the road near the burning Huey.

Khaled slipped out and ran crouching toward where he'd seen the headlights. At first, there were no shots. A few feet later, he spotted the white Explorer, much too visible in the darkness.

"Over here, Mark," Khaled called cupping his mouth with his hands. He saw Mark start toward him. Gunfire rang out.

"Down!" Khaled shouted and then felt his right upper arm take a hit, spinning him around and knocking him to the ground.

Ah, shit! he said to himself as he scrambled behind a tree trunk. *Not now, damn it!*

He shrugged out of his coat quickly before the shock wore off. He tugged on a shirtsleeve. He tried unsuccessfully to rip it off to make a bandage.

"Here, let me," Mark said as he crawled up beside him. Mark grabbed the sleeve and cut it with a sharp jackknife he always carried. Mark tied the sleeve around Khaled's arm making a crude tourniquet and tightened it with a small tree branch to slow the bleeding.

"Coming in," Mark said quietly, cupping his mouth, trying to be as subdued as possible. No luck. There was another hail of bullets all around them, but high.

Alvarez threw two grenades in the direction of the muzzle flashes. The explosions provided cover for Mark and Khaled as they ran in a crouch to the dense grove of pines.

"Here ya go," Sifton said to Mark, handing him four grenades. "How's your throwing arm? You're part of our artillery now."

"I pitched a little baseball in Afghanistan," Mark said grinning.

"Hallelujah!" Sifton replied with a broad smile. "I figured you might come in handy. Welcome aboard!"

Their introductions were interrupted by a heavy outburst of firing. Twigs, pine needles, tree bark and pine cones rained down on them. They guessed correctly more of Rhamir's fighters had arrived. Suddenly two ATVs and the dune buggy came down the road. The lights of all three were turned in their direction.

The four defenders realized a major assault was about to begin.

They divided the remaining grenades. Alvarez and Mark took the M4's. Khaled had the AK-47. Sifton grabbed his service revolver in his left hand and Alvarez checked the load for him.

Then everything went deathly quiet. Mark took advantage of the lull to put down his weapons and phone Sorensen. He quickly briefed his boss who then patched the call through to the Kirtland operations center. Mark described their situation and location, and the enemy's positions. He used the road, his white Explorer and the burning Huey as reference points. He also told them the terrorists had ATV headlights pointing in their general direction. Gunners on board the two incoming Huey's would have clearly defined targets as well as guidance from the satellite surveillance.

As Mark and Sorensen were speaking, the two Huey's roared up the road high above them, heading east. Seconds later, the helicopters banked around low and began strafing the jihadists' positions across the road. The choppers made repeated runs, back and forth, taking turns with their twin 7.62 mm machine guns.

A few minutes later both Huey's headed east, up the road 500 yards and out of harm's way. The four defenders heard the helicopters set down. At the same time, there were cries of agony and shouting from the enemy. Then they heard the sound of a dune buggy pulling away, headlights off.

"I'm going after those buggers," Mark said. "You're staying put, Khaled."

"So are you, Tiny," Alvarez said to Sifton. "That's an order, Sergeant."

"Yes sir, sir!" Sifton replied with a little sarcasm and a lot of reluctance.

Alvarez and Mark grabbed their weapons. Both pocketed extra ammo clips and two grenades each, and headed toward the road. The scattered remains of two ATVs greeted them. There was no sign of the dune buggy. The two men counted nine bodies. The rest had scattered. Mark and Alvarez shouldered their weapons and each picked up an AK-47 abandoned in the dirt on the shoulder of the road. They fired a couple of rounds to make sure the weapons were serviceable. They pocketed spare clips of ammunition.

"Hold it! Don't move or I'll shoot you dead right where you stand!"

The loud command came from behind them. Mark and Alvarez dropped the weapons and raised their arms.

Damn it! Mark thought. *How'd those assholes get behind us? Surely, it's not going to end like this.*

"Who are you?" the voice demanded. "Identify yourselves, right now!"

The voice didn't sound like a terrorist.

"I'm Special Agent Mark Tremblay of the FBI," Mark said. "And he's Lieutenant Hugo Alvarez from Kirtland Air Force Base. Who the hell are you?"

"All right, you two guys," the voice said, chuckling. "Fer Christ's sake, Alvarez! You coulda got your ass shot off!"

Mark and Alvarez turned. In the dawning light, they saw four pilots, obviously from the two helicopters. They stood in the middle of the road, M4's pointed skyward. Alvarez went over and shook hands then introduced Mark. They called Khaled and Sifton over.

One of the airmen said three Sea Stallion helicopters were due shortly. Their orders were to land separately, two in a clearing a few miles southeast of the jihadists' camp, and the other a few miles northwest. On board were more than 50 combat-ready Marines with orders to surround the terrorists and take them into custody. They were authorized to use lethal force if fired upon.

The pilots offered one of their Huey's to take Khaled and Sifton back to the base for medical attention. With their initial mission completed, one of the choppers and the satellite relay were to become spotters for the roundup of the jihadists. The one chopper was available to transport the two injured men to Kirtland. And it would be back in time to provide backup. Mark and Alvarez walked with their injured comrades over to the helicopters. They met the FBI agent from Albuquerque walking up the road towards them, his SUV blocked by the helicopters on the road.

Moments after the chopper with Sifton and Khaled lifted off, the heavily armed six-member NMSP tactical unit also arrived. Mark and Alvarez briefed them. They now had 12 men, all with body armor and well armed. They started down La Jara Road on foot toward the ISIS camp.

Rhamir and his terrorist followers were about to be on the receiving end of a classic military pincer movement.

Chapter 47

ISIS Camp

It didn't take long to discover just how elusive Rhamir could be.

The helicopter gunships had no sooner finished their strafing runs than Rhamir, apparently sensing the turning tide of battle, had headed back to the terrorist camp.

By the time the Marines arrived at the camp, Rhamir was long gone. He and two elite fighters he used as bodyguards were in a nondescript four-wheel drive pickup equipped with a powerful engine racing along back roads heading for I-40.

He didn't know where Shahid was and didn't much care.

*

Columbus, NM

Rhamir met his nuclear bomb team the next day east of Columbus, NM. The plan was to disappear across the Mexican border a few miles south. But first, Rhamir had a few other things up his sleeve.

"We will proceed immediately!" Rhamir told Shokar, Barehi and Chegini over lunch in Tres Salsas Restaurant in Columbus.

His bodyguards were told to eat in a separate booth. Even though he'd ordered them to say nothing, he didn't want to risk the nuclear bomb team learning about the raid on the Albuquerque camp from a careless comment. It could discourage them. Stories likely would be appearing in the news media soon enough. He was certain most of the jihadists at the camp had been killed, wounded or captured. The Islamic Army of America was crumbling.

Rhamir's backup plan was now in play.

He ordered his nuclear team to rush back to New York, put the nuclear weapon in place, and then set a timer that had come with the device. They were to set the timer for five days, enough time to reach the Mexican border by car. There, the team would rejoin Rhamir. He'd also told his 'real' deputy, Fahim Tahir, to meet him there. The small group would escape into Mexico using a tunnel built by a local gang to smuggle drugs. They'd also used it to smuggle weapons into America for his Islamic Army.

Rhamir had $1,300,000 in large bills with him neatly stacked in a briefcase. The money would finance the start of a new Islamic Army based in Mexico City.

However, before slipping into Mexico, Rhamir had something else he was determined to do first.

Chapter 48

ISIS Camp

"Hi Love," Mark said into his iPhone. "We're almost done here searching the ISIS camp. Why don't you and the kids fly down to Albuquerque? We can head out from there for that holiday we've been promising ourselves."

"Hey, I like that!" Paige said. "I'm glad it's over. We'll be packed in a jiffy. Have you found Rhamir?"

"Not yet," Mark replied. "There's a nation wide APB out for him and whoever's with him. He can't get far. My biggest worry right now is we've still not tracked down that nuclear device, assuming there is one and that it made it into the country.

"Listen, my Love, I'm going to be out at Rhamir's camp for a while yet, probably overnight, hoping to find some clues about that device.

"So, why don't you and the kids fly down this afternoon? There's a mid-afternoon flight. You can stay at my motel. I booked an adjoining room for the kids. We can spend some family time together here while I'm not working. Sound good?"

"The best offer I've had in weeks!" Paige said.

The smile in her voice and the inference of longing were loud and clear.

Mark and his team of investigators meticulously scoured the site of Rhamir's camp through the day and far into the night, searching for clues to the whereabouts of the nuclear bomb and evidence about the murder of Farouk Mohammed.

That evening, Mark met his family at Albuquerque International Sunport. He was back out at the camp the next morning and on the phone updating Bjorn Sorensen when he got a call-waiting signal. It was Rhamir; the terrorist leader obviously hadn't learned how to block caller ID.

"Hey, boss, I gotta go!" Mark said. "You'll never guess who's trying to call. It's Rhamir!"

"Call me later," Sorenson replied and hung up.

"I'm not fucking done with you yet!" the voice shouted when Mark answered.

"Rhamir, it's over!" Mark replied. "Give yourself up, man. It's all over. You are going to be held accountable for what you've done. You . . . will . . . be . . . tracked . . . down, and you will be put on trial! Do you hear me?"

"I'll be easy to find," Rhamir shot back. "My men and I are at your motel, holding your pretty little wife and those two brats who ran away from me.

"Now, if you don't do exactly as you're told, I have something special in mind for them. And your wife won't be quite as pretty after we give her a face wash with hydrochloric acid. Here's what you're going to do. I want a helicopter with sufficient size, range and fuel to fly 10 people to Mexico. I will release your family when we land on the other side of the border. You have two hours."

The phone went dead. A sick feeling grabbed Mark's heart.

"We've got a problem," Mark told the investigators. They included the FBI, State troopers,

Albuquerque city police and military police from Kirtland Air Force Base.

"Abdul Rhamir is holding my wife and kids at the La Quinta Inn near the airport," a visibly shaken Mark told them. "He's demanding a chopper with a range capable of flying him, a bunch of his men and my family to the Mexican border. He claims he will release Paige and the kids when he lands at the border.

"Frankly, I don't believe he will."

Two hours later, cars had been removed from the La Quinta parking lot so a Huey from nearby Kirtland AFB could land near Fuddruckers Restaurant. Before the Huey arrived, more than 75 law enforcement and military personnel had quietly and secretly moved in to surround the motel. Snipers were positioned in facing rooms at LaQuinta Inn, and on the roofs of LaQuinta, Residence Inn, Fairfield, Towne Place and AmericInn.

A distraught Mark watched through the tinted windows of Fuddruckers as the helicopter landed. His room where Paige and the kids were being held overlooked the parking lot. He'd heard nothing more from Rhamir, who obviously would have heard the chopper arrive.

"Standby," said a voice in his earpiece. The Albuquerque Police Department was providing its tactical channel. "One or more of the suspects are expected to emerge with three hostages momentarily.

"Snipers," the voice commanded. "Watch for clear shots, but hold your fire unless authorized. We must have three clear shots. Acknowledge."

Mark heard a chorus of 'Roger One', 'Roger Two', 'Roger Three'. He felt relief but he also felt an urgent need for action.

The door to his ground level motel room opened. Paige stood in the doorway. Her face was filled with terror. She kept looking over her shoulder. Mark assumed she was checking on Edward and Caylyn. Suddenly, she was pulled back from the doorway, and then emerged again. This time, Rhamir was behind her, his arm around her neck, almost lifting her petite body off her feet. He kept glancing nervously back and forth.

So that's what that miserable son of a bitch looks like! Mark thought.

Rhamir paused. His two bodyguards emerged, each carrying one of the children on one arm and an AK-47 in the other hand. Rhamir looked around again, and then glanced toward the Huey. Its nose was facing slightly away from him. The near side door was closed. He could see the other was open. Still holding Paige by the hair from behind, he pushed her toward the open door, motioning his bodyguards to close up tightly to his back. As the six people approached the helicopter, the bodyguards put Edward and Caylyn down on the parking lot so they could crouch over to avoid the rotors, still turning slowly.

"Two targets clear," Mark heard.

"Hold your fire!" came the command. "Wait until all three targets are clear! Await my command!"

Edward was forcing one bodyguard to drag him toward the helicopter. His reluctance served to separate them slightly from his sister and the other bodyguard.

Mark saw what Edward was up to. *Smart kid*, he thought.

The tight group began to head around toward the front of the helicopter, the adults bent over. Without warning, Paige fell heavily, appearing to have tripped over a skid.

Two shots rang out. Both bodyguards fell. Edward grabbed Caylyn's hand and ran around the back of the helicopter toward Fuddruckers.

Rhamir guessed what was happening. He quickly stepped over Paige and headed toward the nose of the chopper, effectively blocking possible sniper shots. He pulled a 357 Magnum from his waistband and swung it towards Paige. His obvious plan was to shoot Paige then hop in the chopper to get away.

"Hey, Rhamir!" Mark shouted as he ran across the parking lot toward the chopper. "You fucking coward! Shoot me, if you dare, you miserable offspring of a camel!"

The distraction was enough. Rhamir swung the .357 towards Mark. Suddenly the windshield on the pilot's side of the chopper developed a big hole, as multiple shots were fired from an M4 inside the cab. Rhamir's chest erupted into bloody hamburger. He was dead before his body hit the ground.

"Atta go, Chief," Sgt. Will Sifton said. "Now we've two damaged chopper to explain."

"Thanks, Tiny," Lt. Hugo Alvarez replied. "And the pleasure was all ours."

Chapter 49

Danbury, CT

The alliance ops team and support personnel had been invited to Douglas and Jennifer's spacious home office in Danbury for an update.

"I sure would like to know how that miserable son of a bitch got away from us at the camp," Mark mused. "I guess we'll never know."

Paige was sitting next to Mark, perched on a low maple two-drawer filing cabinet, holding his left arm tightly as he briefed them on details of the final roundup at the extremists' camp and the scary events at La Quinta Inn in Albuquerque.

"We counted 14 bodies," Mark said. "Nine were recovered where the two Huey's strafed the ISIS assault on our location. The Marines took out five more in firefights near their camp, and then Rhamir and two others were shot at the La Quinta. With those arrested, that accounts for 53.

"Oh, by the way, Rhamir's mother is in custody," Mark said. "We're confident she's the one who allowed Edward and Caylyn to escape; seems like a nice enough old lady. Apparently, she fell asleep while guarding the kids. I wouldn't be a bit surprised if she deliberately let herself fall asleep. Anyway, she's been trying to be helpful, answering through an interpreter all the questions from our guys. We're not sure she has much of an idea what else had been going on. I hope the folks at Justice go easy on her."

When Mark finished, his grandfather piped up:

"Your family was damned lucky," Paul said, glancing sideways in time to catch Paige nodding her agreement. She was still holding tight to Mark's left arm. "And some of your own antics, Mark, were not all that prudent if you ask me."

"I know, Grandpa," Mark replied with a smile, failing in his half-hearted attempt to sound contrite. "Bjorn's already chewed me out, okay?"

His boss nodded, pursing his lips in feigned sternness, a smile breaking through.

"Never mind me . . . what about the two of you?" Mark said, with an accusing look. "Grandpa, I've heard stories about you and Uncle Doug . . . you two were not exactly shy violets in your day, either."

Douglas and Paul exchanged glances; neither wanted to go there. They shook their heads with ill-concealed pride for Mark. Bjorn broke the silence and changed the subject.

"I just got a text," he said. "As you know, arrests are being made all over the country, thanks to this alliance of yours. I must say I still don't quite believe it – the mob, law enforcement, the Pentagon, and civilians! Working together? Never thought I'd see it. But by God it's working!

"Based on the latest reports, your alliance has been responsible directly or indirectly for the arrests of more than 175 people – the so-called leaders, guerillas, other extremists, trainers, recruits and wannabe lone-wolfs. Some of them are as young as 16 years old, for Christ's sake!"

Bjorn continued: "I want you to know also that tips from your contacts have led to the seizure of over 2,800 pounds of PETN as well as a transport truck filled with bulk chemicals to make more of the stuff. On top of that, the FBI, and state and local police forces have seized 351 AK-47s, 137 Uzi's, a dozen .30 caliber machine guns, 215 sets of body armor and more than 127,000 rounds of ammunition. It's damned obvious those sons of bitches were preparing for a war all right.

"Let's not forget in all our excitement we still face one huge threat," he added. "There's no sign of that nuclear bomb. We're still looking hard for it. No one we've arrested will admit knowledge of it. One possibility is that a team of Rhamir's jihadists has it and is still planning to set it off somewhere.

"Law enforcement and the military across the country are on full alert and actively searching for them and the nuke. We need that alliance network to redouble its efforts to help us track that thing down."

While Bjorn was speaking, Douglas's wife Jennifer appeared at the door of the den with a strange look on her face. She gestured with her thumb, chest high, trying to signal surreptitiously that someone was behind her.

"It's alright, Miss," Joe Caprionni said as he brushed carefully past her and walked into the den like he owned it. Caprionni was leaning heavily on a cane in his right hand.

The group looked up at the slightly stooped, grey haired old man. He was perfectly groomed and elegantly dressed. Everyone recognized him. All were startled except Paul, who showed a hint of a smile, taking it all in stride. Through his surprise, Mark noticed Caprionni had gained a little more weight, much needed. The cane was new.

The boss of bosses over organized crime in New York and much of New England walked over to Paige, took her right hand, leaned over and kissed it with a gentlemanly flourish. Paige was obviously surprised, flattered and pleased. Then she quickly pulled her hand away, remembering here was the mafia boss who just a few months earlier had ordered Mark's murder.

"I've been looking forward to meeting you, young lady," Caprionni said, his voice dripping with Italian charm. A warm and endearing smile enlivened his still-handsome face. "Thank you for sharing your husband for this vital cause. Our nation has much reason to be grateful to him."

Paige was still recovering from surprise when the aging mafia don turned, and still leaning on his cane, walked slowly over to Paul, and said:

"It is a privilege to meet you, Mr. Winston. I was not surprised to learn Mark is your grandson. You are a man of honor, of principle. For many years, I have been hearing good things about you and your many accomplishments. I want you to know, sir, that your wisdom and integrity have rubbed off on your grandson. You must be very proud of him."

Caprionni extended his hand. Paul stood, reached out and accepted it, saying:

"May I say it's a surprise and a pleasure to meet you, Mr. Caprionni. And yes, we are very proud of Mark. Thank you."

While they were talking, Mark recovered from his surprise over Caprionni's unannounced arrival. He was curious how the mafia boss had found out they were in his uncle's den. He managed to blurt out:
"What an unexpected surprise, Mr. Caprionni! Is there something we can do for you, sir?"
"Yes there is, son," the mafia elder replied warmly, turning to face him. He took a few steps toward Mark and said:
"Look . . . I'm gonna be 80 years old in three weeks. I am, that is my wife and I have been thinking it is time for a change. For us, you understand. So, maybe you can help me with that. Can you tell me, where do I find a good lawyer outside of the families? You know? Someone with, ah, with no connections, you understand?
"I'm gonna retire, you see, and I wanna stay outta jail. Maybe it would be good for my wife and I, maybe we should get away, you know . . . maybe that witness protection thing you people have!"
Everyone shared the surprise that flashed across Mark's face. Caprionni was implying he would be willing to give testimony on what he knew about La Cosa Nostra in return for immunity for himself and his wife.
"It's over," Caprionni said before anyone could recover enough to speak up.
"It's all over," he repeated, his voice weary and resigned. "There is no one with honor to continue the path we have taken, here or back home. Maybe that is a good thing. It is our own fault, you see. By our indulgence, we have made our children complacent, lazy. And they know nothing of respect.

And then there are our grandchildren. They want no part of who we are and what we do. They are becoming doctors and dentists, accountants and teachers, and some are building legitimate businesses. I can see this is the future of our families, not our way of life as it has been.

"I speak only for myself, my family, you understand. Not for the others. Not for The Commission. Some feel as I do. I know this. Some do not. It is for them to decide. They do not know what my wife and I are doing. They will find out soon enough."

Before anyone could respond, Paige's iPhone signaled a text. She read the message and stepped out of the den into the hallway to make a call.

When she returned her face was pale and had a haunted, almost haggard, look.

"Okay," Mark said. He recognized the look on her face. "What is it, Love?"

"I just got a report from our alliance office in New York," she said. "NYPD got a tip this morning from an employee of a Prescott affiliate to check out a mini-van in Times Square. The employee had walked past the van for two days on her way to work. The van had been backed into an ally, behind a makeshift fence.

"Hold onto your hats, folks," Paige continued. "Inside that van was the missing nuclear bomb! I'm serious! That two-megaton bomb! Something went wrong or it would have detonated by now. My God! Can you imagine what a horrible disaster?

"NYPD had the vehicle towed to an impound lot and opened. A black tarp was covering something in the back. The cops thought it could be a body. Under the tarp, they found a device with a time clock attached. That put them on alert. The time had run out but the timer was still turned on. They called the bomb squad. A couple of US Army bomb experts were in the city for training with their NYPD counterparts. They figured out what it was. They helped disarm the timer and remove the detonator.

"The Army's bomb experts say that corroded electrodes in the detonator caused the device to malfunction. They said the corrosion was consistent with the effects of saltwater on copper.

"Thank God for that!" Paige added. "The device is being flown out to the Nevada desert as we speak. It's going to a nuclear research facility where it will be examined and dismantled."

"You can be sure word of this has reached the White House," Mark said. "A bunch of people at the top of the FBI, the CIA, Homeland Security and elsewhere are going to be answering some very serious questions about how this could have happened in America."

The room had grown silent as those gathered contemplated the horrendous tragedy seemingly averted by the good fortune of Nature.

"May we come in?" a woman asked at the door.

Mark recognized the voice. It was his mother's, Catherine Tremblay. Mark's head snapped up.

"Mom!" he said. "Come in, of course, by all means! Welcome! What brings you here?"

"Someone wants to speak with you, Mark," she replied gently.

Mark's father, oil executive Philip Tremblay, followed Mark's mother into the room and stopped beside her. Everyone was visibly uneasy. They knew the history.

"Mark," his Dad began, stepping toward Mark. "Son. I came here to tell you personally, how very proud I am, how proud we all are, of you. I will admit I've been remiss for not saying that to you much sooner. I apologize for my pig headedness.

"I understand now, son, and respect the calling you have chosen as your life's work. What you have accomplished makes abundantly clear America has been made much safer for all of us. You are to be congratulated – that one so young can teach the rest of us so much."

Mark opened his mouth to reply. His father raised his right hand, palm out. He wasn't finished.

"I know that we disagreed when you joined the Navy," his father continued. "I was wrong trying to decide your future for you. That right belongs to you. I understand that now. You and I lost valuable years because we are both strong willed men. I came here to change that. I hope you feel the same way, son."

Mark looked intently at his father, glanced over at Paige, who smiled, and then he walked across the room, his right hand extended. His father grasped it. They embraced. Paige, his mother and Jennifer made no effort to stop tears from tumbling down their faces. The three women hugged tightly. Paul and Anne walked over and joyfully hugged their daughter, Catherine, and the reunited father and son.

The room erupted in applause and cheers. Everyone knew about the strained relations between Mark and his father, Philip, and despite their sadness had said nothing. Now, it was behind them.

Mark turned to Paige and asked, "Now, my love?"

Paige smiled knowingly and replied, "Yes!"

Mark picked up his iPhone and pushed a button. He spoke into the phone: "You can come in now."

The couple stood. Mark put his arm around Paige and said to the group:

"Uncle Doug doesn't know this, but there was another reason for all of you to attend this meeting today."

As he spoke, Emile Bilodeaux came through the door of the crowded den. He was holding Caylyn's hand in his left hand. Edward was on his right side, feeling much too grown up to have his hand held. Hey, he was almost seven years old.

"Are we correct that your many talents include being a wedding commissioner?" Mark asked. "That you are authorized to perform marriages in the State of Connecticut?"

"That is correct," Emile said, a smug look on his face. "I hold dual citizenship. I was born near Hartford, and grew up in Montreal."

Mark's mother Catherine caught the drift quickly. Her eyes began to sparkle. Her right hand rose to her mouth in anticipation.

"Aunt Jennifer?" Mark said. "Paige has something to ask."

Paige said: "Since my parents are in Costa Rica and can't be here, will you be my bridesmaid?"

"I would love to!" Jennifer replied excitedly.

"Just a minute!" Douglas said. "I thought you two were already married."

"Well, yeah," Mark said. "But it was just the two of us at city hall then. We wanted to do it again, do it right, like it's supposed to be done with family and friends around."

"Catherine?" Paige turned to Mark's mother. "I would be so very pleased if you would be my Matron of Honor."

"Oh, yes! Yes!" Catherine said proudly. "I only wish your parents could be here!"

There was silence as Mark walked toward his father.

"Dad," he said. "I need a best man. Would you?"

"Of course, son," Philip replied. The two men embraced again.

*

The next morning, Mark and Paige and the children arrived at Kennedy International Airport. Paige was holding Caylyn's hand and Edward had a firm grip on Mark's.

"I'm excited!" Paige said. "Finally, we're off on our honeymoon! And all this terrorism fighting is finally over."

Oh how I wish it really was over, Mark thought. He smiled longingly at his young wife. He decided he wouldn't spoil their vacation by telling her the truth – that the battle against domestic terrorism was far from over.

The young family of four cleared security at Kennedy's executive flight center and then walked out toward the Prescott Enterprises corporate Lear Jet. Its destination was known only to Mark and Paige, the flight plan center and the pilots. Edward and Caylyn didn't much care.

Postscript

Civilized peoples have been fighting modern forms of terrorism for decades, and yet the battle has just begun. The number of terrorist organizations continues to grow and their influence is expanding. Every one of those cesspools of depravity must be taken seriously. Make no mistake: they are not Muslim nor are they the prophets of Islam they claim to be. They are apostates – in their own words, non-believers – perverting and abusing an honorable religion in order to camouflage their barbaric behavior. And they are united in one goal – the destruction of our way of life.

An important part of our individual contributions to eradicating this growing threat is for each of us to question the myths that many of us have acquired from well intentioned but often-misinformed sources including the Internet, news media, even friends and family. Doing so will ensure that we serve the best interests of our communities, and thus ourselves. Surely that's the intelligent thing to do.

However difficult as it may be, let us get it through our heads that clinging to prejudices as if they were truths only serves to further the goals of terrorists. The fact is, ISIS has perfected the art of preying on our primordial instincts, to make us fear those who we do not know and to ridicule that which we do not understand. How tragically unfortunate it is that otherwise rational peers among us have been driven in this way to demonize all Muslims, and thereby unwittingly serve the goals of terrorists.

These psychopaths must surely love it when we behave so unwisely, for there is ample evidence that the terrorists themselves have created many of the myths that appear to be anti-terrorist, yet have been crafted to serve their purposes. Similarly, they have learned how to use social media effectively to further their interests, and have manipulated the western news media with unparalleled skill into serving them as their propagandists. Video coverage on TV of those gruesome beheadings, mass slaughters and burnings of people alive – need more be said?

We would do well to avoid branding as enemies those with beliefs different from our own, until we have in hand incontrovertible evidence that they are indeed adversaries. Would it not be wiser for us to invite to become allies those whom we may be tempted to improperly accuse of wrongdoing? Would that not also be the intelligent thing to do? The color of someone's skin, their religion and their manner of dress or way of life are evidence only of diversity, nothing more. Different is only different, until proven otherwise.

Acknowledgements

Much is owed to many for their support in the creation of this novel. First among these is my amazing wife Sharolie Osborne. Her patience, tolerance and encouragement have been indispensable, for while writing is a solitary experience, so it is also for those close to the writer.

I owe special thanks to Trevor Apperley, Keith Critchley and Tim Young. It was Keith's foresight, creative mind and encouragement that inspired the journey that has culminated in The Ultimate Threat. I am equally indebted to Trevor and Tim for providing the benefit of their extraordinary editing skills and insightful critiques.

My deep gratitude also to Endeavour Press Ltd. of London, UK, for taking a chance on a debut author. The courage and professional leadership exhibited by this innovative publisher are among the reasons why the publishing industry continues to flourish during a time of much change.

A host of early readers are also due my sincere thanks for their suggestions, and for enduring those early drafts. Warm thanks to Judy Bader, Michael Flood, Jan and Jared Joynt, Kent O'Connor, Hugh Philip, Lorelei Piotto and Betty Ann Stimson. Your helpful advice contributed more than you may realize to the final product.

As always, errors and oversights are mine alone.

--James Osborne